# DARING TO LOVE THE DUKE'S HEIR

Janice Preston

MILLS & BOON

First Published in Great Britain 2019
by Mills & Boon, an imprint of HarperCollins*Publishers*
1 London Bridge Street, London, SE1 9GF



ISBN: 978-0-263-26915-4

MIX
Paper from
responsible sources
FSC C007454

This book is produced from independently certified FSC™ paper
to ensure responsible forest management.
For more information visit www.harpercollins.co.uk/green.

Printed and bound in Spain
by CPI, Barcelona

To Lynn.

Thank you.

# *Chapter One*

*March 1817*

Raindrops rattled on the roof of the carriage that carried Miss Liberty Lovejoy and her sister Hope through the dark, slick streets of a rain-drenched London.

'Liberty. I beg you…please do not do this. Gideon will never forgive you.'

Liberty wrenched her attention from the passing streets and resolutely swallowed down her own burgeoning doubt. She didn't want to do this, but she had to. *Someone* must save Gideon from himself.

'I have to do something, Hope. Gideon is running amok and it is all the fault of Lord Alexander Beauchamp. Gideon will be grateful to me for saving him from the results of his own folly. Eventually.'

'Well, I do not think you are fair to embroil me without warning,' said Hope tartly. 'You *said* we were going to Hookham's. I would never have agreed to accompany you if I knew you intended to visit Alexander's father, of all people. He is a *duke*, Liberty. People like us do not just call upon a duke.'

Hope's reaction did not surprise Liberty—she had given up expecting support from either of her sisters when there was any unpleasantness to deal with. They had been so young when their parents had died within days of one another and they had come to rely on Liberty and her twin brother, Gideon—just nineteen at the time—to take charge. Uncle Eustace was worse than useless…far too selfish to stir himself, even though he had been appointed their guardian. It was no wonder her entire family took Liberty for granted.

'If you are afraid to come in, you may remain in the carriage while I speak to the Duke. *I* cannot afford the luxury of fear.' Oh, but how she wished she could order Bilk, their coachman, to turn the carriage around and drive back to their rented London house. 'It is my responsibility as the eldest—'

'You are the eldest by a mere five minutes, Liberty Louisa Lovejoy, and *Gideon* now happens to be an earl.'

'His conduct is more reminiscent of an overgrown schoolboy than a peer of the realm,' retorted Liberty.

Since Liberty's twin brother had unexpectedly acceded to the Earldom of Wendover last autumn his behaviour had grown increasingly exasperating. Was it really asking too much of him to help her to secure their sisters' futures instead of careening around town and frittering his newfound prosperity on wine, cards and horses and in the pursuit of females who were no better than they should be? Besides, she missed Gideon and how they had worked together to ensure the survival of their family.

'Well, I would say that being an earl makes him senior to you, do you not? Do not forget we are all reliant on his goodwill now if we do not wish to be banished back to Eversham with Uncle Eustace. I think it is very generous of Gideon to fund a Season for all three of us at the same time.'

Liberty clenched her jaw. If Hope only knew how much persuasion it had taken for Gideon to agree to his sisters coming to London in the first place...left to himself, she had no doubt her twin would have been content for his sisters to remain hidden away at Eversham for ever while he lived the high life to which he now felt entitled.

She stared out of the window, seeing neither the grey streets they passed nor the people hurrying along beneath their umbrellas, wrapped in coats and cloaks against the dreadful dark, cold and wet weather that had assailed the entire country for the past year. If it were not for Hope and Verity she would much prefer to still be at home, running the house for Uncle Eustace—her late mother's unmarried brother who had always made his home with the Lovejoys—and living in quiet obscurity.

But Hope and Verity, at one-and-twenty and nineteen respectively, deserved a chance to better themselves in life. After their parents' deaths there had been neither opportunity nor funds for the younger Lovejoy sisters to even dream of a come out, not until the unexpected death of a distant cousin and his two sons in a house fire and Gideon's sudden preferment.

'And do not forget what Mrs Mount said.' Hope's words broke into Liberty's train of thought. 'It is bad etiquette to call on your social superiors before *they* have left their card with *you*.'

Mrs Mount was the lady they had hired as duenna during their sojourn in London. The daughter of a viscount and now the widow of the younger son of an earl, she had many acquaintances within the *ton* and was thus perfectly placed to help steer the Lovejoy girls through the mysteries of polite society. Well, perfectly placed if Liberty chose to follow her advice. Which, in this instance, she did not.

'It is a certainty that the Duke of Cheriton is never likely to leave his card for us,' said Liberty, 'so I do not see that I have any choice if I am to persuade him to control his son's wild behaviour.'

'I cannot believe that a duke will take kindly to a country squire's daughter lecturing him on how he should control his son. Libby—it is not too late. Please, let us go home and I promise I will help you talk some sense into Gideon.'

'But we have tried that, Hope, many times, and he ignores us. I fear his new status has gone to his head and that he will never be the same again.'

She was not even certain she much liked the man her twin had become. He had become secretive and thoughtless, and the closeness that had bound the two of them together throughout their childhood now felt as though it hung by the most fragile of threads.

*It breaks my heart, this distance between us.*

Liberty slid one gloved hand inside her woollen cloak and pressed it to her upper chest, rubbing in a soothing, circular motion, but the familiar hollow ache remained, as it had for the five years since her childhood sweetheart, Bernard, died.

Being back in London had resurrected those dreadful memories and, with them, the guilt. If only she hadn't been so selfish by accepting the offer from her wealthy godmother to sponsor her through a London Season. If only she had stayed at home, Bernard and her parents might still be alive. At the very least she would have been able to say goodbye to her husband-to-be. A knot of disquiet had taken root in her stomach since their arrival in London…a nagging reminder of her selfishness and her failure.

Well, she would not fail Gideon, or the girls. And if it meant calling on a duke unannounced, then so be it.

In an unexpected gesture, Hope clasped Liberty's hand.

'You cannot protect all of us all the time, Liberty. Gideon is a grown man. I know you miss the old Gideon, but he will come to his senses, you'll see.'

'But what if he does not? What if I sit by and do nothing and he ends up destroying himself? And that's quite apart from the damage his wild behaviour will do to you and Verity.'

Their background would be hurdle enough without Gideon casting a deeper shadow over them. Papa had been a gentleman, but Mama had been the daughter of a coal merchant—that whiff of trade would be a difficult barrier to overcome, according to Mrs Mount.

The carriage rocked to a halt.

'This must be it,' Hope said, her voice awed. 'Goodness!'

Liberty was momentarily distracted as thunder growled in the distance, a stark reminder of the most terrible day in her life—the day she had learned that not only both her beloved parents, but also Bernard, had succumbed to the outbreak of cholera that swept through their village while Liberty had been enjoying dress fittings in London in preparation for her debut. She had not even glimpsed the inside of a ballroom before receiving that urgent summons to return home.

She thrust down the memory that still had the power to bring hot, stinging tears to her eyes and peered through the rain that streamed down the window. She gulped. *This* was Beauchamp House? It was huge. Magnificent. Intimidating. It was not a house, but a mansion. Stretching for five wide bays, it would swallow several houses such as their modest rented abode in Green Street. A new surge of doubt as to her plan swept over Liberty, but she had come this far and she wouldn't allow herself to back away now. She gathered her courage, flung open the carriage door, grabbed her oilskin umbrella and, opening it, thrust it out of the door into the deluge. Lightning flickered and she braced herself for the next rumble of thunder. Was the storm getting closer? There were several seconds before the sound reached her ears—it sounded more distant than before and she released her pent-up breath. She gave herself no time for further qualms. Bilk handed her down and she hurried up the steps to the imposing front door of Beauchamp House, which remained firmly shut.

She lifted the brass knocker—so highly polished it gleamed even in the unnatural yellowish-grey afternoon light—and let it fall. Then she waited, irritation clambering over any nerves she felt at facing such a powerful nobleman. What was taking so long? 'Where—?'

'Might I be of assistance?'

She whipped around. A carriage was drawing away from the front of the house, presumably after depositing this man…her darting gaze settled on his face, half-shielded by his own umbrella, and she gasped, her stomach clenching with anger. She held fast to her courage and straightened her spine even though her knees quaked. This close, she was only too conscious of Lord Alexander Beauchamp's daunting presence—his height and the width of his shoulders spoke of a powerful man.

'I have come to speak to your father about your behaviour.'

He stiffened, his dark brows slashed into a forbidding frown. 'I *beg* your pardon?'

As she opened her mouth, he held up his hand,

palm forward, effectively silencing her. 'Apart from the fact that you and I have never met, madam, I regret to inform you that the Duke is not in residence.' He brushed past her to the door.

'We may indeed never have met, my lord, but I know who you are.' Liberty set her jaw. She'd recognise Lord Alexander Beauchamp anywhere, even though she'd only ever glimpsed him in the distance as he gaily led her brother astray. 'The knocker is on the door.' She summoned her very haughtiest tone. 'That means the family is in residence.'

'A member of the family, maybe, but that member is not my father. Now, if you will excuse me? You might relish being out in such weather, but I can assure you I do not.' The door began to open. 'I suggest you put your grievance into writing. If you have it delivered here it will be forwarded on to my father for his attention, you have my word.'

*The word of a rackety rakehell!*

The door opened fully to reveal a liveried footman.

'Sorry, milord,' he said breathlessly. 'I was downstairs when I heard the knock.'

'No need for apologies, William. This—' Liberty stiffened, detecting the faint curl of his upper lip as His Lordship looked her up and down '—*person* wished to speak to my father. I have advised her to write to him.'

He handed his dripping umbrella to the servant and strode into the hall. Despair spread its tentacles through Liberty, squeezing her lungs. Coming here to confront the Duke had been a risk, but at least she would have had an opportunity to use her powers of persuasion. A letter could be all too easily dismissed. It was true she had never met Alexander, but perhaps if he knew who she was…? If she could appeal to his better nature…?

'Lord Alexander! Please!' She tried to dodge around the footman, who foiled her attempts using His Lordship's still-open umbrella. 'Wait, I beg of you.'

Once she succeeded in knocking aside that umbrella, she could see His Lordship had stopped and now faced her, a look of weary resignation on his face. Encouraged, she discarded her own umbrella on the doorstep and rushed towards him, darting around the still-protesting footman.

'Please. May we talk? I am Gideon's sister.'

His brows snapped together, forming once again a dark slash across his forehead. 'Gideon? Who is Gideon?'

'Lord Wendover.'

'You have my sympathy.'

Liberty bridled. 'If you think so little of him, why do you spend so much time together?'

He looked beyond her. 'William—take the

lady's coat and bonnet, if you please. Ask Mrs Himley to send wine and cakes to the drawing room, and find a maid to sit with us—' He looked Liberty up and down before fixing his gaze on her face. The chill in his light-coloured eyes sent a shiver through her. 'For propriety's sake,' he continued. '*You* might have no compunction about calling upon your social superiors not only uninvited but also unchaperoned, madam, but a man cannot be too careful.'

The nerve of him! 'My sister is in the carriage outside,' said Liberty, shedding her dripping cloak. 'She was too afraid to come in and speak to your father.'

'Too afraid or too sensible? I suspect the latter. Perhaps you would be wise to pay more attention to your sister's instincts.' His bored tone sent Liberty's temper soaring. 'Invite her to join us, William, if you please. She cannot wait outside. But I shall still require a maid,' he called after the departing footman.

He eyed Liberty again, from head to toe, and she squirmed inside. She had donned her best Pomona-green bombazine afternoon dress for this visit to the Duke, but His Lordship's impassive inspection made her feel as though she was dressed in rags. It was not the height of fashion—she had been unable to reconcile herself to wasting money on new gowns when she had a trunk full of barely worn dresses and accessories from five years ago—but it was respectable.

'One cannot be too careful.'

*He means for himself! He is not concerned with* my *reputation, only that I might try to entrap him!*

Liberty squared her shoulders and elevated her chin. 'The drawing room, sir?' She was proud of the haughty tone she achieved.

Utterly unruffled, he strolled to a nearby door and opened it. 'This way, ma'am.' *His* tone conveyed bored amusement.

She swept through, head high. How dare he treat her as though she were of no consequence? Although, she had to admit it was humiliation that spurred her rage. Undoubtedly, to a duke's son, she *was* inconsequential. He followed her inside the elegantly furnished room with its vermilion-painted walls above white-painted wainscoting, its high ceiling with elaborately moulded cornice and three tall windows dressed with delicately sprigged floor-length curtains.

'You are suffering under a misapprehension.'

She started at the voice behind her. She halted her inspection of the room and turned to find him closer than she anticipated. Nerves fluttered deep in her belly as she got her first good look at his pale silvery-grey eyes and the utter confidence they conveyed. And why should they not? Not only was he the son of one of the most powerful Dukes in the land but he was sinfully, classically handsome with a straight nose, sharp cheekbones and a beautifully sculpted mouth above a determined chin. Those silvery eyes of his seemed to penetrate deep inside her and yet they were as opaque as a silver coin, revealing no hint of his thoughts.

She stepped back, dragging her gaze from his. His beautifully tied cravat—how Gideon would appreciate such skill in *his* valet!—sported a simple gold pin in the shape of a whip and his olive-green superfine coat hugged wide shoulders and well-muscled arms. Beneath that form-fitting coat he sported a grey-and-white-striped waistcoat that did nothing to hide the heavy muscles of his chest. Her eyes travelled further, skimming the powerful thighs encased in cream breeches. He had the look of a Corinthian...the name given to gentlemen who enjoyed and excelled at physical sports such as riding, boxing and fencing, according to Gideon.

The face of a Greek God, the body of a warrior and a duke's son. How could one man have so many advantages in life? Her gaze snapped back to his face, the sight of those powerful thighs imprinted on her brain. He was watching her. By the quirk of his lips, her perusal of his person amused him. Mortified at being caught studying him as a sculptor might study his subject, Liberty swallowed and then sucked in a deep breath. That did nothing to calm her nerves. Male and spicy, his scent filled her and those butterflies in her belly fluttered even more.

She forced a scowl to her face. This was Lord Alexander Beauchamp: the devil who was leading Gideon astray. She tilted her chin and looked down her nose at him, but the look that satisfactorily quelled the most persistent of tradesmen dunning for payment made no impression on His Lordship, judging by the arrogant lift of his eyebrows.

'Misapprehension, my lord?'

'Indeed.'

His deep cultured tones penetrated all the way inside her, stirring yet more fluttery sensations as she felt the full force of his attention.

'Allow me to introduce myself.' He bowed, the action somehow mocking. 'Avon, at your service. Miss…?'

His words jerked her from her irritation. 'What did you say? Who is Avon?'

'Alexander is my brother. My *younger* brother. I am the Marquess of Avon, hence Lord Avon.' His head tilted. 'Do you require an explanation of courtesy titles? I understand you and your brother were not raised in aristocratic circles.'

Liberty's face burned. Mrs Mount had warned

them that their background would swiftly become common knowledge in the *ton*. No doubt His Lordship also knew her grandfather was a coal merchant. Without volition, her chin rose even higher than before.

'I am not ignorant of such matters, sir. If Gideon ever has a son, he will take Gideon's next highest title, Viscount Haxby, as a courtesy title to use as his own until Gideon's death, when he will become the Earl of Wendover.'

'I am relieved you have learned something since your brother was elevated to the peerage. The fundamental etiquette of introductions appears to have passed you by, however. It is customary to introduce oneself in return.'

Infuriated that he was right, her face scorched even hotter. Lord Avon might resemble one of the marble statues she had admired at the British Museum last week, but he was as patronising and pompous as any man she had ever had the misfortune to meet.

She stiffened her spine and again looked down her nose. 'I am Miss Liberty Lovejoy.'

## *Chapter Two*

Dominic bit back the sudden urge to laugh. Liberty Lovejoy? What parent would saddle their daughter with such a name? They had no choice over surname, to be sure—he was well aware Lovejoy was the family name of the Earls of Wendover—but what was wrong with naming their daughter Jane or Mary? Liberty Lovejoy—she sounded like some kind of actress. Or worse.

Still...he controlled his amusement and bowed. 'And to what do we owe the pleasure of your visit, Miss Lovejoy?'

He found himself scrutinised by a pair of intelligent, almond-shaped eyes. They were extraordinary and he found himself being drawn into their depths. They were the dark blue of the summer sky at midnight, with golden flecks in the irises and fringed with thick golden-brown lashes. Tawny brows drew together in a frown and her lips, soft pink and lush, compressed. He waited for her reply, controlling his visceral reaction to Miss Liberty Lovejoy. He was well practised in that art—his position as heir to a wealthy dukedom as well as his honour as a gentleman meant he simply did not indulge in idle flirtations.

'Your brother is tempting *my* brother into entirely inappropriate and wild behaviour and I came here to dem—*beg* your father to stop your brother from leading Gideon astray.'

Her velvety eyes glowed with fervour and he didn't doubt her genuine concern. His heart sank at the news that Alex might be falling back into his old, wild ways. He had already heard tales circulating about the newly ennobled Lord Wendover and his readiness to sample every entertainment available to a young, wealthy man about town, but Alex's name hadn't arisen in connection with them. The last he had heard, Alex was living at Foxbourne Manor in Berkshire and making a success of his horse breeding and training establishment—gaining a reputation for providing high-quality riding and carriage horses.

'Please be seated, Miss Lovejoy.' Dominic indicated a chair by the fireplace.

With a swish of her skirts, she settled on the sofa. Mentally, he shrugged. He would allow her that small victory. He studied his visitor as he strolled across to sit by her side—his scrutiny, his pace and his choice of seat specifically intended to ruffle her feathers. A man had to have some fun, after all.

Her gown looked new, but was outmoded by a few years, with its high neck and ruff of triple lace, and he couldn't help but notice how beautifully it clung to her curves. His pulse kicked, but Dominic controlled his surge of desire for this voluptuous woman. He prided himself on his self-control. In every area of his life. He sat, half-facing her, noting the crease of a frown between her tawny eyebrows and the tension in the lines around her mouth.

'I trust you have no objection to my sitting next to you?'

He allowed one corner of his mouth to quirk up and was rewarded by Liberty's subtle but unmistakable shift along the sofa, increasing the distance between them. The faint scent of roses drifted into his awareness—the scent of his late mother, remembered from his childhood—and all thought of teasing Miss Liberty Lovejoy vanished, swamped by a swirl of memories.

His mother had been on his mind more and more lately—ever since he had decided that this was the Season he would choose a wife. It was time to marry. Time to produce an heir. Time to fulfil the vow he had made all those years ago after his mother had died. He straightened, rolling his shoulders back. The sooner he addressed

Miss Lovejoy's concerns, the sooner he could get on with compiling a list of candidates suitable for his bride.

'Tell me why you believe Alexander to be in any way responsible for your own brother's behaviour,' he said. 'Is he not his own man?'

She drew in a sharp breath but, before she could reply, William appeared in the open doorway.

'Miss Hope Lovejoy, milord,' he said.

Dominic stood. A young lady bearing a familial resemblance to Liberty Lovejoy entered the room, her cheeks blooming a becoming shade of pink. Out of habit, Dominic registered her appearance with one sweeping glance. Pretty. Golden-haired. Delicate features. Taller than her sister, with a trim figure, enhanced by the latest fashions. He couldn't resist glancing once again at Liberty and making comparisons. No. He wasn't mistaken. It would appear Liberty was a woman prepared to make personal sacrifices to ensure her younger sibling enjoyed every advantage. Was it that same trait that had driven her to come here and confront his father? That took some courage. His opinion of Liberty Lovejoy rose. Just a notch.

He bowed to Hope and directed his most charming smile at her, fully aware it would further vex the still-smouldering Liberty. 'I am pleased to make your acquaintance, Miss Lovejoy.'

Hope would prove popular with the gentlemen of the *ton*, he had no doubt. And she was fully aware of the effect of her beauty upon members of the opposite sex, he realised, as she rewarded him with a coquettish smile and a swift, apprais-ing glance through her long lashes. A poorly sti-fled *hmmph* from Liberty reached Dominic's ears, stirring another urge to laugh which he manfully resisted.

'I am Avon. Please be seated.' He gestured to the place on the sofa he had recently vacated. 'Your sister and I were about to discuss the reason for this visit. Ah, Betty, Thomas, thank you.' A maid had come in with a dish of macaroons, fol-lowed by another footman carrying a tray bearing a bottle of Madeira and three glasses. 'Please be good enough to pour the wine, Thomas. Betty—will you sit by the window once you have served our visitors? You may remain until our visitors leave. Thank you.'

Liberty glowered at him, clearly irritated by the implication that her motives for this visit might differ from her stated reason. But, from a young age, Dominic had known his duty was to choose a suitable, well-brought-up lady as his future Duchess and it was now second nature to avoid any risk of getting trapped into an unsuitable alliance through carelessness.

Hope had now settled next to Liberty on the sofa and so Dominic moved to stand by the fireplace while he waited for the wine to be served.

'So. To continue with the reason for your visit, Miss Lovejoy—you lay the blame for your brother's wayward behaviour at the door of *my* brother?'

She raised her gaze from the contemplation of her glass. 'Yes.' She bit delicately into a macaroon.

Dominic frowned at her brusque reply.

'Why?' Two could play at that game.

The pink tip of her tongue as it rescued stray crumbs from her lips did strange things to Dominic's pulse rate. Irritated, he willed his body under control. Simple lust—not difficult for a man like him to resist. Yet he could not tear his gaze from her mouth as she chewed in a leisurely fashion, her fine tawny brows drawn together in a frown of concentration.

'Gideon has never been on the town before,' she said eventually. 'He is a…a…greenhead, I think is the word. He is being led astray by your brother, who appears intent on introducing him to every vice known to man.'

*I sincerely hope not.* Reading the earnestness of Liberty's expression, Dominic doubted she had the first idea of the full extent of the vices available in London to eager young bucks with money to burn. But he trusted Alex not to return to his past reckless behaviour. Didn't he? He made a mental note to check up on his brother's activities. If he felt Alex was in danger of sliding back into his old, wild ways, he would nip that in the bud before their father and stepmother came up to town.

'I am sure Alex is simply helping your brother to find his feet in town,' he said. 'I fail to understand why you feel he needs your protection. What would he say if he knew you had come here to speak to my father?'

Liberty's cheeks bloomed red. 'He would object, of course.'

She was honest, at least. His opinion lifted another degree.

'Then you will do well to allow him to determine his own path. No man would take kindly to his sister trying to control him. I presume you are older than him?'

'We are twins but, yes, I am the elder.'

'Twins? No wonder he objects to your interference. Heed my advice, Miss Lovejoy, and allow your brother to be his own man.'

Her lips parted as she inhaled. Her breasts rose, drawing Dominic's gaze like a lodestone. His pulse quickened and his cravat suddenly felt too tight. The room too warm. He swallowed down his reaction even as he acknowledged that Liberty Lovejoy's natural, curvaceous femininity was more attractive to him than any of the painstakingly elegant ladies of the *ton*. He could never act upon such attraction, however—as the sister of an earl and a lady, she was off limits other than for marriage. And she was definitely not marriageable material. Not for him.

He had sworn at his mother's death, when he was eight years old, that he would do his duty and make her proud of him.

*Never forget, Avon—you will be the Duke one day. You must never bring your heritage into disrepute. Make me proud, my Son.*

He'd spent his life striving to fulfil her expectations. He had never felt good enough for her while she was alive—other than that one hint of affection he had glimpsed from her, on the day she died—but now, this Season, he would finally prove to her that he was worthy. Besides, it was what was expected of a man in his position, and he owed his father that much, too. His bride must be perfect in every way: bloodlines, upbringing, behaviour.

And Liberty Lovejoy fitted none of those requirements. Not one.

Unsettled and irritated by his visceral reaction to this woman Dominic lowered his gaze to where her hands were gripped together in her lap, her kid gloves stretched taut over her knuckles. He choked back his exasperation. It was not Liberty's fault he found her so…enticing. Her distress at her brother's behaviour was tangible and the urge to comfort her took him by surprise. He softened his tone.

'What your brother is doing is not so very unusual, Miss Lovejoy. Most young men on the town for the first time behave somewhat recklessly. But they soon settle down and I am convinced your brother will, too.'

'But I must stop him before he squanders his entire inheritance.'

'Are his debts so very ruinous?' He would have thought Wendover's estates were wealthy enough, even after the disaster of last year's harvest.

Liberty's lips pursed.

'*I* am certain you are right, my lord.' Hope smiled at Dominic and fluttered her lashes. 'As you might guess, my sister does have an unfortunate tendency to imagine the worst. We do not know the scale of his debts as Gideon, *quite rightly*—' she cast a quelling look at her sister '—refuses to discuss—'

'He is out until all hours and sometimes he does not come home at all.'

The words burst from Miss Lovejoy as she swept her hand through her hair, scattering hairpins and leaving bits of hair the hue of dark honey sticking out sideways from her scalp. Two locks unwound to drape unnoticed over her shoulder.

'And when he does, he is so…so distant. So *secretive.*' Her voice rang with despair. 'We have always shared everything, but he will not confide in me…the tradesmen haven't been paid…there is a stack of bills awaiting his attention, yet when I begged him to pay them, all he would say is that he must pay his gambling debts first as a matter of honour. He lost two hundred pounds at hazard last night. Two *hundred*!'

Her horror at such a loss was clear, but her words convinced Dominic that she was worrying over nothing. Her lack of understanding of the ways of the aristocracy was hardly surprising when she had not been raised in such circles.

'That does not sound so very bad to me.'

'Not so very bad? *Two hundred pounds?*'

He'd intended to reassure her. Instead she was looking at him as though he'd suddenly sprouted a second head.

'Well, no. The Earldom of Wendover is a wealthy one with properties in Buckinghamshire and Suffolk, if I remember rightly. It can stand a few losses at the gaming tables. I am convinced you are worrying over nothing, Miss Lovejoy. You will see. Your brother will eventually settle down.'

'But…the tradesmen. Gideon flatly refuses to pay them. He says they can wait. He never used to be so…so careless of other people, but whenever I remonstrate with him, all he will say is that is how everyone in society carries on.'

Dominic shrugged. 'Many do.'

He did not do that himself. Neither did his father. But he could not deny that many gentlemen considered tradesmen to be at the bottom of the list of debtors to be paid.

'It is your brother's prerogative to pay the tradesmen who supply your household as and when he chooses, just as it is the tradesmen's prerogative to cease supplying such late-paying customers if they choose. In my experience, most tradesmen elect to continue enjoying the patronage of their aristocratic clients for the prestige it brings them.'

'That is *appalling*.'

He agreed. It was one of the many habits of the higher echelons of society that he disliked, but he would not admit as much to Miss Liberty Lovejoy as she sat on his father's sofa passing judgement. She seemed determined to believe the worst of his world, including blaming *his* brother for *her* brother's misbehaviour.

'Can you not ask your brother to stop encouraging Gideon? *Please*, my lord.'

Dominic passed one hand around the back of

his head, massaging the tight muscles at the top of his neck. 'Even if I were inclined to speak to him on this, I can assure you Alex would likely do the exact opposite of what I asked of him.'

And, now he came to think of it, that was no doubt the exact reason Gideon was behaving as Miss Lovejoy had described.

'Perhaps if you trusted your brother to make his own decisions instead of—how did you put it?—*remonstrating* with him, he would mend his ways that much sooner.'

Liberty surged to her feet.

'So it is *my* fault, is it, Lord Avon?'

Dominic didn't answer, distracted by her curvaceous figure as she paced the room, her skirts swishing. She really was magnificent.

'*If* you would do me the courtesy of replying to my point?'

Her voice dripped sarcasm. Furious with himself for ogling her in such an ill-bred manner, Dominic blanked his expression and calmly met her glare. If looks could kill, or even maim, then he would be prostrate on the floor even now. The impulse to prod her further was irresistible. He raised one brow in deliberate provocation.

'You may have noticed, my dear Miss Lovejoy, that calmness, elegance and poise are three of the qualities most desired in the young ladies of our world. There is a very good reason for that and I would advise you to nurture such traits in your own behaviour.'

Her eyes narrowed. 'What do you mean?'

'Only that too much vigour and…er…*passion* are not the done thing, you know.'

He smiled kindly at her as she continued to look daggers at him.

'You, sir, are no gentleman.'

'I am merely trying to give you a hint as to how to go on in society, Miss Lovejoy.' He folded his arms across his chest, enjoying her chagrin. 'And, might I add, sarcasm does not become you. Am I correct in assuming that you and your sister will be making your debuts this coming Season?'

Liberty turned to her sister. 'Come, Hope. We are wasting our time expecting any assistance from His Lordship.' She glared again at Dominic. 'I shall write to your father, as you suggested, sir, in the hope that he possesses the conscience you so clearly lack.'

Hectic pink flushed Hope Lovejoy's cheeks as she shot a furious look at her sister. She stood and smoothed out her skirts, then dipped a curtsy as she smiled apologetically.

'Do please excuse us for invading your home, Lord Avon,' she said. 'Good afternoon.'

Dominic bowed. 'No apology is necessary. Good afternoon, Miss Hope Lovejoy.'

He then glanced at Liberty and guilt thumped

him hard in the chest at the despair that dulled those extraordinary eyes. He stifled a sigh.

'I shall have a word with Alex and make sure he and Wendover are not getting in too deep, Miss Liberty Lovejoy—' and her name still made him want to smile '—but other than that there is little I can do. Alex will not take kindly to any attempt by me to tell him how to behave.'

Gratitude suffused her features.

'But I am still convinced you are worrying over nothing,' he added.

'I thank you nevertheless, my lord.'

Liberty's face lit with a more-generous smile than his offer warranted and, before he could stop himself, he found himself responding. He blanked his expression again and crossed to the bell pull. Liberty Lovejoy provoked strange emotions in him—emotions he did not care to examine too closely—but he was reassured by the knowledge their paths would rarely cross. Wendover, as a peer—even a hellraising peer—would find acceptance everywhere, but his sisters, raised in obscurity and with a grandfather in trade, would likely only frequent the fringes of society.

William, thankfully, answered his summons promptly.

'Please see the ladies out, William.'

He bowed again, avoiding eye contact with either of his visitors, then stood stock still after they had gone, staring unseeingly at the closed door, wondering how one voluptuous, sweet-smelling woman had stirred such unaccustomed feelings within him. He had always kept his emotions under strict control, as behoved his father's heir. Alex and their younger sister, Olivia—before she had wed four years ago—had always been the lively, mischievous ones of the family, but Dominic had grown up with the weight of expectation on his shoulders. It was his duty to make his father proud, to uphold the family name and to always behave as befitted a future duke.

Also, strangely, he felt compelled to protect his father—a nonsensical-seeming notion when one considered how powerful Father was. But Dominic recalled his mother's death all too clearly, and how Father had suffered from guilt. Dominic had seen and heard things no eight-year-old boy should ever see and hear and, by shouldering the responsibility of being the perfect son and the perfect heir, he had vowed to shield his father from further distress.

He shook his head, as though he might dislodge those memories and the thoughts they evoked, clicking his tongue in irritation. He swung round to face the room. Betty hovered not five feet from him, having been unable to get past him to the door as he stood there like a mindless idiot, blocking her exit.

He frowned and moved aside, motioning for the maid to leave, his promise to Miss Lovejoy—it *had* been a promise, had it not?—nipping at him. He would speak to Alex.

'Betty?'

'Yes, milord?'

'Is Lord Alexander currently in residence?'

Dominic did not live at Beauchamp House, preferring the privacy of his own town house when staying in London. He had travelled up to town yesterday from Cheriton Abbey and had merely called at Beauchamp House to warn the staff that his father's butler, Grantham, would be arriving shortly to prepare the house for the arrival of the Duke and Duchess and to find out what day his sister, Olivia, and his brother-in-law, Hugo, were due to arrive in London.

'No, milord.'

'Ask downstairs if anyone knows where he is staying in London, will you please?'

Betty nodded and then scurried past him out of the room.

# *Chapter Three*

That glimpse of kindness in Lord Avon just before they left almost changed Liberty's impression of His Lordship. Almost, but not quite. That one final concession was simply not enough to wipe out the many black marks against him, and Liberty, crotchety and restless after that interview, was in no mood to forgive. She clambered into the carriage behind Hope and sat down before knocking on the roof with her umbrella as a signal to Bilk to drive on. As soon as the carriage was in motion, Hope swivelled on the bench to face Liberty.

'I was never more embarrassed,' she said. 'Do you *never* stop to think of the consequences of your actions on me and Verity? Lord Avon is the most eligible bachelor in the *ton* and Mrs Mount had grand hopes that one of us might catch his eye. She told me the family estates in Devonshire are *vast*, but now you have ruined our chances because you will *never* listen to *anybody*. You always think you know best. Oh! To think! I might have been a duchess.'

'A marchioness, Hope. Lord Avon's father is very much alive and well. And do please stop dramatising everything. That man would never seriously consider either you or Verity as suitable…he was utterly contemptuous about us not being raised with the expectations of moving in high society.'

'But we have our looks on our side. Why, Lord Redbridge called me an Incomparable the other day! And, oh, Liberty! Isn't Lord Avon the most handsome, well-set figure of a man you have ever seen?'

'Hmmph. A person might think that, if she cared for the Corinthian type, but he is also arrogant, haughty, conceited—'

Words failed her but, next to her, Hope unexpectedly giggled.

'He *has* made you cross, hasn't he, Liberty? Do you not realise all those words have the same meaning?'

Liberty pursed her lips. 'Unfeeling. Rude. Superior—'

'Superior means the same again,' crowed Hope.

'Well, we can't all have a way with words like you, Hope.'

Now Hope was relieved of the necessity to earn a little money by teaching in the local school, she either had her head buried in a novel, or was madly scribbling poetry and plays, while Verity was rarely seen without a sketchbook in her hands.

They were happy to leave the practicalities of running the family to Liberty—a responsibility she had taken on after their parents died, having promised her dying mother that she would look after the family and keep them safe.

'Well, it matters not what your opinion of His Lordship may be, Libby, for I am very certain he would not consider *you* as marriageable after the way you spoke to him.'

'I said no more than the situation warranted.' Liberty turned aside and stared pointedly through the window as she continued her diatribe against Lord Avon inside her head.

*How dare he look down on us? Just because we weren't raised in the lap of luxury it does not mean we are worth less as people.*

She glanced down at her gown. Admittedly, it was not today's fashion, but it had hardly been worn, and surely it was wasteful not to make use of the gowns made for her five years ago.

*At least His Precious Lordship can't fault Hope—her gown is the very latest fashion!*

The carriage pulled up outside the Green Street

town house they currently called home. Lord Avon might have tried to divert her by claiming the Wendover estates could stand such losses as two hundred pounds a night—even thinking of such a loss made Liberty feel quite faint—but Gideon's inheritance did not even include a house in London and his country house needed complete rebuilding, which would cost a fortune, so she was right to worry about money. Someone had to. She'd wager Lord Avon had never had to worry about money, with a father who was a wealthy duke. They were clearly so vastly rich and so elevated on the social scale that ordinary people's fears simply did not register with them.

Hope jumped from the carriage and scurried to the door, leaving Liberty to follow. As she shrugged out of her pelisse and handed it to Ethel, their housemaid, Hope's tones of outrage floated down the stairs.

'And, *would you believe*, she dragged me to the house of none other than the Duke of Cheriton to confront him about his son's behaviour.'

Liberty sighed.

'Thank you, Ethel. Has Miss Hope ordered a tea tray?'

'Yes, miss.'

Liberty trod up the stairs, reluctance to face her sisters and Mrs Mount slowing her steps. Of course they would all three disapprove of what she had done, but what choice did she have?

She had kept to her word to Mama, working hard to help keep their small family estate solvent. Gideon—who had inherited the estate from Papa—had left university and thrown himself into the life of a country squire and farmer. He'd never complained. She'd thought he was content enough.

Gideon and she…they had been a true partnership through those hard years. But then, last year, summer had never materialised and harvests had failed the length and breadth of the country, leaving many in hardship and the poorest starving. Gideon had become morose and withdrawn, worrying about the survival of their family home. And then had come the most unexpected news of all. Lord Wendover and his entire family—distant family members they had never even met, so obscure was the connection—had perished, leaving Gideon as the nearest male relation and thus the new Earl of Wendover.

Gideon had changed. It had been as though he had been incarcerated in a prison, and freedom had taken him and turned him from a hard-working, considerate brother into…a stranger. That familiar hollow ache filled Liberty's chest and she rubbed at it absentmindedly, tears burning behind her eyes. Her beloved brother. The other half of her. Her twin. They'd always shared a close bond but now…she feared he was lost to her for good.

*What does Lord Avon know? Supercilious, over-privileged, condescending...* He seemed to think this behaviour was normal. Well, Liberty knew Gideon as well as she knew herself and this was as far from normal for him as it was possible to be. It *had* to be the influence of Avon's wicked brother.

Head high, she walked into the drawing room and a deathly silence. Before she had taken a seat by the fire, however, all three occupants spoke at once.

Hope, accusing. 'I told them what you did.'

Mrs Mount, regretful. 'My dear—how could you possibly think that a wise course? If only you had sought my advice. You know how important it is for you all to get vouchers for Almack's—this sort of transgression will do nothing to help your cause.'

Verity, condemning. 'Isn't that just like you, Liberty—charging in without a thought as to how your actions will reflect upon the rest of us?'

Liberty sat down and arranged her skirts, then folded her hands in her lap.

'If you have all *quite* finished—I did what I thought needed to be done and I shall not apologise for it.'

She sensed the others exchanging glances, but

she kept her attention on the flickering flames and concentrated on keeping any tell-tale tears at bay as she hoped Lord Avon would not spread the story of her visit far and wide. She had taken a risk, but she was growing desperate and she felt so alone. Where else could she turn for help? Even Godmama was gone now, having passed away last year. The alternative was to ignore Gideon's ever-wilder behaviour and simply pray he would come to his senses. Well, that approach might have been Mama and Papa's solution were they still alive—they had always put their total faith in God and the Bible—but Liberty had long ago stopped trusting in Divine intervention. Where had God been when first Bernard, then Papa, then Mama had all succumbed to the cholera, even though Liberty had spent the entire journey home from London in desperate prayer? Nowhere, that was where.

No. It had been worth the risk to visit the Duke, even though only his arrogant son had been in residence. Lord Avon had given his word to speak to Alexander, although his warning that his brother would be unlikely to pay any heed rang in her ears, reviving her feeling of utter hopelessness.

Ethel brought in the tea tray and Verity poured the cups and handed them round. Liberty accepted hers and sipped, relishing the slide of the hot tea as it soothed her paper-dry throat.

'What did the Duke say?' Mrs Mount's tentative enquiry broke into Liberty's circling thoughts.

'Ah.' Liberty placed her half-drunk cup carefully in its saucer. 'He is not in residence. We did, however, speak to his son, Lord Avon. Lord Alexander's older brother. Do you know him?'

'Yes, of course, although not as well as his father. He and I are of an age, you know—such a tragedy, his first wife dying like that...but there! That's all in the past now. Avon, now...he is a very different man to his brother—very serious and correct. And he is the most eligible bachelor in the *ton*.' Her reproving look scoured Liberty. 'I did harbour hopes he might develop a *tendre* for one of your sisters, but that is now a lost cause. Avon's behaviour is very proper. Beyond reproach. I dare say he was shocked at a young lady having the temerity to call upon him without prior introduction and unchaperoned to boot.'

Liberty shrugged. 'Firstly, I was not unchaperoned. Hope was there and there was a maid in the room, too. And secondly, I should not care to even hazard a guess as to His Lordship's thoughts.'

She recalled the slide of his gaze over her figure—for a split second she had seen desire flare, before he masked his expression. The thought sent a quiver of heat chasing across her skin.

'Hope,' said Mrs Mount reprovingly, 'is not an adequate chaperon for you, nor you for her. And so the visit was a waste of time and a risk not worth taking?'

'Not entirely. He did offer to speak to his brother, but he did not give us much hope that Lord Alexander will pay him any heed.'

'Is the Duke coming to town? If anyone can control Lord Alexander, it will be him.'

'Lord Avon did not say. Maybe…should I speak to Lord Alexander myself?'

'Nooo!' three voices chorused.

Mrs Mount shushed Liberty's sisters with a wave of her hand before fixing Liberty with a stern look. 'You have done what you can, my dear. I really think you must allow Gideon to come to his senses in his own time. And he will. I am sure of it. In the meantime, we should concentrate on the upcoming Season and finding you three girls suitable husbands. Once you are married off and have families of your own, you will have more important matters to occupy your thoughts.' Her grey eyes raked Liberty. 'Are you *certain* I cannot persuade you to have a new gown or two made, my dear? That one does look sadly outmoded.'

'Mrs Mount is right, Liberty,' said Hope. 'Verity and I have had so much and you've barely spent a penny on yourself. You deserve something nice. Surely you can bring yourself to order one gown?'

Liberty recognised Hope's peace offering—their family squabbles never lasted long, thank goodness. She recalled Lord Avon's initial perusal of her. Despite Gideon's assurance that he could *'stand the blunt'*, as he put it, Liberty had been unable to bring herself to squander even more money on herself. Now, however, she found herself eager to prove to His High-and-Mighty Lordship that the Lovejoys could be respectable.

'Very well. One evening gown,' she conceded. 'But not to catch a husband. I have told you. I shall never marry. Bernard was my one and only love and I shall remain true to his memory.'

The words were automatically spoken. When Bernard died, she had sworn never to look at another man, never to contemplate marriage. But over the past year she had come to accept the truth. She was lonely. Even with her entire family around her, she was lonely.

That hollow, aching feeling invaded her again and she rubbed absently at her upper chest.

But she was still afraid to admit her change of heart out loud…afraid to fully acknowledge that she dreamed of finding someone to love who would love her in return…afraid that no man could ever take Bernard's place. It was safer to keep that daydream locked inside. That way she would not have to face anyone's pity if she failed to meet such a man. That way, she could keep her pride.

'Still hiding behind the sainted Bernard, Sis? Isn't it time you looked to the future instead of forever harking back to the past?'

That careless drawl shot Liberty to her feet. 'Gideon!' She rushed to him and grabbed his upper arms, scanning him quickly: his drawn, pale features; the dark shadows beneath his eyes; the dishevelled evening clothes. The lingering smell of alcohol and…she wrinkled her nose… cheap perfume and—there was no other word for it—*bodies*. Activities she did not wish to think of. She released her brother and stepped back.

'You have been out all night.'

He quirked a brow and a faint smile lifted the corners of his mouth. 'I have indeed.'

'You need a bath.'

His eyes narrowed. 'So I do. And I have sent word for water to be heated. Not that it is polite for you to mention such a matter.'

'But—'

'But nothing, Liberty. You are not my keeper.' He moved past her. 'Good afternoon, Mrs Mount. Hope. Verity. I trust you are all well?'

All three returned his smile and his greeting

but, before he left, Hope—after a sympathetic smile at Liberty—said, 'We do miss you when you stay out so very much, Gideon. Will you dine with us tonight? We have no invitations.'

In truth, invitations for the Lovejoy ladies to attend evening events were still a rarity. Mrs Mount had reassured the girls that the Season had barely begun and that once Easter was over many more families would come to town and the invitations would, hopefully, start to arrive. Currently only one invitation adorned their mantelpiece—to a rout at the home of Sir Gerald and Lady Trent, Sir Gerald being a cousin of Mrs Mount.

'Can't. Sorry.' Gideon turned to the door. 'A bath and a couple of hours' shut-eye, then I'm off to the theatre.'

'We could go with you,' said Liberty. 'We could hire a box.'

His look of dismay clawed at her, leaving her feeling raw and, somehow, exposed. 'I'm not going to the theatre with my *sisters*. Good God! Where's the fun in sitting in a box when I could be down in the pit where all the fun is? Tell you what, Sis—if you're that keen on seeing Mary the Maid of the Inn, I'll reserve a box for you another night. Just tell me when you want to go. You've got Mrs M. to chaperon you and you'll soon have beaux flocking around you if it's male company you're pining for.'

With that, Gideon marched out of the room, leaving the three sisters—and Mrs Mount—looking at one another in despair.

'I still say it's just the novelty of it all that has turned his head,' said Mrs Mount in a faint voice as the sound reached them of him bounding up the stairs. '*Surely* he will come to his senses?'

Liberty did not reply. She returned to her chair and stared at the fire, her mind awash with ideas as plans spiralled to the surface and then sank again as her common sense scuppered them. Finally, realising she was getting nowhere, she went to consult Mrs Taylor about dinner that evening. It went against the grain but, somehow, she must control her penchant for taking action and trust that Lord Avon would be true to his word and do something to curb his own brother's wild ways.

# Chapter Four

The next day was dry but cold after the thunderstorm and Dominic, following a sparring session with Gentleman John Jackson in his saloon on Bond Street, strolled to White's for a glass of wine and a bite to eat. On arrival, he picked up *The Times* and appropriated a quiet table in the corner of the morning room, hoping the open newspaper would discourage anyone from joining him. He had important matters to attend to this Season, like selecting a wife—a well-bred young lady with the poise and the correct upbringing suitable for a marchioness, a society hostess and, one day, a duchess. His purpose in coming up to town in advance of the rest of the family was to make a decision about his bride-to-be and here was as good a place to plan his strategy as any.

After being served, he drank a little wine, took one bite of the cold beef and horseradish sandwich and then settled back into the chair, holding the paper but not actually reading. He'd written a list of names last night. Seven in all. He wasn't interested in a bride straight out of the schoolroom—his Marchioness would already have some town polish with, preferably, at least two Seasons behind her. The highest families were in no hurry to marry off their daughters—they took their time and selected the very best husbands, usually with a view to allying with a powerful family. A huge dowry wasn't a prerequisite for his perfect bride; he was more concerned with their breeding and background as well as their conduct. These were essential qualities for a lady who would, at some time in the future, occupy the role of Duchess of Cheriton and give birth to the Eighth Duke.

Seven names were too many…he must cut his list to three or four ladies, then he could concentrate on making his final choice, but discreetly; it would not do to raise expectations in the ladies themselves or in society in general. He was under no illusion, imagining himself so perfect that any female would swoon at his feet. It was not conceit, but realism…any one of the ladies on his list would jump at the chance of marrying into the Beauchamps, one of the most powerful families in the land.

He lay down the paper, hooked one hand around the back of his neck and rubbed, sighing. He would be happy when it was all over and he could get on with his life. In his mind's eye he saw his future stretching ahead of him, and he felt…nothing. No excitement. No anticipation.

Unbidden, Liberty Lovejoy crept into his thoughts and he dismissed her with a silent oath. Wasn't it bad enough she had invaded his dreams last night…erotic, enchanting dreams that had him waking bathed in sweat and in a state of solid arousal? A woman such as Liberty Lovejoy had no place in his future—to marry well was his duty and his destiny, as it had been Father's. Dominic was fortunate that *he* had not been obliged to wed at eighteen as Father had done, when his own father was in failing health and worrying over the future of the Dukedom. *Father* had put aside any personal inclination by doing his duty and marrying Dominic's mother, the daughter of a marquess and the granddaughter of a duke. The current Duchess—his stepmother, Rosalind—might be the daughter of a soldier and the granddaughter of a silversmith, but that did not affect the aristocratic lineage of the Dukes of Cheriton.

At least Dominic was six and twenty and had some experience of life, but sometimes—although he would never admit as much, not to anyone—the responsibility lay heavy on his shoulders. Almost without conscious thought, he withdrew the list of names from his pocket, unfolded it and read the names. If he could cross off three names, that would make—

'Mind if I join you, old chap?'

Hurriedly, Dominic folded the list and shoved it back into his pocket. He looked up into the bright blue inquisitive gaze of Lord Redbridge and inwardly cursed. Of all men, it had to be Redbridge. One of Alex's friends, he was an inveterate gossip and Dominic could only hope he hadn't deciphered any of the names on his list. He smiled and gestured to the chair next to his, then reached for his sandwich and bit into it. His leisurely luncheon was about to change into a hurried repast.

Redbridge had no qualms in admitting he had recognised at least two of the names on that sheet of paper and proceeded to not only tease Dominic about its existence, but also badger him about the other names.

'There must have been half a dozen on there at least, Avon.' His eyes were alive with curiosity. 'You can tell me, you know. Soul of discretion and all that. It'd do you good to talk about it. Alex is always sayin' you're too buttoned up for your own good.'

Dominic knocked back what remained of his wine and stood up. 'Your imagination is running amok, as usual, Redbridge. Now, if you will excuse me…?'

Redbridge didn't take the hint. He stood, too, and exited the coffee room by Dominic's side. 'Are you thinking of getting leg-shackled then? Oh, my life—the ladies will be in a flutter! There'll be neither time nor attention for the rest of us poor sods once the word gets out…it'll all be about Lord Avon and his list!'

He nudged Dominic with a sharp elbow and grinned hugely. Dominic stifled the urge to grab his neckcloth and slowly choke the wretch. Instead, he halted and turned to face his companion. They were close to the front door of the club by now and Dominic was damned if he'd put up with the man's inane chatter all the way to his front door.

'I'll bid you good afternoon here, Redbridge. And I will repeat what I have already said—your conjecture over that list is entirely wrong. My sister arrives in town today and she asked me to list any ladies I can think of who came out in the past two Seasons, as she will not have made their acquaintance. The truth is as mundane as that. And if—' he thrust his face close to Redbridge's '—I happen to hear *any* rumours to the contrary, I shall know precisely whose door to knock upon. Are we clear?'

Redbridge's mouth drooped. 'Perfectly.'

Dominic pivoted on his heel and strode for the door, anger driving him to reach home in record time. He barged through the front door of his leased town house, his temper frayed and his nerves on edge. He knew better than to believe Redbridge would keep such a juicy morsel to himself. Half the *ton* thrived on gossip and this, he knew, would be avidly passed from mouth to mouth. He would have to tread very carefully indeed not to reveal any preference for any of the many eligible ladies in town, but at least there were now two names he could cross off his list—the two Redbridge had read. Dominic would avoid those two as he would avoid a rabid dog and concentrate his efforts on the remaining five.

'Brailsford?'

'My lord?'

His man, who fulfilled the roles of valet, butler and footman in his bachelor household, appeared like magic from the kitchen stairs.

'Send word to the mews for my curricle to be ready for three-thirty. I intend to drive in the Park.'

'Will you require Ted to accompany you, sir?'

'Yes.' He would need a groom up behind if any of the five ladies were in the Park: to hold the horses if he got out to walk or to add propriety if he took one into his curricle to drive her around the Park. He felt heavy…his heart a leaden weight in his chest. But this was his duty; his destiny. And he would not allow himself to shirk it.

At three-forty, Dominic steered his matched bays into the Park and sent them along the carriageway at a smart trot. Ted perched behind him on the back of the curricle, ready to take charge of Beau and Buck if needs be. As Dominic drove, he scanned the walkers they passed and the small knots of people who had gathered to exchange the latest on-dits. The Season was not fully underway and wouldn't be until after Easter, but many families were already in town to attend to essential dress fittings and other preparations. He eased his horses back to a walk as he spied Lady Caroline Warnock in a stationery barouche, next to her mother, the Marchioness of Druffield. A couple they had been talking to had just walked away as Dominic drew his curricle alongside and raised his hat.

'Good afternoon, ladies.'

'Good afternoon, sir.'

Lady Druffield honoured him with a regal smile as her daughter bowed her head, her own smile gentle and gracious.

'Good afternoon, Lord Avon,' Caroline said. 'A pleasant afternoon for a drive, is it not?'

'Very pleasant, following yesterday's thunderstorm.'

A delicate shudder passed through Caroline. 'I do not care for the loud bangs or the lightning.'

Lady Druffield patted Caroline's hand. 'Such things are bound to play havoc with your sensibilities, my dear. As they would with any lady.'

Unbidden, yet again, an image of Liberty Lovejoy surfaced. *She* had not been undone by a mere thunderstorm. He could not imagine Lady Caroline standing under a dripping umbrella, nor dodging around a determined footman. He bit back a smile at the memory and he couldn't resist a gentle challenge.

'But there is something delightfully elemental about a good storm, is there not?'

He raised an eyebrow at Caroline, whose serene expression did not waver.

'Of course, my lord. You are so right—a good storm can be most exciting.'

Lady Druffield nodded in approval at her daughter's response, but impatience already plagued Dominic. He was so easily bored by this sort of dance with words…talking about nothing…being polite and mannerly…and females who hung upon and agreed with every word he uttered. But it was the game they all played, him included. And it was not Caroline's fault—she had been raised to be the perfect lady and that was what he wanted. Wasn't it?

'It is an age since we last met, sir,' Caroline said. 'Was it at…?'

She hesitated, her head tipped to one side, a smile hovering around her lips and her fine brows arched. Dominic complied readily with her hint… it would be unladylike for Caroline to admit she recalled their last meeting but he, as a gentleman, was expected to remember the exact place and circumstances.

'It was at Lord Silverdale's house party in February, if memory serves me correctly, my lady.'

'Ah, yes, indeed.' Caroline settled her dark brown gaze on his face.

'I am delighted to renew our acquaintance,' said Dominic.

Caroline smiled and her lashes swept low as she cast her gaze to her lap, where her hands rested in tranquil repose. 'As am I.'

He might as well begin his campaign. 'Would you care to take a turn around the Park in my curricle, Lady Caroline? With your mother's permission, of course.'

Another gracious smile. Not once had she revealed her teeth. Nor had any of those smiles reached her eyes. He wondered if she might show a little more life out of earshot of Lady Druffield. Dominic directed his most charming smile at that lady.

'But of course. It will be perfectly proper with the groom up behind, Caroline. And I can trust His Lordship to remain in the Park…he will take every care of you, I make no doubt.'

Dominic tied off the reins while Ted ran to the horses' heads, enabling Dominic to climb from the curricle and assist Lady Caroline from the barouche and into his curricle. Then he leapt aboard.

'I will deliver her back to you safe and sound, my lady.' He gave Beau and Buck the office to proceed and they set off at a trot, the vehicle dipping as Ted sprang up behind.

The first person Dominic saw was Liberty Lovejoy. From the direction of her purposeful stride he could only surmise she had been heading straight for him, presumably with the intention of interrupting him despite the fact he was already engaged in conversation. He did not slow his horses. He had nothing to tell her, in any case, because—and guilt coiled in his gut—he had been putting off his promise to speak to Alex. He hadn't forgotten it—he hadn't been *able* to forget it because, since she had erupted precipitously into his life yesterday, he had been quite unable to banish Miss Liberty Lovejoy from his mind.

Liberty's accusing gaze pierced him as the curricle drew level with her and she raised her hand, as though to stop them. Dominic tipped his hat to her, but did not slow. There was nothing to say and he did not want to say it in front of Caroline.

'That lady looked as though she wanted to speak with you,' said Caroline, looking over her shoulder at Liberty. 'I do not believe I have made her acquaintance…is she someone?'

*Someone.* Dominic held back his snort. What did that even mean? Well, he knew what it meant, but it did not stop him disliking that too widely held presumption that only 'their' sort of people were anyone.

'She is the new Earl of Wendover's sister.'

'Oh. I see.' Those three words were sufficient to convey Caroline's opinion. 'Mama warned me to be wary of his sisters. She said they are not really our sort of people. How do you know her?'

'I do not know her.' Officially, her visit to Beauchamp House had never taken place and Dominic had never met either Liberty or her sister. Their transgression of the rules would not become common knowledge through him. 'I know her identity because my brother is friendly with Wendover.'

'I see.' Caroline folded her hands on her lap. 'I wonder what she wanted to speak to you about.'

'I doubt very much she wanted to speak to me. I am certain you are mistaken.'

'Yes, of course. That must be it.'

As luck would have it, two of the other ladies whose names were on Dominic's list—Lady Amelia Carstairs and Lady Georgiana Buckleigh—were promenading that afternoon so, after delivering Caroline back to her mother, he endured two further circuits of the Park. Not one of the three put a foot wrong or spoke a word out of place. He should be thrilled. Any one of them would be the perfect wife for him. There was little to distinguish between them so far and once he had also renewed his acquaintance with Lady Sarah Patcham and Lady Sybilla Gratton, he would decide which one of them to concentrate on. Then, as soon as his father arrived in London, Dominic would make his offer.

Two days later Liberty stood to one side of the Trents' crowded salon with Mrs Mount, and plied her fan, sipping from the wine glass in her other hand. Although the weather was chilly the number of people packed into the modestly sized room for the rout party, combined with the heat from dozens of candles, made the room insufferably hot and stuffy. And the tightness of her corset wasn't helping, she silently admitted. When she had dressed for the rout in the least outmoded of her evening gowns, it had proved a touch too snug across the bosom, and so she had donned her sturdiest corset and ordered Lizzie—the maid she shared with Hope and Verity—to lace it as tightly as she possibly could in order to ease the fit of the dress. Now the disadvantage of that was becoming clear as her breathing grew shallower.

To distract herself from her increasing discomfort, she focused her attention on her sisters—so charming and pretty, their golden hair shining with health—and she watched with pleasure as young gentlemen vied with one another for their attention. They weren't bad girls, just a little thoughtless at times, and she knew her tendency to take charge made it easy for them to leave any difficult or awkward matters to her.

Gideon, of course, had declined to escort them and his valet, Rudge, had confirmed his master's intention to visit the Sans Pareil Theatre once again, causing dismay to ripple through Liberty. She feared she knew the attraction of that particular theatre, recalling how Gideon had waxed lyrical over a certain actress called Camilla Trace.

She leaned towards their chaperon.

'I am hopeful the girls will both attract offers before the Season is out, Mrs Mount.'

'Dear Hope and Verity...their popularity is unmistakable,' said Mrs Mount, 'but I must implore you not to risk a scandal with any more ill-advised visits, Liberty. I saw Lord Avon a few minutes ago and it seemed to me that, when he noticed you, he deliberately avoided this area of the room.'

'Avon is here?'

Her pulse kicked—surely just at the prospect of finding out if he had kept his promise? She'd spied him only once since her visit to Beauchamp House, in Hyde Park. She'd tried to catch his eye but, although he acknowledged her, he had driven his curricle straight past her.

'I wonder if he has spoken to his brother yet?' She craned her neck to try to see over the throng of people, but it was impossible. 'I shall go and ask—'

'No!' Mrs Mount caught hold of Liberty's hand, restraining her. 'Did you not hear what I said? Or perhaps you misunderstand the meaning of his action? He *turned away* when he saw you. You *cannot* approach him. He is the most eligible bachelor in the *ton*. Eyes follow him wherever he goes and tongues will always find stories to spread about him. Merely to approach him is unthinkable and if he were to *cut* you…oh, my dear, the tales would spread like wildfire and they would scorch your sisters' reputations in the telling. The gossip columns in the newssheets would not spare your blushes—the upstart twin of the new Earl of Wendover making an overt play for the Marquess of Avon…oh, heavens!' She plied her own fan vigorously to ruddy cheeks. 'Do you not understand? Your situation renders it even more imperative that your conduct is above reproach.'

Anger smouldered inside Liberty, heating her still further, and she felt as though she had a furnace inside her. She drank more wine and then tugged discreetly at her neckline in a vain attempt to allow some cooling air to reach her skin. Each breath she drew seemed shallower than the one before.

'But I am not interested in Lord Avon in the way you imply,' she said. 'You know I am not. I am concerned only about Gideon and I wish to know if Avon has spoken to his rascally brother yet.'

'I know, my dear.' Mrs Mount patted Liberty's hand without loosening her grip upon it. 'But you can do nothing about it until he decides to tell you. And he will *not* do so here—he will no more risk awakening speculation by singling out an unattached female than he would strip off his jacket and cavort about in his shirtsleeves. Proper conduct is everything to His Lordship, particularly this Season, if that rumour is true.'

'Rumour? What rumour?' Despite her dire need for fresh air, or a chair to sit on, or both, Liberty was distracted by this titbit.

'It is said that he has compiled a shortlist of eligible young ladies who meet the standards he has set—breeding, upbringing, ladylike conduct—and that he will make his selection before the end of the Season.'

The hushed awe of Mrs Mount's words stirred resentment inside Liberty. No wonder Avon was so top-lofty with people hanging upon his every word and treating him like some kind of god.

'A shortlist? I presume you mean for a wife. Why on earth does he need a *shortlist*?'

'Avon's bride must possess the very best blood-lines, perfect manners and be of exemplary character. Only the best will do for a man in his position and to be the mother of a future duke.'

The suppressed excitement in Mrs Mount's voice irritated Liberty even more.

'You make the poor girl sound like a glorified brood mare,' she muttered.

Really! Had people nothing more to worry about? What about all the poverty in London? Children in rags living on the street while their so-called betters lived in luxury. People like Avon were in a position to help and yet, instead of helping those worse off than him, he put his time and effort into making pathetic *lists* in order that any bride he might choose was *worthy* of him.

'So you do see why it is imperative that you do not put a foot wrong in any further contact with His Lordship, do you not, Liberty?' Mrs Mount's anxious enquiry brought Liberty's attention back to her. 'Not so much for your sake, but for Hope and for Verity.'

'You are not suggesting that His Lordship might consider—'

'It is unlikely, my dear, but…one never can tell what might happen when a pretty girl catches a gentleman's eye. Avon is expected to look much higher for his bride—at the very *least* the daughter of an earl—and she will be a young lady who has been properly prepared from childhood for her role as the wife of a peer of the realm. But your sisters, especially dear Verity, are so very pretty—one never knows what might happen. A list may always be added to.'

Mrs Mount's voice appeared to fade. Goodness, it was so hot. Liberty plied her fan with renewed vigour as she stared at her chaperon's mouth, concentrating fiercely in order to make out her words.

'And the lucky young lady of his choice will be a future duchess. It is worth keeping our hopes alive for such high stakes.'

Liberty put a hand to her forehead. The room seemed to sway and she was aware of Mrs Mount staring anxiously at her.

'Liberty? My dear? Are you quite well? Oh, dear.' Mrs Mount clutched at Liberty's arm. 'Are you sickening for something? Do you need to leave? Only, it would be such a shame…'

Liberty gritted her teeth in a desperate attempt to remain upright. She thrust her empty wine glass at Mrs Mount. 'I am not sickening for anything. I need air. Watch the girls, will you, Mrs Mount?' Desperate now to get out of the room, she headed in the direction of the door, weaving in and out of the chattering groups of strangers, until her way was blocked by a tall figure with a pair of wide shoulders in a dark blue swallowtail coat. To either side of those shoulders were people, pressed closely, clearly hanging on every word uttered by the gentleman. Liberty screwed her eyes shut, wafted her fan over her heated skin, sucked desperately at the stale air, then opened her eyes and prepared to negotiate her way around the group, for it was obvious she could not barge through the middle of them. She shuffled sideways until she spied a gap. Perspiration now dampened her forehead and she could feel it gather on her chest and trickle into the valley between her breasts. She frowned, concentrating on placing one foot in front of the other as she edged through that gap. She was close to the door now—she could see it above people's heads—and she blindly aimed for it, desperate now to get away from this crush of people.

'Well! Of all the—'

'I say! That was my foot!'

'I'm sorry.' The words came on a gasp. 'I cannot—' Horror filled her as her knees buckled.

A strong arm encircled her waist from behind. A deep voice barked, 'Stand aside. She's swooned.'

She desperately wanted to deny it—she had never swooned in her life—but all she could manage was to turn into that embrace, her head tipping forward until her forehead rested against a solid chest. She breathed in a clean smell of soap and starch, mixed with a pleasing masculine scent.

Then she knew no more.

## *Chapter Five*

Dominic stared in disbelief at the swooning woman in his arms, her head tipped into his chest. How in hell had this happened? He tightened his hold around her as she sagged. There was no other word for it—her head lolled back on her neck and he was certain her legs were no longer supporting her. He tightened his arms again, instinctively taking note of her womanly curves and her soft flesh.

He peered down into her face and recognition speared him. Miss Liberty Lovejoy. Her eyes were closed, her golden lashes a feathery fan against her creamy skin; her cheeks were flushed pink; her lips…plump and rosy…parted to reveal small, white, even teeth. And the urge to press his mouth to hers took him completely by surprise.

He tore his gaze away and scanned the faces

that surrounded the two of them, noting the various expressions.

Eager—they were the gossips! Disgruntled—the young ladies who aspired to his hand. Envious—the rakes and…well, more or less every male within touching distance, damn them. As if he would relinquish her to *their* tender mercies. Speculative—he would soon put a stop to *that*! And concerned…

He focused on the nearest of those faces. Lady Jane Colebrooke, whom Dominic had known since childhood. Jane's family were neighbours of the Beauchamps in Devonshire—she was a kind girl with not a spiteful bone in her body.

'Lady Jane, would you come with me, please? I shall need your assistance.'

He bent down and slid one arm behind Miss Lovejoy's knees and hefted her up into his arms, cradling her like a baby. He felt something inside his chest shift as her rose scent curled through his senses and his exasperation melted away. However much she had defied the conventions when she had called on him, he knew it was from love for her brother. His own family were large and loving and he could not condemn a woman who put her family first.

'Yes, of course, my lord.' Jane bent to scoop Liberty's reticule and fan from the floor.

Dominic headed for the door, slicing through

the crowd which parted before him—like the Red Sea before Moses, he thought sardonically. Through the door and out on to the landing—the fingers of his left hand curving possessively around the soft warmth of her thigh. Jane kept pace with him and thankfully refrained from bombarding him with inane comments or pointless conjectures. Then the pitter-patter of footsteps behind them prompted a glance over his shoulder.

*Just perfect!*

Not the lady—presumably the Lovejoy girls' chaperon—he had seen Liberty with earlier, nor either of her sisters. Any one of those would be welcome at this moment. No, they were being pursued by two determined-looking young ladies, both of whom happened to be in Dominic's final five. He had little doubt that their reasons for following him had everything to do with currying his favour and absolutely nothing to do with a desire to help a stricken fellow guest. In fact, he had overheard Lady Amelia being particularly scathing about 'those common Lovejoy girls' earlier that evening.

*At least with them here as well as Jane, I cannot be accused of compromising anyone.*

A servant directed them to a small parlour.

'Send a maid to assist, if you please,' said

Dominic, 'and tell her to bring a glass of water and smelling salts.'

He gently deposited Liberty on a sofa and Jane snatched an embroidered cushion from a nearby chair to tuck under her head while the other two hung back and stared, doing absolutely nothing to help.

'Lady Sarah!'

The Earl's daughter started. 'Y-yes, my lord?'

'If you have come to assist us, be so good as to fan Miss Lovejoy's face. She appears to have been overcome by the heat.'

Lady Sarah moved forward, but thrust her fan into Jane's hand. With a wry flick of her eyebrows at Dominic, Jane wafted the fan, the breeze lifting the curls on Liberty's forehead. Her colour was already less hectic, but Dominic's hand still twitched with the urge to touch her forehead and check her temperature. He curled his fingers into his palm and stepped back, yet he could not tear his gaze from her luscious figure. The fabric of her gown—the colour of spring leaves—moulded softly to every curve and hollow, revealing far more than it should: her rounded thighs; the soft swell of her belly; the narrow waist above generous hips; and above that…good Lord…those gorgeous, bountiful breasts…

Dominic quickly shifted his gaze to Liberty's

face, uncomfortably aware of both Lady Sarah and Lady Amelia watching him closely.

Liberty's lashes fluttered and her lids slowly lifted to reveal two dazed eyes that gazed in confusion into his before flying open in horror. She struggled to sit and Dominic instinctively pressed her back down. Her skin was like warm silk, smooth and baby soft and he longed to caress…to explore…to taste… The hairs on his arms stirred as his nerve endings tingled and saliva flooded his mouth. Good God…how he wanted to—he buried that thought before it could surface.

'Lie still!'

She collapsed back at his barked command, eyes wide, and he snatched his hands away.

'Who should I request to attend to you, Miss Lovejoy?'

'Mrs Mount.' Their eyes met and his heart thudded in his chest as his throat constricted. 'She is our chaperon. Thank you.'

She half-raised her hand and he began to reach for it before recalling their surroundings. Their witnesses.

'My Lord Avon, you may safely leave Miss Lovejoy in our care.' Lady Amelia inserted herself gracefully between Dominic and the sofa. 'This is no place for a gentleman.'

*Our* care?

He controlled his snort of derision—he'd seen

precious little care from either Amelia or Sarah—but he knew she was right. This was no place for him and Liberty *would* be safe in Jane's hands, he knew. Jane, still gently fanning, caught his eye and again flicked her brows at him, clearly sharing his cynical reaction.

'I have hartshorn here.' Lady Sarah, on his other side, reached into her reticule.

'Good. Good,' he said, retreating. 'Make sure she remains lying down. I shall send a footman to alert Mrs Mount. Jane, is there anything else you need?'

Both Amelia and Sarah shot resentful glances at Jane. Mentally, he scratched their names from his list although he would still pay them some attention, if only to divert the gossips from identifying the three names that remained.

'No, thank you,' said Jane. 'I am sure Miss Lovejoy will soon recover.'

Dominic strode for the door, every step between himself and all that temptation lifting a weight from his shoulders. He had purposely avoided her tonight. He had seen her across the room with a spare-framed woman in her mid-forties and he'd taken care to keep his distance—partly for propriety's sake, when they had not, officially, been introduced, and partly through guilt because he still had not fulfilled his promise to speak to Alex. And the reason for that, he knew, was because his innate cautiousness was screaming at him to keep his distance from Liberty Lovejoy. But, try as he might, he had been unable to entirely banish her from his thoughts and he knew he must remedy his failure as soon as possible.

For the first time he wondered if she had seen him, too, and had purposely swooned to force him to catch her. He cast a look over his shoulder. Eyes like midnight-blue velvet followed his progress from the room. No. He did not believe her swoon was faked—she hadn't even glanced his way as she stumbled blindly through the group that surrounded him and, if he was absolutely honest with himself, there had been half-a-dozen fellows closer to her than him, any one of whom could have caught her when she swooned.

Except… His jaw clenched as he reviewed his actions. He might not have consciously recognised her but, by the time she collapsed, his feet had already moved him to her side, putting *him* in the perfect position to catch her.

He paused outside the room, still thinking. His head began to throb. *Good grief…*he rubbed his temples. He hadn't even known she existed three days ago, but she'd been on his mind ever since and now here he was—the instant he saw her again—playing the hero like an eager young pup in the throes of first love. He scowled as he scanned the landing. All his life he had avoided any behaviour that might give rise to gossip or speculation. He had always been far too conscious of his position as his father's heir and the expectations he placed on himself.

He beckoned to the same footman he had spoken to before.

'Please find Mrs Mount and ask her to attend Miss Lovejoy in the parlour at her earliest convenience.'

He was damned if he'd take the message himself—the more distance he kept between himself and the Lovejoys the better.

*The sooner I make good my promise and speak to Alex about her dratted brother, the better.*

His enquiry as to Alex's whereabouts had elicited not only the information that his younger brother had taken a set of rooms at Albany, St James's, but also that he often frequented the Sans Pareil Theatre, on the Strand, in the company of a group of young noblemen, the new Earl of Wendover among them. He felt a twinge of envy at Alex's ability to make friends so easily—a trait that had somehow always eluded Dominic.

He returned to the salon. He had no particular urge to rejoin his earlier companions, but he must—he could not allow the other guests' last sight of him to be of him carrying a swooning female from the room. He made polite conversation for twenty minutes or so and, once he was confident enough people had noted his return, he took his leave.

Too restless to go home and prompted by the events of the evening, he headed for Sans Pareil in search of Alex, determined to discharge his promise to Liberty as soon as he possibly could. From the floor of the theatre he scanned the boxes, finally spotting his father's close friend, Lord Stanton and his wife, Felicity, Dominic's second cousin. He ran up the stairs and slid into a vacant seat behind them.

'Mind if I join you?'

Felicity's head whipped round and a huge smile lit her face. 'Dominic! Of course. We're delighted to see you. But you have missed the play, you know. There is only the farce left.' Her eyes twinkled. She knew very well that most people preferred the farce to the serious drama, which was why the theatres always showed the farce last in the programme.

'I'm not here to watch either—I'm looking for Alex. Have you seen him?'

Stanton leant forward, searching the pit below. He pointed. 'There he is,' he said, 'with Wolfe and Wendover.'

Felicity also leant forward. 'Wendover? Is that the new Earl? Oh, yes. I see—the man with the golden hair? I've never seen him before, although

I have, of course, heard the gossip.' She settled back into her seat. 'Such a dreadful thing to happen—the previous Lord Wendover and his entire family perishing in that fire.' She shuddered. 'It's frightening.'

Stanton took her hand. 'Try not to think about it, Felicity Joy. You mustn't upset yourself.' Then he twisted in his seat to face Dominic and lowered his voice. 'The entire house was gutted, I hear. It is beyond repair. Wendover will have to rebuild.'

Was that why Liberty was so anxious about money? The knowledge that the family seat would need to be completely rebuilt?

'Have you heard how the fire started?'

'The bed hangings in the main bedchamber caught fire. Wendover and his lady were in bed. They didn't stand a chance—the house went up like a rocket, with all those dry old timbers to feed the flames.'

Dominic suppressed his own shudder. Fire… it was a terrifying prospect, and an ever-present danger with candles and lanterns supplying light and with open fires where an unwary soul might find their clothes catching alight and going up in flames. There were new innovations, with gas lighting now more common in London streets, but there was widespread distrust at the idea of employing the new technology in private homes.

Felicity looked at them, frowning. 'What are you two whispering about?' She narrowed her eyes at Stanton and shook her head. 'You should know better than to try to hide unpalatable truths from me, Richard.'

Her husband laughed. 'I wouldn't dare,' he said, with a wink at Dominic. 'But this is not hiding. It is *protecting.* You know the tragedy that occurred, but you do *not* need to know the details, my sweet.'

Felicity pouted, then smiled. 'You are right. As you so often are, my darling husband.'

A laugh rumbled in Richard's chest. 'If you believe that last remark, Dom, my boy, you do not know women. Or, more particularly, wives. We men might hold the titles, property and wealth, but, in a marriage, it is the wife who holds the power.' He captured Felicity's hands and kissed first one palm, then the other. 'My heart. Your hands.'

His smile confirmed his happiness at being in such thrall to Felicity and Dominic was happy for them. He was very fond of Felicity—they had worked together closely for years, supporting and funding Westfield, a school and asylum for orphans and destitute children—and he remembered only too well the traumas of the early months of Richard and Felicity's arranged marriage. Would he be so fortunate in his marriage of convenience? He mentally ran through his shortlist and doubts erupted. Not one of them, from his observations, had Felicity's kind heart and sincerity. He shifted uneasily in his seat and tried to quash those doubts.

*I'm not looking for love. Nor for a comfortable wife. I want a lady suited to the position of a marchioness; someone with the perfect qualities to be a duchess in the future and capable of raising a son who will one day be a duke. Someone of whom my mother would approve and a daughter-in-law to make my father proud.*

That had always been his destiny. From a young age, his mother had drummed into him his responsibility as his father's heir and his duty to marry a lady worthy of the future position as the Duchess of Cheriton. It was the price one paid when one was firstborn.

His situation was entirely different to that of the Stantons.

He dragged his thoughts away from his future marriage to concentrate on the reason he had come to the theatre. If he could set Miss Lovejoy's mind at rest about her brother, then hopefully he could move on with his plan without distraction.

Liberty's brother was easy to pick out in the auditorium below, with his hair the same shade as Hope's—a golden-blond colour, two shades lighter and much brighter than Liberty's dark honey hue. Dominic watched him. He was behaving much as every other young buck in the pit—whistling and calling at the hapless performers and, during those times the onstage drama failed to hold his attention, boldly ogling the theatre boxes and any halfway pretty occupants. So far, no different to how most young men behaved when they were out with other young men and without the civilising influence of ladies to curtail their antics.

Alex, Dominic was interested to see, was more subdued—indeed, he looked almost bored, gazing in a desultory fashion at the surrounding boxes. He gave every impression of wishing he was anywhere but where he was. Whatever jinks the three young men were up to, Alex was not the ringleader.

Dominic leaned forward. 'What do you know of Wendover, Stan?'

'Not a great deal,' Stanton replied. 'A gentleman's son, but his mother was some sort of merchant's daughter. He attended Eton, but left Oxford early after his father died. He has three sisters and I've heard it was a financial struggle for them after their father's death. He's a lucky man, inheriting so unexpectedly. Why do you ask?'

'He and Alex were pally at Eton and I've been told that Alex is encouraging Wendover in some wild behaviour. I'm worried Alex will slip back into his old ways.'

'How old is Alex now?'

'Five and twenty. Old enough to know better.'

Alex had always been a difficult youth, but Dominic, and the rest of the family, had believed the worst of his wildness was in the past.

'I didn't even know Alex was in town,' said Stanton. 'I heard Wendover's new-found fortune has gone to his head and, looking at them now, I should say he is the instigator, not Alex or Wolfe. It is Wendover's first time on the town—he's bound to kick out. I shouldn't worry too much, Dominic.'

How perfect if Stanton was right and it was Gideon trying to lead Alex and Neville astray. Dominic would enjoy putting Liberty straight… although…there was still the effect of Wendover's behaviour on his sisters' reputations—they would face enough of a struggle to be accepted in society, with their maternal grandfather being in trade, without a rackety brother to further taint the family.

He stood. 'I'll go and talk to him, nevertheless. I think you are right, but it won't hurt to make certain.' He shook Stanton's outstretched hand and bent to kiss Felicity on the cheek.

Down on the floor of the theatre, he stood at the back until the end of the play, keeping a close watch on Alex, Neville and Wendover. As the audience began to leave, he moved to meet the three men.

Alex's eyes met his. A smile was swiftly masked.

'Dominic.' Alex nodded casually.

'Alex.' Dominic kept his nod just as casual. 'Why did you not let me know you were in town?'

He cringed inwardly as soon as he said the words. There was nothing he could have said more likely to provoke Alex into a fit of the sullens, as their aunt Cecily used to call them.

Alex shrugged. 'I don't need your permission to have some fun in my life, do I?'

Dominic bit back the urge to cuff his brother's ear as he might have done when they were lads.

'No, of course not. But if I'd known I could have let you know Olivia, Hugo and the twins arrived yesterday.'

They'd been due to arrive the day he'd met Liberty at Beauchamp House, but had delayed their journey a couple of days when one of the twins was poorly.

Alex's eyes lit up. 'Are they staying in Grosvenor Square?' Dominic nodded. 'Good. I'll call on them tomorrow.'

Dominic then turned to Neville Wolfe, a friend of Alex's since boyhood.

'Wolfe. How do you do? Are your family well?'

Neville grinned and shook Dominic's hand. 'Very well, Avon. Very well.'

Dominic shifted his attention to Gideon, Lord Wendover. Miss Liberty Lovejoy's twin brother. The family resemblance was strong—the same stubborn chin and the same blue eyes. He wondered idly if Wendover's irises were likewise flecked with gold before jerking back to the realisation that he was staring mindlessly at the man. He thrust out his hand.

'I don't believe we've met. I'm Avon… Alex's brother.'

Gideon shook Dominic's hand. 'Wendover. Good to meet you, Avon, but… I beg you will excuse me—I'm due backstage.'

His words slurred and Dominic could smell the gin on his breath, but at least neither Alex nor Wolfe appeared foxed. Gideon was quickly absorbed into the throng of people slowly shuffling out of the theatre.

Alex muttered a curse. 'I'll call on you tomorrow, Dom. I have to go now. C'mon, Nev.'

He followed Gideon but, as Neville began to move, Dominic grabbed his arm.

'Hold hard there, Wolfe.'

Neville halted, but looked pointedly at Dominic's hand on his sleeve. Dominic released his grip.

'Give me a moment,' he said. 'I just want to be sure he's safe.'

Understanding dawned on Neville's face. He'd been friends with Alex for a long time and had stood by him through difficult times and wild behaviour. 'There's nothing going on that need trouble you, Avon. We're tryin' to watch out for Gid, that's all. He's got the bit between his teeth—taken a fancy to Camilla Trace and we're trying to stop him doing anything stupid like promise to marry her when he's in his cups!'

Camilla Trace was a beautiful and popular actress currently appearing at the Sans Pareil.

'Is Alex in danger of following Wendover's path?' At Neville's startled expression, Dominic elaborated. 'I don't mean falling in love with an actress. I heard Wendover's getting in deep and I'm worried Alex might get drawn back into high-stakes games.'

'Don't worry, Alex won't lose sight of what's important to him—he values his horses too much to put his business in jeopardy.' Neville clapped Dominic on the shoulder. 'Leave it to me to watch him.'

Dominic watched the other man go, his brows knit in a frown. Neville Wolfe and Alex had been partners in crime throughout their youth—what if they *both* slipped back into their old ways? With neither Father nor Uncle Vernon in town, it was up to Dominic to keep Alex safe. So, while Alex and Neville watched over Gideon, Dominic would watch over his brother. From a distance. Because one thing was certain—if Alex got wind of what Dominic was up to, he would just as likely dive headlong into any and every vice that presented itself to him. Simply to prove he was his own man.

Dominic sighed and made his way to the door into the backstage area. He entered and immediately spied a cloaked and hooded figure lurking in a doorway up ahead. He adjusted his grip on his ebony cane, which handily concealed a sword, but the figure did not move as he passed.

He'd taken two steps past before the scent of roses reached him, sending the hair on the back of his neck on end. He pivoted round to face… Miss Liberty Lovejoy.

# *Chapter Six*

Liberty gasped as a vice-like grip encircled her upper arm. The thick wool of the cloak she wore did little to disguise the strength in those fingers. Heart pumping with fear, she raised her eyes to her assailant and the breath whooshed from her lungs.

'You scared me half to death. What are you doing here?'

Dominic did not answer. His fingers tightened, then he was dragging her with him, opening doors at random, muttering apologies, until he found an empty room. He whisked her inside and released her, pushing her to the far side of the small, cluttered space. A lamp illuminated the interior, revealing clothing strewn over a chair and brushes and pots of face powder and rouge scattered upon a table with a mirror fixed on the wall behind it—a mirror that reflected Dominic's furious expression as he glared at the back of Liberty's head.

She squared her shoulders and pivoted to face him. 'How dare you manhandle me?'

She strode for the door, but his hand covered hers on the handle before she could open it. She tugged her hand free and turned to face him, her back to the door. He was close. Too close. And his expression had, somehow, transformed from fury into… Stillness. Focus. Like a cat waiting to pounce. Heat shimmered in those silvery eyes.

Liberty swallowed—hard—as her pulse hammered. His body was against hers, all unyielding muscle and spicy, musky, masculinity. Her stomach fluttered and liquid heat pooled in her core. She could not tear her gaze from his as he propped his hands against the door, one either side of her shoulders, pinning her. His scent surrounded her, sending waves of pure longing crashing through her—a feeling she hadn't experienced since Bernard had died. And just like that, she broke free of his spell. She shoved at his chest, ducked beneath one of his arms and stalked to the furthest corner of the room. Her breathing steadied the more distance she put between them…he remained by the door and did not follow her.

'What are you doing here?' He growled the question out.

Liberty elevated her nose. 'I asked you first.'

*No doubt he is here to visit his amour. That's what gentlemen do, is it not? Keep company with lightskirts and actresses and the like?*

And that's exactly what she feared Gideon was doing here now. Wasting his time and his money on an actress when he should be thinking about securing his new position as a peer. He would need an heir. He wouldn't meet a suitable wife backstage at a theatre!

'I am a man. I can do as I please. My reputation is not at stake.'

'And *my* reputation matters not when it comes to my brother's well-being.'

His narrowed gaze pierced her. '*Your* reputation might be of little consequence to you, but what about your sisters' reputations?'

'What of them?'

'If you are seen, not only will *you* suffer, but your sisters will be irretrievably tainted. Is that really what you want?'

Her bravado was shrinking fast. She had been unable to settle after their return from the rout, so worried was she about what Gideon was up to. She had taken a calculated risk in coming here tonight, sneaking out of the house, persuading Bilk, their coachman, to drive her to the theatre by telling him that Gideon had asked her to meet him there, and entering such a place unescorted.

A scandalously improper way for a lady to behave, but she had persuaded herself she would not be noticed.

Now, though, she was well and truly caught, and her disgrace would rebound on Hope and Verity if Lord Avon chose to reveal it.

But she refused to beg for his help again, not when he had failed to keep his earlier promise.

'Well, I *have* been seen now, so I have nothing left to lose, have I?' She dipped a curtsy, intending the gesture to be ironic. 'If it is your intention to expose my conduct, I cannot stop you. If it is not, then please allow me to leave so I can find Gideon.'

His lips firmed. 'You asked why I am here. I shall tell you. I have come to see what your brother is up to and to ensure that his bad example does not corrupt my own brother.'

'Oh! That is outrageous! It is *your* brother leading mine astray.'

He raised one brow, making her itch to slap him. Smug, superior know-it-all.

'I hate to contradict a lady, but my observations thus far indicate the exact opposite.'

Their gazes remained locked for several fraught seconds until Dominic's shoulders relaxed and one corner of his lips—his beautifully shaped mobile, enticing lips—lifted.

'Liberty—'

She opened her mouth to object, but held her silence when he raised his hand, palm forward.

'It is shocking for me to call you Liberty, but acceptable for you to wander alone backstage at a theatre?'

His lips twitched. They really were fascinating lips. What would it be like to kiss him? To feel his lips moving over hers? His tongue in her mouth, sliding against hers?

*Oh, dear God. Forget scandalous. I am utterly depraved.*

She moistened her dry lips. His eyes darkened. A pulse in her neck fluttered wildly and, without volition, she pressed shaking fingers to it. A vain attempt to suppress it? Then his gaze lowered and her nipples peaked in immediate response. She swallowed again and tugged at the edges of her cloak, pulling it across her chest in a defensive gesture.

Dominic hauled in an audible breath, his broad chest swelling and then deflating again as he released his breath.

'Let us begin again, Miss Lovejoy.'

His tone meant business. His very stance meant business. Despite herself, Liberty paid attention. This was not a man to defy, not in this mood.

'I am here at this theatre to see what *both* of our brothers are up to.'

Despite herself, she rather liked that—it was nice to have someone on her side, someone to rely on, if only for a short while. Although she would die before she admitted it to him.

'How did you know they would be here?'

'I asked the servants. They tend to know everything, you know—they seem to have their own methods of finding things out and of spreading the word. You would do well to remember that.'

Her thoughts flew to Bilk. She had sworn him to secrecy, but could she trust him? Liberty bit back her doubts. It was too late now. Unconsciously, she raised her chin.

'Continue,' she said.

Drat him. There was that barely concealed smirk again.

'I have spoken with all three of them—my own brother and Mr Wolfe are watching over your brother to ensure he does nothing…stupid.'

'Stupid? Like…what?'

'Like making rash promises.'

Liberty pondered his words. 'Promises? To whom?' They were in a theatre…that must mean… 'As in…promises of marriage? Offers? Oh, dear God.'

She rushed for the door, but Dominic grabbed her arm as she brushed past him. Liberty struggled to free herself.

'Let me go! You mean one of these floozies, don't you? A common actress. I have to stop him.'

A tug unbalanced her and suddenly she was in his arms, held for the second time that night against the solid comfort of his chest. She felt herself relax into him, despite her panic over Gideon. It felt good, to feel a man's arms around her, to feel protected, even if for a split second.

'You can do nothing.' His voice rumbled in his chest, vibrating through her. He gripped her shoulders and set her away from him, gazing down at her. 'Gideon will heed his friends' advice and opinions more readily than that of his sister. Leave it to us.'

'Leave it to the men, you mean. You think because I am a female that my opinions count for nothing.'

That infuriating brow rose once again. 'I think that because you are his sister, your opinions will simply drive him into contrary behaviour. Take my advice, Miss Lovejoy. Use your time wisely and channel your energies into finding respectable husbands for yourself and your sisters.'

'I do not seek a husband for myself,' she muttered. Pride would not allow her to admit her private dream of finding love again. Especially to him.

'Then concentrate on your sisters' futures, if

that is the case. Leave your brother to me. It is all under control.'

She raised her gaze to his. Those silvery eyes shone like polished steel. She could see herself reflected in them, but she could read nothing of the man within. They were like a mirror. What secrets did he hide? Or maybe he had none. Maybe he was exactly what he appeared to be—a handsome, straitlaced nobleman who never succumbed to spontaneity and always behaved with utmost propriety, as Mrs Mount had said.

'Why should I put my trust in you? What do *you* care what Gideon does?'

'I shall keep my eye on your brother simply to ensure Alex does not follow him into reckless behaviour and harmful habits.'

'But you are not watching him now. You are here with me.'

'That is true, but I happen to know both Alex and Mr Wolfe are with Gideon so he is in no imminent danger of making a complete cake of himself. Now, will you allow me to escort you home, Miss Lovejoy?'

'There is no need. I shall take a hackney.'

Earlier, she'd had no qualms about how she would get home, anticipating that Gideon would feel honour-bound to escort her. Now, for the first time, she realised her predicament, but pride, again, forbade her from admitting as much to His Lordship.

His eyes narrowed. 'Refusal is not an option. *That* was not a question.'

'It sounded exactly like a question to me.'

A muscle leapt at the side of his jaw. 'I was being polite.'

'Be that as it may, I am in no need of your escort. Just think how your reputation will suffer if we are seen together.'

He sighed. 'I told you before that sarcasm does not become you, Miss Lovejoy. Your choice is twofold. Either you allow me to take you home. Now. Or you and I shall go and find your brother and see what he has to say about his twin sister snooping around the nether regions of a theatre. The choice is yours.'

'My lord… I have no wish to sound ungrateful, but you cannot simply order me around. Besides, I have no wish to disrupt your evening further than I already have.'

His sensual lips thinned into a firm line. He spun to face the door, grabbing Liberty's right hand as he did so. He drew it firmly between his left arm and his ribcage and then crooked his elbow, clamping her arm in place. He strode for the door and she found herself stumbling in his wake, unable to resist his strength.

'My lord… Avon! Stop!'

'No.' The word was gritted out. 'No more talk. Pull up your hood.' They left the room and he slammed to a halt. 'Do it,' he growled, 'or I'll do it for you. Unless you *want* to be recognised?'

The sight of a figure emerging from a nearby door spurred her to obey. She pulled up her hood, tugging it forward to cover her face and, without another word, Avon headed towards the rear of the theatre, towing Liberty behind him. She kept her gaze to the floor, avoiding eye contact with anyone they passed, then they were out of the door, into the chill night air, with raindrops pitter-pattering on her hood and, when she risked glancing up, her face.

'Keep moving and don't look at anyone,' Dominic muttered. 'Maiden Lane is no place for a lady.'

He walked briskly, rounded a corner and then another, and she recognised the Strand and the front of the theatre, where a town coach and pair waited, a coachman at the horses' heads. The waiting man whisked sacking from the horses' backs as Liberty found herself bundled unceremoniously into the vehicle. Avon leaned inside as she perched on the edge of the seat.

'Where do you live?'

'Green Street.'

He withdrew and she heard him call, 'Webster. Green Street, please.'

The carriage dipped as Dominic climbed inside. He stripped off his gloves and hat and cast them on to the opposite seat before settling next to her, his hip and thigh touching hers. She inched away from him, until her own hip was pressed against the padded side of the coach, still stiffly upright, wondering how it had happened that she had been removed from the theatre without catching even one glimpse of Gideon or discovering what he was up to. And how she was now in a carriage, alone with a man she barely knew.

'I presume you have fully recovered from your swoon earlier tonight?'

'Yes, thank you.' It infuriated her that he'd seen her behave in such a feeble way. 'I do not make a habit of swooning. It was excessively stuffy in that room.'

'It was.' His amused tone set her hackles to rise. 'I did not, however, notice any other ladies swoon.'

She had no answer to that. It was true. And the episode had undermined her determination to have only one new gown made. She had no choice now. She would need more. She only hoped Gideon could afford it.

'How can I be sure Gideon is safe?'

'You cannot be sure. Not completely. But you have to understand there is nothing you can do. You are a female. You simply *cannot* follow him around to spy on him. Perhaps you should instead learn to trust him? And besides—' Dominic swivelled on the seat to face her '—tell me truthfully. What exactly did you intend to do if you caught Gideon behaving recklessly?'

'I… I do not know, for certain. I suppose I would try to persuade him to leave and to return home with me.'

'I see.'

The simple scepticism in those two words spoke volumes. In the silence that followed Liberty began to realise the futility of her plan—what *had* she thought she might achieve?

'And your chance of success would be?'

Liberty slumped back against the squabs.

'Very well. You are right. He would refuse. We would argue.'

'And the result would be that the distance you spoke of between you and your brother would widen further.'

That was the last thing she wanted. She missed sharing things…*life*…with Gideon; missed having him to lean on; she missed his company. And she was terrified he would make some drastic mistake and blight his life. She rubbed at her aching chest while the guilt lay heavy in her stomach. She had failed Bernard and her parents. She could not fail Gideon, too.

Dominic faced forward again, folding his arms

across his chest. Liberty waited for the 'I told you so' or 'How could you be so stupid?', but no recriminations were forthcoming. After several excruciating minutes of silent self-recrimination, she exhaled sharply.

'I am sorry.'

He cocked his head. 'Sorry for what?'

'My behaviour. I know it is not what is expected of a lady, but I—I could not go to bed and sleep without trying to do *something*.'

'I do understand. Gideon is your brother and your worry for him overrode everything else.' A long, quiet sigh escaped him. 'Lest you forget, I have a brother, too, and, although he is not as wild as he used to be, he is still not an easy man to understand or even, sometimes, to like.' He leaned forward, his forearms propped on his knees and his gaze on the floor. 'Our sister has been known to get herself into some difficult scrapes in an effort to protect Alex—often without regard for the consequences. In that respect you remind me of her.'

He looked at her. 'For the Beauchamps all that is in the past and Olivia is a respectable married lady now. If you will take my advice—concentrate your efforts on your sisters even if you have no wish for marriage yourself. I meant what I said earlier—if you bring disgrace upon yourself, your sisters will suffer. They will be tainted for life.

You already start from a lowly position in society and there will be many who will relish any disgrace as it will reinforce their view that inferior breeding will out.'

Liberty bristled at being lectured. 'A view you yourself agree with, I am given to understand. I've heard you have a list of perfect ladies suitable for a future duke and that breeding comes right at the top of your requirements.'

'Only insofar as it affects my choice of bride,' he retorted. 'It is my duty as my father's heir to marry well, but I do not hold such views in general.'

'Because everyone below you is so far beneath your notice?'

She felt the full force of his stare. 'Not at all,' he said, stiffly. 'As it happens, I'm involved—'

Liberty waited, but he did not continue. 'You're involved...?'

'It is of no matter.'

He faced forward again and they lapsed into silence. Within a short time, Liberty felt shame creep through her. She had been unfair, needling him in that way. For all he was infuriating, he *had* been trying to help her.

She swivelled slightly so she could study him. She could just about make out his profile in the gloomy interior of the coach. As they passed the occasional street lamp, she could make out lines of strain running from his nose to his mouth.

'Do you really believe your brother can be trusted to bring Gideon back to his senses, my lord?'

He hooked one hand behind his neck, further obscuring her view of him. At first she thought he would not answer her, but then he abruptly released his neck and lowered his arm, shooting her a sidelong look.

'I believe so.' He twisted to face her then, and touched her hand. '*You* may trust *me*, however. I shall keep an eye on both Alex *and* Gideon.'

And she did trust his word.

'Thank you. You are more generous than perhaps I deserve.'

His eyes glittered as they passed another street lamp. 'Generous?' He reached out, and touched her face with one finger, tracing her cheekbone, raising a shiver in its wake before he withdrew it. 'You needed help and I have been in a position to provide it.' His teeth gleamed as he smiled and her heart tumbled over. 'Twice. As I said, you remind me of my sister...oh, not in the way you look, but in that stubborn determination to make sure the people you love are safe. How could I not help?' He leaned forward, gazing out of the window. 'We are here. Green Street. Which house is it?'

'A little further along, on the left-hand side.'

She felt dazed. What had happened to the pompous lord she had met at Beauchamp House? Dominic rapped on the carriage ceiling and it halted. He climbed out, then turned to hand her out.

'Pull your hood up again,' he whispered. 'I will watch to see you safely inside the house, but I won't escort you to the door in case we are seen. I hope we are now agreed that your reputation is important, if only for the sake of your sisters.'

'Yes. Thank you again.'

His eyes gleamed briefly, then he raised her hand to his lips. 'You are most welcome, Miss Liberty Lovejoy.'

# Chapter Seven

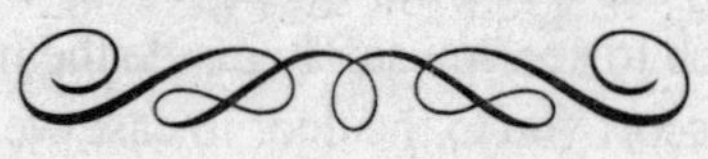

A sense of urgency—of events slipping out of his grasp—drove Dominic to head straight for home and for his sitting room.

'I shan't need you again tonight, Brailsford,' he said to his man. 'You get off to bed.'

'Can I fetch you something to eat before I go, milord?'

Dominic consulted his gut. 'No. I'm not hungry.' Actually, he felt a little nauseous…sort of uneasy…a churning, unsettling sensation. Apprehension, that was it. Well, it was hardly surprising when he was about to make such a momentous decision. 'But you may pour me a brandy before you go, if you would.'

Dominic crossed the room to his writing desk and, opening a drawer, he extracted a sheet of paper. He had no real need of the list—the names that remained were indelibly inscribed into his memory. There was no chance he would forget any of them. But he nevertheless carried the list over to his favourite chair—a deeply buttoned green-leather-upholstered wing chair—and waited while Brailsford poured a glass of brandy, set it on the small table next to his chair and stirred the slumbering fire into life before refuelling it. Dominic did not look at the list until the door had shut behind Brailsford, then he scanned the names before steadily working his way through them again, from the first name to the fifth. Amelia and Sarah, of course, he had taken against, leaving three. For each name—Caroline, Georgiana and Sybilla—he conjured forth a mental image of the lady in question, mentally reviewing what he knew of each one: her family connections, her qualities, her conduct. Any one of them would be suitable for the Marchioness of Avon, and for the future Duchess of Cheriton, although he hoped that last would not be for a very long time. No one lady stood out among the others, but Georgiana was, he knew, afraid of horses. Did he want a wife who was afraid of horses? And Sybilla wasn't even in town yet.

'Lady Caroline Warnock.'

He closed his eyes, recalling the sweet sound of her singing at a musical recital last Season. Her voice had raised the hairs on his arms. He opened his eyes again and mentally shrugged.

She had a beautiful singing voice. It was as good a reason as any. Her attitude towards Liberty the other day had irritated him, but it was, he knew, no different to the attitude of many in the *ton* to those whom they considered of inferior breeding and upbringing. That was settled, then. Although no one but he would know—he would pay equal attention to all five original names but, as soon as Father came up from Devonshire, Dominic would make his offer. He did not doubt Caroline would welcome an offer from him—she had been raised with a view to taking her place as the wife of a high-ranking aristocrat.

The sound of the door opening disturbed his thoughts.

'I told Brailsford to leave me to find my own way.' Alex sauntered across to the brandy decanter and poured himself a generous glassful. 'You don't mind, do you?' He raised the glass as he wandered across to the fireplace and sat in the matching wing-back chair set on the opposite side to Dominic's.

'Be my guest. Oh. Wait. You already have.' Dominic reached for his own glass, raised it in a silent toast to his brother, drank, then returned it to the side table. He placed his list next to the glass before eyeing Alex. 'I didn't expect to see you again tonight. To what do I owe this pleasure?'

'My insatiable curiosity. Saw you leaving the back door of the theatre with a woman and, if my eyes weren't deceiving me, it was Wendover's twin sister—the interfering and irritating Liberty.'

Dominic frowned. 'I didn't think you'd seen us. And I didn't know the two of you had even met.'

'We haven't…but I've seen her from afar and I recognised her, before she pulled up her hood. That description, by the by, is verbatim from her ever-loving brother.'

Sympathy for Liberty bloomed in Dominic's chest. He drank some brandy then shifted in his chair, unsettled, staring into his glass as he swirled the amber liquid around. He'd come in here determined to finalise his future and to forget Miss Liberty Lovejoy and now here was Alex, stirring up her presence all over again.

'So I was right. It was her.'

The softly spoken comment jerked Dominic from his thoughts. He looked up to find Alex watching him with a knowing look.

'Is she the reason you came to the theatre? What were the pair of you doing backstage?'

Dominic tilted his glass and drank again, considering. Then he set his glass down again and steepled his fingers in front of his mouth, his joined forefingers resting against his lips.

'It was coincidence. But I do know she is worried about her brother. I saw her there and I persuaded her to leave. That is it.' This subject needed changing. 'More importantly, what are you up to with Wendover? You're not slipping back into old habits, are you?'

'No.' Alex sipped his brandy. 'Lucky for you it was me that saw you.'

Silently damning his brother's tenacity, Dominic asked, 'What d'you mean?'

Alex's eyes gleamed, crinkling at the corners. He was unmistakably a Beauchamp, but he was the only one of the three children who had inherited their late mother's colouring—thick mahogany brown hair and golden-brown eyes that always reminded Dominic of a tiger he had seen at the Exeter Exchange when he was a boy. Now, those eyes mocked Dominic, whose jaw clenched.

'Careful you don't get caught, that's all,' Alex drawled. 'I doubt the luscious Liberty would tick many of the qualities on the list of the perfect bride for the perfect heir.'

Alex left his chair in one fluid motion and, before Dominic realised his intention, he snatched the list from the table. Dominic surged to his feet.

'Alex!'

Alex spun away and scanned the names. Then he thrust the paper at Dominic and subsided back into his chair. Gritting his teeth, Dominic folded the list and put it in his pocket before sitting back down, steeling himself for the ribbing he sensed was coming his way.

'I was hoping the existence of that list was a daft rumour.' Alex recited the five names, his voice soft and almost sorrowful. '*Really*, Dom? They're the best you can conjure up?'

'What are you talking about, you numbskull? They come from the very best families in England and every one of them has been properly raised and educated to take her place in society and to be the perfect choice for a nobleman's wife.'

Alex drained his glass and went to refill it, and topped up Dominic's while he was up.

'There's not one of 'em with an ounce of warmth or spark,' he said once he regained his seat. 'Yes, they're perfect ladies, but they're so icy and correct they can freeze a fellow with just one look.'

'Alex...you know I have always planned to marry a lady worthy of being a future duchess. I need to choose my bride carefully.'

Alex simply held Dominic's gaze.

Goaded, Dominic said, 'I never took *you* for a romantic. I should have thought you would approve of marriages of convenience.'

'This isn't about me. It's about you.' Alex scrubbed his hand through his hair, a slight flush washing across his cheeks. 'You always seem so…alone, somehow. I don't want to see you alone in your marriage as well,' he added, his voice gruff.

Dominic stared at his brother. How unlike Alex to trouble himself over someone else, even a member of the family. That thought unsettled him far more than Alex's words and he shifted uncomfortably in his chair.

'Do you remember Liv and I used to call you Lord Earnest after…after…?'

'I remember.' Dominic knew he meant after their mother's death, but they never talked about it. Ever. He supposed they'd been too young to fully understand what had happened at the time and it had become something of an unwritten rule. He couldn't even remember his father or Aunt Cecily really mentioning it, except as a fact. They had never *talked* about it. 'Someone had to be the responsible one. I am the eldest…it was my duty to help keep you and Livvy out of trouble, as it is my duty to marry well.'

'You take care that sense of duty don't choke you, Brother.' Alex sipped again at his brandy. 'I look at you sometimes, Dom, and all I see is the perfect heir to the Duke of Cheriton—the man you present to the world. And I wonder about the man inside and about *his* dreams and desires.'

Dominic's heart pounded uncomfortably. 'You're talking utter rubbish.'

His brother might be a year his junior—and he might have spent his youth bouncing from one scrape to another—but there were times when he appeared much, much older than his years. It was all right for Alex…*he* wasn't burdened by the weight of duty and expectation. *He* wasn't the heir.

Dominic had never questioned that duty—it was the way of their world. He was destined to follow the example set by his father, when he had married their mother for the good of the Dukedom.

'The family have it all wrong, Dom. They've spent years fretting about me, watching over me. But it's *you* they should be worrying about. I don't believe any of those women will make you happy. You are allowed to be happy, you know.'

Dominic stared at his brother as those words sank in, stirring unfamiliar feelings that, somehow, tightened his throat until it felt as though he had tried to swallow a lump of dry bread. He was not used to this sombre and, somehow, sorrowful version of Alex; where was his devil-may-care brother who took mockery to new heights?

He thrust down the unfamiliar surge of emotion and unclenched his jaw. Never would he reveal how that simple comment had reached deep inside him and wrenched at his soul. He drew in a deep breath before forcing a hearty laugh.

'All this is an excellent ruse, Alex, but you won't divert me that easily.'

Alex shrugged. 'Not trying to divert anyone. Just telling it as I see it.'

Dominic straightened his spine, now thoroughly irritated with himself for succumbing to Alex's mood and allowing him to raise doubts in his mind. 'I spoke to Wolfe earlier.'

Alex's eyes narrowed. 'He said.'

'What's your game with Wendover? Tell me you're not getting in too deep. Is everything truly all right?'

'Why wouldn't it be?'

'Alex…'

Alex's eyes glittered. He tossed back his brandy and rose to his feet. 'Worry about your own future. Not mine. *One* day maybe my family will see me as something other than a boy looking for trouble. 'Night, Avon.'

Dominic sat for a long time after Alexander left, that same nervy apprehension churning his stomach relentlessly even as he reassured himself that Alex didn't have a damned clue what he was talking about.

The following morning, Dominic called at Beauchamp House, to take his brother-in-law,

Hugo, to Jackson's boxing saloon for a sparring session. It was Olivia and Hugo's first visit to London for the Season since the birth of their two-year-old twins, Julius and Daisy, and he found them waiting for him in the first-floor salon. After greeting Olivia with a kiss, Dominic said, 'Ready to go, Hugo? We'll soon get you back in condition.' He jabbed at Hugo's abdomen. 'Seems to me you've gone soft since you married.'

Hugo laughed, but Olivia leapt to his defence. 'He has not gone soft, Dominic! I'll have you know—'

She stopped as the door opened again and Alex strolled in. Dominic's heart sank as their eyes met. Their conversation of the night before was unfinished and Alex, he knew, would have no hesitation in raising the subject in front of Olivia and Hugo.

'Alex!' Olivia flew across the room to embrace him. 'Oh, I am so happy to see you! *Why* have you not been to visit us for such an age?'

'Hey! Steady on, Sis! You near to knocked me flying—you're no slip of a girl nowadays, are you?' Alex held her away from him and looked her up and down, mischief glimmering in his eyes. 'But still as much a hoyden as ever.'

'Oh, do stop teasing, Alex.' She reached up

to tidy her black hair, re-pinning it haphazardly. 'I'm a respectable matron now, don't you know.'

He grinned. 'I'll accept matron, but respectable?'

She punched his arm. 'I am a mother! Of course I am respectable!'

Alex kissed her cheek, then greeted Hugo and Dominic, who took the opportunity to suggest to Hugo it was time they left.

'Something I said, Brother?' said Alex. 'Or something I *might* say?'

Dominic shrugged. 'I thought you and Livvy would appreciate the chance to catch up.'

'Oh, we'll have plenty to talk about,' drawled Alex, casting himself down on the sofa. 'See you later, Dom. Don't take out *all* your frustrations on Hugo, will you?'

Dominic didn't trust himself to answer—not without causing an argument. He strode from the room and waited until he saw Hugo's tall form descending the stairs before he left the house and climbed into his carriage. Hugo settled by his side and the carriage moved off.

'Well?' he said eventually, unable to stomach the continuing silence. 'I suppose Alex told you?'

Hugo raised one dark eyebrow. 'That you intend to select a bride this Season? Yes, he did. Congratulations.'

'You might say that like you mean it.'

Hugo huffed a laugh. 'As if you care for my opinion. I warn you, though, Livvy is hell-bent on meeting the ladies on your list.'

He'd been afraid of that.

'I've warned her not to interfere, but I have no doubt you'll know her verdict once she's met them all.'

'No doubt.'

Silence fell, and Dominic gazed from the window as the carriage turned into New Bond Street, idly watching the people they passed. Then he stiffened as he caught sight of Ma Prinks, shabbily dressed as ever, carrying a wailing toddler. Dominic rapped on the ceiling and the carriage halted.

'What is it?' Hugo leaned over to peer out of the window.

'I know that woman and I know her game.'

Dominic leapt from the carriage and strode back towards Prinks, who halted the minute she saw Dominic, her scowl morphing into an ingratiating simper.

'You're a long way from your usual haunts, Ma. What are you up to?'

'Not up to nuffin, milor'. Just takin' my young nipper for a walk, see?'

Dominic studied the child, pale-skinned and red-haired, with puffed-up eyes and snot trailing from its nostrils, and then eyed Prinks's dark hair and swarthy face.

'Yours, is it?' It was impossible to tell the sex of the child.

'His pa was ginger.'

'I don't believe you, Ma. Are you up to your old tricks again?' He glanced at Hugo, standing by his side. 'Ma Prinks here has a talent for "finding" young 'uns and using them to gain sympathy and money from passers-by.'

'You never cease to amaze me by the company you keep, Avon,' drawled Hugo.

Dominic frowned as he noticed the interest of people passing them by. Fortunately, it was still before noon and most of the *haut ton* had not yet started to shop, but he had no wish to continue drawing attention.

'Did you think Bond Street might give you easy pickings, Ma?'

The woman snorted. 'So it would if certain nobs would keep their conks out of poor folks' business.'

'Did you steal him?'

'No! I never! 'Is ma's dead, in't she, and 'is father's nowhere to be found. I'm doin' him a favour, see? At least wi' me he'll get fed.'

Dominic held out his arms. 'Give him to me, Ma. I'll make sure he's cared for.'

'You got no right—'

'Hand him over, or I'll hand *you* over to the constables. I'm sure the magistrates will be even more interested than me to hear how you came by the boy.'

She thrust the child at Dominic, not even waiting until he had him securely before releasing him. 'Tek 'im,' she snarled. 'Plenty more where 'e came from.'

By the time Dominic had the boy in a secure hold, Ma Prinks was striding away. He sighed.

'She's right,' he said to Hugo. 'We do our bit at Westfield, but it simply isn't enough. There are just too many children.'

He led the way back to the carriage and, once inside, he looked down into the infant's face. Two blue eyes stared back. Then Dominic checked his limbs. Two arms. Two legs.

'At least this one appears unharmed. The last one she had was blind.' His heart clenched at the memory. '*Deliberately* blinded, to gain more sympathy and thus more alms. It's a filthy business.'

'That…' Hugo's voice choked. He cleared his throat. 'That is atrocious. He looks the same age as our twins. When I think…' Again, his voice failed him and he cleared his throat again. 'What now?'

'I'll take him straight out to Westfield. The Whittakers will take him in and then Peter will make enquiries just in case anyone *is* missing their child. I don't hold out much hope, though.' He smiled wryly at Hugo. 'Sorry. It looks like we'll have to postpone our session. But we can drop you off at Jackson's if you wish. I'm sure someone there will spar with you.'

'No.' Hugo's voice was thoughtful. 'I'd rather come with you, if you've no objection. I have a sudden urge to discover what it is you do at this school of yours.'

Three days later, Liberty sat with Mrs Mount at one end of Lord and Lady Twyford's ballroom, absorbing the gowns and the jewels, the elegant dancing and the smiling faces, tapping her foot in time to the music from the quartet sitting on the dais at the far end of the room and just…just… *enjoying* being there.

This was the first truly prestigious ball she and her sisters had been invited to attend, courtesy of the unflagging efforts of Mrs Mount to inveigle invitations for the Lovejoy sisters who were indeed viewed as upstarts by many members of the *haut ton*. Liberty hoped and prayed this ball would be the first of many. It was her sisters' first opportunity to mingle with the highest in society and they had already proved a draw for several eligible gentlemen eager for introductions. Hope—her blue eyes shining with excitement—

had been led out for the first dance by the youthful Lord Walsall and Verity's card was also full although Liberty would have preferred a less… seedy-looking partner for her youngest sister's first dance. The gentleman, who had been introduced by Lord Twyford himself as Lord Bridlington, looked forty if he looked a day and there was a gleam in his sleepy-lidded eyes as he leisurely inspected Verity's person that Liberty could not quite like. Still, she consoled herself…it was just one dance.

Gideon and Lord Alexander Beauchamp were also gracing the ball with their presence which meant Liberty could relax and enjoy herself rather than fretting over what her twin was up to. The rules that governed high society, she had decided, were hopeless as far as females were concerned. Even *she* hesitated to follow Gideon to some of the haunts he frequented. But she had found an unlikely ally in Gideon's valet, who was as determined as Liberty to prevent his master from committing social suicide, and Rudge was proving a satisfactory spy, informing Liberty of Gideon's intended destination every evening. But every time Liberty was tempted to throw caution to the winds and follow Gideon, Dominic's words would echo in her memory.

*It is your sisters who will suffer. They will be tainted for life.*

She was infuriated at finding herself controlled by his words even in his absence but, because she knew him to be right, she could not disregard his warning. Nor had she found it easy to banish Dominic himself from her thoughts. For the first time since Bernard's death she was attracted to a man but, in a hopeless twist of fate, it was to a man who—although she could see he found her attractive in return—would never in a million years act upon that attraction. He was not only heir to a powerful duke, but he had set out a list of essential qualities for his perfect bride to help him make his choice. Liberty suppressed a snort. His choice, indeed. As if he just needed to snap his fingers and any female he selected would simply fall at his feet.

She banished Lord Avon from her thoughts. It was Lord Alexander she must apply herself to for, as far as she could see, his bad influence on Gideon continued unabated despite what Dominic claimed. Now she had seen him at close quarters Liberty wondered how she had ever mistaken Dominic for his brother. Their facial characteristics were similar, to be sure, but Alex was nowhere near as intimidating as his brother. Not quite as tall, not as solid, nor as *dark*…as brooding.

*Nor is he as handsome.*

The latter observation whispered through her

thoughts before she could prevent it. She swatted it away and distracted herself by watching Gideon as he partnered one of Lord Twyford's daughters. Her hand rose to her chest, as though to fill the hole there…the void that yawned deeper and darker the more her twin seemed to reject her.

Again, she gathered her scattering thoughts and redirected them to Alex, who was also dancing. Gideon had already declined to introduce her to him, but she was determined to find somebody who would. Maybe a direct appeal to him might work after all? She wouldn't know until she tried. Lord knew, she'd made no progress in bringing Gideon to his senses over the past week and although she'd seen Lord Avon a few times, driving or riding in the Park, he had done no more than tip his hat to her so she had no way of knowing if he had kept to his promise to watch over their respective brothers.

She scanned the Twyfords' ballroom for the umpteenth time, searching for *anyone* who might introduce her to Lord Alexander Beauchamp. Of a sudden, her pulse kicked. Across the floor, through a gap in the dancers, she spied a face she recognised—Lady Jane Colebrooke, standing with a beautiful young woman with shining black hair and a tall, dark gentleman.

# *Chapter Eight*

'Mrs Mount.' Liberty leaned towards their chaperon. 'Lady Jane Colebrooke is over there—I should like to renew my acquaintance with her and to thank her again for her kindness. I shan't be gone long.'

Mrs Mount nodded and smiled, then resumed her conversation with the matron sitting on her other side. Liberty stood and shook out the skirts of her new violet gown—one of three she'd had made after the disaster at the Trents' rout—before making her way around the edge of the room. She slowed as she reached Lady Jane and her companions and, as she hoped, Lady Jane noticed her.

'Miss Lovejoy! How do you do?'

'Why, Lady Jane. What a happy coincidence. I had hoped I might see you, to thank you again for your kindness.'

Lady Jane blushed. 'Oh, it was my pleasure. Might I introduce you to Lord Hugo Alastair and his wife, Lady Olivia? Miss Lovejoy is Lord Wendover's sister,' she said to Lady Olivia. 'We met when she was overcome by the heat at a party last week—I merely leant my assistance when requested by your brother, Avon.'

*Brother?* Liberty's breath seized as cool silvery-grey eyes—the mirror of Avon's—slowly assessed her. Of all the rotten luck—she could hardly beg an introduction to Lord Alexander when his sister was within earshot. Liberty curtsied again, this time a little deeper. Lady Olivia, after all, was the daughter of a duke and would no doubt expect her due. And Lord Hugo must be the son of a high-ranking aristocrat, she realised, as he bowed with a charming smile.

Mrs Mount's efforts to drum lessons of aristocratic precedence into the three Lovejoy sisters had not been for nothing because Liberty now knew that only the sons of marquesses and dukes had the courtesy title of 'Lord' affixed to their Christian names, so Lord Hugo must at least be the son of a marquess. Or marquis as some of them chose to be known. But Liberty still couldn't quite fathom why sons of earls were not called 'Lord' when their sisters were afforded the title of 'Lady'. This world was still a confused muddle of rules and details that had never touched upon her or her life before, but to which she must now conform.

Lady Olivia's gaze fixed on Lady Jane. 'I am all agog, Jane. What happened? And how came Dominic to be involved?'

'Livvy.' There was a note of warning in Lord Hugo's voice. He smiled at Liberty. 'I apologise for my wife's inquisitiveness, Miss Lovejoy.'

'Oh, *pfft*, Hugo. Jane knows me too well to take offence and I am sure Miss Lovejoy will forgive my curiosity about what my brother gets up to when I'm not around to keep an eye on him.' Lady Olivia grinned at Liberty. 'Jane's family estate adjoins our father's in Devonshire. We grew up together and dear Jane is well accustomed to the Beauchamps' ways, are you not, Jane?'

It struck Liberty that, for all their high birth, these aristocrats seemed less stuffy than many of the lower ranks of the peerage she had encountered since their arrival in London. *They* did not appear to view her as a person not fit to associate with.

Jane smiled. 'I am. As to the other night, all I recall is seeing Miss Lovejoy walking towards the door and then she seemed to stumble over someone's foot before…well, her knees simply buckled. And Dominic…he was quite the hero. He must have been quick to notice something amiss because, even though he was on the far side of our group, he was the first to reach Miss

Lovejoy and he caught her before she could fall to the floor.'

Liberty kept her attention on Jane although she felt the weight of Lady Olivia's silver-eyed stare. Nerves quaked in her stomach. Would she think it had been a deliberate ploy on Liberty's part? A trick to attract Avon's attention? That particular rumour had already reached the Lovejoys' ears, but Liberty knew any attempt at denial would sound like too much protestation.

'And he asked you to go with him to protect Miss Lovejoy's reputation?'

'I believe it was with a view of protecting his own reputation.' The tart words blurted from Liberty's lips before she could stop them. Horrified, she clapped her hand to her mouth but, to her amazement, Olivia laughed.

'That sounds just like Dominic—his behaviour must always be above reproach. Does your brother attend this evening, Miss Lovejoy? I do not believe I have ever met him—this is our first time in town for over two years.'

'Yes. He is dancing in the same set as your brother Alexander...the man with the golden hair.'

'Oh, he is very handsome, is he not? I can see many girls losing their hearts over that head of hair!' Olivia grinned. 'Do you envy him? Oh! I do beg your pardon. I did not mean to be rude.

Your hair is very pretty, but it is not quite so… um…eye-catching, is it?'

Liberty smiled back. 'I take no offence. I am used to my brother garnering all the attention. We are twins and when we were children people would stop and exclaim at his angelic appearance—'

*'Twins?'*

'Why, yes.'

'Hugo!' Olivia nudged her husband. 'Did you hear that? Miss Lovejoy and her brother are *twins*.'

Lord Hugo smiled indulgently. 'I heard her say so, my love.'

'Miss Lovejoy! Will you do me the honour of calling on me at Beauchamp House tomorrow? I should deem it a great favour.' Olivia's eyes shone with excitement. 'We have two-year-old twins—a boy and a girl also. I should appreciate hearing from you direct what it is like to grow up as a twin.'

Liberty was happy to accept. She liked what she had seen so far of Lady Olivia and who knew what advantages Hope and Verity might gain if Liberty and Olivia were to become friends?

'I shall be happy to call upon you, but you must realise I have no experience of growing up *not* a twin so I am not sure I can be of much help.'

'Oh, I am sure you can. Shall we say two

o'clock? You must come, too, Jane. I long to hear how things are at home.'

'I am sorry, Livvy, but I cannot. Stepmama wishes me to remain at home every single afternoon in case of gentlemen callers.' She sighed, sending a rueful smile Liberty's way. 'She is determined to see me married this year, before my stepsister makes her debut next Season.' She lowered her voice. 'Unfortunately the only gentleman who ever calls on me is Sir Denzil Pikeford and my fear of displeasing Stepmama is not yet as great as my fear of marrying a drunkard with scant manners and even less conversation.'

Olivia pulled a face. 'Pikeford? You have my sympathies!'

The music stopped and the dance ended, and Liberty was happy to see Lord Alexander heading in their direction. This would save her from having to beg an introduction. As he neared, he was joined by Lord Avon and Liberty's heart performed a lazy somersault as his gaze swept over her. What would he think, finding her here with his sister and brother-in-law after their last encounter at the theatre? His impassive features gave nothing of his thoughts away and, without volition, Liberty plucked at the low, round neckline of her new violet ball gown—a neckline that exposed rather more of her décolletage, shoulders and back than she was used to. She stopped that nervy fidgeting as soon as she realised what she was doing, but she was grateful she had given in to Mrs Mount's persuasion and had some new gowns made, even though the cost had set her nerves jangling. They jangled again now, but for a completely different reason, as the Beauchamp brothers neared.

Liberty watched Olivia greet both of her brothers with a kiss…she really was very different from so many members of the *ton* with their painfully correct behaviour. Liberty found herself looking forward to her visit the next day.

Olivia drew Liberty forward. 'You have already met my brother Dominic, of course, Miss Lovejoy.'

Avon's eyes met hers and the question in their silver-grey depths prompted Liberty to elaborate. 'Jane has been regaling your sister with the story of how she and I met, my lord.'

'Ah, yes. I trust you are fully recovered, Miss Lovejoy?'

'Thank you, sir. I am.'

'And have you met my other brother, Alexander?' Olivia said. 'Alex, this is Miss Lovejoy.'

Liberty found herself the object of a quizzing stare from Alex's tawny eyes before he inclined his head. 'Miss Lovejoy. We have not formally met, but I am acquainted with your brother, Wendover.'

'I am aware of it, my lord.'

She knew her tone was a touch terse and a frown flicked between his brows, but he did not respond. Instead, his eyes moved on to his older brother, his gaze mocking. 'I'm surprised you're wasting your time with us, Dom. Haven't you an agenda to follow? Important decisions to make?'

Avon's eyes narrowed. 'Not here, Alex.'

'Your list is an open secret, Brother. No need for coyness. Did you know about it, Jane?' Jane nodded, somewhat reluctantly it appeared to Liberty. 'Have you heard of it, Miss Lovejoy? Lord Avon's list?'

Finding herself the centre of attention, Liberty swallowed, suddenly as nervous as Jane had looked. 'I have heard a mention of it,' she admitted.

Alex shrugged. 'Common knowledge, Dom. They're taking bets at White's.'

'In that case...' Dominic straightened the cuffs of his black swallowtail coat '... I shall go and attend to my...er...*agenda*, as you so elegantly phrase it, Alex.'

'No! Wait!' Olivia clutched at Dominic's sleeve. 'Don't do anything hasty, Dominic. I should like to at least meet these girls before you decide.'

A smile curled Avon's lips, but there was no humour in it. 'You wish to inspect my choice of potential bride, Sis?' He swept the room with a searching glance. 'You wish me to introduce you?' He crooked his arm. 'Come, then. Let us proceed.'

Liberty watched the byplay, fascinated by this glimpse into the undercurrents that swirled around the Beauchamps. The hint of sarcasm in Dominic's tone had brought fire flashing into his sister's eyes and Liberty was aware of Lord Hugo watching intently, with the focus of a cat waiting to pounce. She didn't doubt he would intervene to protect his wife if needed. Alex, on the other hand, now stood back. It was as though, having lit the fuse, he was waiting to enjoy the fireworks.

Liberty had always imagined other families were calm and polite in their dealings with each other. It appeared she was wrong. Maybe the Lovejoy family wasn't so different after all, with their petty squabbles. But there was no denying the strong bond between the Beauchamps and she prayed the bond between her and Gideon would prove resilient enough to be repaired.

'I have no wish to meet them in a noisy ballroom,' Olivia snapped. 'How can I talk to them properly or get to know their characters?'

'Their characters are none of your concern, Olivia. It will be my decision. Not yours.'

'*Pffft!* You know what I mean, Dominic.' She bit her lip, then stepped closer to him, putting her hand on his arm, her voice softer. Pleading. 'Of *course* it is your decision, Dom, but I want to help. Let me help. Please.'

A muscle ticked in his jaw. 'Very well. I shall drive you in the Park tomorrow and make the introductions.'

'Perfect! Are they all in town?'

Olivia was all smiles again and Lord Hugo relaxed. Alex, strangely, also looked satisfied, although Liberty would have sworn he had deliberately stirred trouble between his brother and sister in order to enjoy the ensuing argument.

'Yes, they are all here. And will no doubt be on parade in the Park at the fashionable hour,' he added in a cynical undertone.

'You never know, I might find you another lady to add to your list.' A frown darkened Dominic's brow, which Olivia blithely ignored. 'You may call for me at four o'clock. Miss Lovejoy is calling at two to meet Julius and Daisy. Did you know she and Wendover are twins as well?'

'I did know, but I don't understand why you should believe that has any relevance, Liv. Neither your two nor Miss Lovejoy and her brother are identical twins and—from the behaviour of the twins I have observed at Westfield—the non-identical twins appear to be much like any other family members who are close in age—they bicker much of the time and yet woe betide anyone who dares to upset the other.'

'Pooh! You cannot compare Julius and Daisy to the children at Westfield—heaven knows what traumas those poor mites have been through. Besides, Liberty *wants* to meet the twins, don't you, Liberty?'

'I…' Liberty—busy puzzling over Dominic's comments about children and Westfield—was caught unawares by the sudden direct appeal to her. 'I…of course, Lady Olivia. I should love to meet them.'

'Olivia! You must call me Olivia, for I foresee that we shall be great friends.' Olivia turned a triumphant smile on her brother. 'There, Dominic. See?'

Dominic shook his head at her. 'I see you are as manipulative as ever, minx.' He grinned at his brother-in-law. 'Thank God she is your responsibility now, Hugo. You should get a medal.'

Hugo grinned back. 'It's as well I thank God every day she's mine as well, then, is it not? Come on, Trouble—dare you be unfashionable and dance with your husband?' He led his beaming wife on to the dance floor.

Liberty felt it the second Dominic switched his attention back to her. 'So…you are to be interrogated about what it is like to be a twin, are you? Poor Olivia. She will go to any lengths, so determined is she to be a good mother.'

Alex smirked and Liberty stiffened.

'*Any* lengths? That includes, I collect, fraternising with someone like me?'

Dominic's lips quirked, but his voice was deadly serious. 'That is not what I meant at all, Miss Lovejoy. You really ought not to belittle yourself in such a way. There was no hidden meaning in my words—I meant exactly what I said. Olivia is determined to be the perfect mother and she drives herself relentlessly. I only hope the twins will not end up spoilt brats.'

'Like their mother,' Alex murmured, earning him a frown from his brother. 'Well, you can't deny she's always been wilful, Dom.'

'And you, my dear brother, should remember her good heart. She helped you out of more scrapes than I care to remember.'

'And led me into enough, too,' grumbled Alex, before straightening, his attention caught by something behind Dominic. Liberty followed his gaze and saw a group of young ladies heading in their direction, their collective attention firmly fixed on Dominic.

'Oh, lord,' Alex muttered. 'Pack alert. I'm off.'

Dominic glanced round at the approaching pack, as Alex had called them. It was an apt description, Liberty thought—like a pack of wolves with tasty prey in their sight. Beyond the tightening of his jaw, however, Dominic did not react.

'Janey…' Alex bowed '…would you do me the honour, etcetera, etcetera?'

'Alex! That is hardly the way to invite—'

'Oh, Janey don't mind, do you?' Alex grabbed Jane's hand. 'She knows me too well—she don't expect me to do the pretty with her! C'mon, let's dance.'

He tugged Jane on to the floor, leaving Liberty with Dominic. They were very soon surrounded by the young ladies, simpering and making eyes at Dominic, who appeared to effortlessly don the guise of the perfect gentleman as he responded with consummate gallantry. Liberty, although she was acknowledged, soon found herself deftly cut out. She stood, irresolute, for a moment but, as she made up her mind to walk away, Dominic raised his voice.

'Miss Lovejoy—pray tell me you have not forgotten our dance?'

She was torn between irritation at being an excuse to escape his coterie of admirers—and how was that different to how Alex had used Jane?—and admiration of his adroit handling of his dilemma. At least he waited for her reply rather than taking her acquiescence for granted as Alex had done with Jane.

She dipped a slight curtsy. 'Of course I have not forgotten, my lord.'

He sent his charming smile around his admirers. 'Please do excuse us, ladies.' He extended his hand. The girls parted and Liberty stepped towards him, trying to ignore the poisonous glances sent her way. She put her hand in his and their eyes met. She felt the jolt way down inside, in the pit of her belly, and heat washed across the entire surface of her skin, including her cheeks which she was certain were scarlet. His eyes darkened and she felt her lips part in response as her tongue darted out to moisten her unexpectedly dry lips. He dragged his gaze from hers.

'Come, Miss Lovejoy.'

His expression blank, his tone was one of world-weary boredom. But Liberty recognised it for the act it was. He led her into the set and she found herself the object of many more envious and a few disapproving looks.

'Are you sure your reputation will survive a dance with me?'

He cocked a brow and his lips twitched. 'Oh, I am tolerably sure it will remain intact.' He placed her next to Olivia in the line of dancers and, before retreating to stand with the gentlemen, he bent his head close to her ear and murmured, 'But please do not swoon again. *That* might take some explanation.'

His breath whispered across her neck, raising shivers in its wake. She smiled, reading it as a teasing remark rather than a reproof. When they first met she'd thought him superior and pompous, but was revising her opinion after he had spoken so movingly about his sister and now upon seeing him with Olivia and with Alex. A man who cared that much for his family couldn't be all bad. She only wished Gideon would demonstrate the same caring attitude.

Among the dancers taking their places for the next dance Liberty saw Hope and Verity and she experienced a tiny glow of triumph at her sisters' shocked and envious expressions when they noticed Liberty's partner.

*Now dare to tell me I've ruined your chances!*

It could only help their standing in society to be accepted by the Beauchamps, but she found herself hoping their acquaintance would prosper for her own sake. She had thoroughly enjoyed being included in their circle this evening and it made her realise quite how isolated she had become since Bernard's death, when she had withdrawn into the cocoon of her family.

She still found it difficult to accept that she deserved happiness. If she hadn't come to London five years ago, might she have spotted the symptoms earlier? She might have nursed them better. Saved them. The only way to make her guilt bearable had been to care for and protect the family she had left. But how could she protect Gideon… save him…when every time she tried to talk to him she ended up pushing him further away?

The music began. It was another country dance—one with which Liberty was familiar—and while she performed the steps mechanically she set her mind to wondering how might she use the Beauchamp connection to further her sisters' chances of meeting eligible men. If she could only persuade Dominic to stand up with both Hope *and* Verity, that would be a real coup. She had realised, since their first encounter, just how many of his peers looked up to Lord Avon, mainly due to his sporting prowess, and neither could she help but notice how many ladies—both young and not so young—fluttered around him, vying for attention. She understood their interest. Not only was he heir to a wealthy duke but he was handsome, he cut a fine, manly figure and he was intelligent.

'Miss Lovejoy? Liberty!'

Startled, she met Dominic's gaze, his silvery eyes like mirrors, as ever—reflecting the world back rather than allowing the light through to his soul.

'It is customary to make at least some pretence of interest in your partner's conversation.'

'Sorry. I was… I was…'

# Chapter Nine

The movement of the dance separated them before Liberty finished her excuse, leaving Dominic even more time to regret not following his instinct to avoid them when he had first seen Liberty Lovejoy with Hugo and Olivia. But then Alex had headed in their direction and he had seen Liberty's eyes light up. Her expressions were utterly transparent—a window to her inner thoughts and feelings—and Dominic's feet had carried him over to the group without a second thought. Who knew what mischief Alex might stir if he felt unjustly accused of leading Gideon astray; his tongue could be sharp and—quite why, he did not know—Dominic felt this compulsion to stay close rather than to walk away.

He'd almost forgotten she was a virtual stranger as he relaxed among his family and fell to bickering with Olivia, as they had in the old days before she had wed. But he had not forgotten Liberty's *presence*. He was viscerally aware of her the entire time, sensitive to the slightest change in her expression and the strange sensations she conjured within him. He could not shake the feeling—no, the certainty—that, somehow, he *knew* her, understood her, could feel her deepest emotions. And he felt…happy. Content.

Until those girls had surrounded them, isolating Liberty as effectively as a well trained sheepdog would cut a single sheep from a flock. Dominic had felt the cloak of his public image fall into place as he became the Marquess of Avon and unaccustomed resentment at those girls had bubbled under his skin when he saw Liberty hesitate, then turn to walk away. Before he could consider the consequences, he was asking her to dance, when nothing had been further from his thoughts or intention. But the pleasure that radiated throughout his body as she placed her hand in his banished his doubts as to the wisdom of his action. Why should he not dance with his sister's friend? Nobody else could see how Liberty Lovejoy fascinated him. As far as anyone else was concerned, it was no different to him standing up with Jane.

But the minute the dance began, those insidious doubts wormed their way once again into his thoughts, fuelled by those memories of his mother, who had been more and more on his mind since his decision that this would be the Season he chose his bride.

*Make me proud, my Son. Society will watch your every move. Never disgrace your position as heir.*

His attempts to quash his mother's voice were not helped by the fact that the innocuous remarks he addressed to his partner were roundly ignored. Liberty appeared more interested in her sisters than in her own partner and he questioned again why he hadn't just left her to Alex's tender mercies. As the steps brought them together again, his irritation got the better of him.

'Well? Have you a reason for ignoring me?'

Even as the words left his mouth he regretted them. It was hardly Liberty's fault he found her so maddeningly irresistible.

Her eyes flashed and her lips thinned. 'I was debating which of those charming young misses were on that list of yours, Lord Avon.'

They parted company, then the steps brought them together again, but before Dominic could speak, Liberty continued, 'I am certain any one of them would make the perfect Marchioness—as long as they possess the requisite bloodlines, of course.'

Her words stung and he retaliated instinctively. 'None of them, for your information. My future wife will not be a female who makes her intentions so very obvious. Discretion and poise—they are the attributes I seek.'

He cringed inside at how very pompous he sounded, but the words were out there and he was damned if he'd humble himself by retracting them.

'As well as *calmness* and *elegance*, if my recollection is correct.' Hectic flags of colour painted her cheeks. 'And now *discretion* to add to your list of requirements.'

'Do not forget poise, Miss Lovejoy.'

'I have not forgotten it, sir, but I am well aware that elegance and poise are one and the same. Did you think me uneducated as well as ill-bred?'

The words hissed out at him from under her breath. The movement of the dance parted them again and he cautioned himself not to further fuel the flame of her temper with any attempt to defend his position. Liberty—as he might have guessed—had no such compunction. She continued as soon as they were close enough for him to hear her. He supposed he should be grateful she waited until none of the neighbouring couples would be able to overhear her tirade.

'I am sorry to disappoint you—although I make no doubt that well-educated is not an essential quality for your ideal wife. I also happen to have an excellent memory. Not this time for the attributes necessary for the perfect Marchioness, but for the *undesirable* traits.'

Again they moved apart and again they came back together.

'Now…let me see…it was most *definitely* no vigour or passion. I can see, however, that none of those insipid young misses would disappoint you in that regard!'

He clamped his jaw tight as the movement of the dance parted them again. What the hell was he doing dancing with Liberty Lovejoy and allowing her to provoke him? All five of the ladies on his original list, together with their families, were present tonight. He would dance with them all, even though Caroline was currently his first choice. That would keep the gossips busy and it would be a far better use of his time.

He and Liberty circled one another, with no opportunity for speech before they parted company yet again. A glance across the ballroom brought Lady Caroline into his line of sight. She was elegant and cool as she performed the steps, smiling serenely as she responded to her partner's comments. He switched his gaze to Liberty—her eyes bright with accusation, her skin flushed, her lips parted and plump, her breasts…*glorious*. His loins tightened. He could not even summon any anger towards her because every word she had said was true. But it didn't change the fact that his bride must be the perfect lady, despite the yearning of every fibre of his being for a woman who was palpably *not* the perfect lady.

Never had he felt so very enticed by any female at a society event. Or by any female anywhere.

He found himself executing a figure of eight with Olivia.

'Are you and Miss Lovejoy *quarrelling*, Dominic?'

Caution whispered through him. If Olivia had noticed, others might, too.

'Don't be absurd!'

Olivia smiled impishly as she circled around him and rejoined Hugo. Dominic and Liberty came together again and this time, before she could speak, Dominic squeezed her hand.

'I apologise unreservedly. Tell me how I might make amends.'

It stole the next wave of invective from her tongue, but the gleam in her eyes warned him that she would take full advantage of his peace offering.

'Will you dance with my sisters, my lord? Please?'

'Your *sisters*?'

Her worry was plain as she sought her sisters among the dancers before directing her gold-flecked midnight-blue gaze back to him.

'Surely that would help us to be more fully accepted?'

He could not bring himself to refuse such a simple, direct request. 'Very well. I shall dance with each of them tonight. But please do not ask me to make a habit of it.'

Her grateful smile caressed him and he cursed the fact that his list was common knowledge. If it were not, he might have delayed finding a wife until next year. But he could not, with honour, back away now speculation over his choice was rife. Or, rather, he *would not* back away. It was one of the standards he set himself as a gentleman—to be true to his word. He knew there could never be more than friendship between him and Liberty, but he might have been better able to relax and enjoy that friendship had the eyes of the *ton* not been watching his every move for a hint as to his intentions.

'I am relieved they have achieved *some* success,' Liberty continued, 'but I cannot help worrying.' She frowned and bit into her plump lower lip, sending sparks sizzling through him. 'I know we are not fully accepted everywhere and I'm afraid that can only get worse if Gideon continues in his reckless ways. If only he would come to his senses…he still won't listen to me.'

'But he is here tonight and behaving impeccably. He looks in a fair way to being smitten with Twyford's eldest girl. That must surely please you?'

She released her lip and smiled again, her eyes crinkling—a smile that was balm to his soul. He kept his expression impassive, again conscious of too many eyes watching.

'Yes, it does. Anyone would be preferable to that actress—I pray he has given her up entirely! And thank you for agreeing to partner Hope and Verity after having danced with me. It is very kind of you.'

'It will help some people to accept you more readily, as will your friendship with Olivia if that continues.'

The dance ended and Liberty took Dominic's proffered arm as they left the floor.

'As I said at the outset, your brother is simply finding his feet in town. I've talked to Alex and I've kept an eye on the pair of them—I have seen nothing for you to worry about.'

Liberty smiled with such trust in her eyes that his heart clenched. How could she affect him so, with just one look? Again, he blanked his expression, delivering her back to Mrs Mount with a wash of relief. Resolutely, he walked away. He would approach her sisters later, after dancing with other partners...partners whose name was not Lovejoy. And, as he had already put Caroline

Warnock to the head of the queue, where better than to start with her?

'Good evening, Lord Avon.' Lady Caroline dipped a graceful curtsy.

'Good evening, my lady.' Dominic bowed. 'May I say how very charming you look this evening?'

'You are too kind, my lord.' Caroline raised her fan and fluttered it, her dark brown gaze clinging to Dominic's face.

'Dare I hope you have a dance available this evening, Lady Caroline?'

'I do, my lord. It is the supper dance, if that is acceptable?'

Dominic was aware of Lady Druffield watching them from her nearby chair with a gleam of satisfaction. Lady Georgiana's mother sat with the Marchioness and was also watching Dominic and Caroline, her expression revealing no hint of her feelings, yet Dominic knew she would be loathing every second of her rival's triumph.

'That is most acceptable,' he said to Caroline. 'Now, if you will excuse me…?'

He did not wait for her response, but headed straight for Lady Amelia and Lady Sarah and secured their hands for dances. Then he scanned the room for Lady Georgiana. His gaze collided with that of Liberty, accusation burning in her eyes. Her thoughts were as plain as if she had shouted them across the ballroom—*You promised to dance with Hope and Verity.* Although such transparency of feelings was frowned upon by most members of the *ton*, Dominic was charmed and entertained by them. And by her. As long as he took care not to single her out—*or to annoy her while we are dancing! I've learned my lesson there!*—he could still amuse himself by teasing her.

He cocked his brow and had the satisfaction of seeing that blatant accusation darken into a glower. He would approach her sisters in his own good time—he would not march to Liberty Lovejoy's command. He caught sight of Lady Georgiana and made his way across the room to discover she was free for the next dance. He led her on to the floor, only to find they were next to Liberty and her current partner, Stephen Damerel, damn his eyes. The man was older than Dominic and the second son of Lord Rushock. He was a decent enough man, but he was a scholar and far too staid for a lively woman such as Liberty.

'My lord? My *lord*!'

Georgiana's petulant tone grabbed his attention. He pushed Liberty and Damerel from his thoughts to concentrate on his own partner, but the dance seemed never ending and, despite his best intentions, he found his gaze straying to Liberty on several occasions. By the time he'd seen her smiling at Damerel in that open, guileless way of hers he was ready to punch something. Or someone. But through it all, he chatted with Georgiana and, at the end of the dance, he felt sure she would have no cause to label him as an inattentive partner.

*One ticked off. Three more to go. Plus Hope and Verity, of course.*

He didn't dare to question himself as to why he was keen to get his duty dances out of the way. He just knew he was. He had no partner for the next and, spying Hope close to where Mrs Mount sat, he grabbed a glass of champagne from a footman carrying a tray, drained it in one and headed in their direction. He arrived at the same moment as Liberty, her hand on Damerel's arm. Dominic nodded at the other man, who returned his nod, bowed to the ladies and then sauntered away.

Dominic turned to Hope. 'Would you care to dance, Miss Lovejoy? If your card is not already full?'

She glanced at Liberty before replying, 'Thank you, my lord. I am engaged for the next two, but the first after supper is free.'

'Perfect. And I believe the one after *that* is a waltz, so…' He captured Liberty's gaze. 'Would you do me the honour of waltzing with me, Miss Lovejoy?'

Her brow creased, puzzlement in her eyes. If

she could have asked him what he was about—which she could not with Mrs Mount and Hope in earshot—he would not be able to tell her because he had no idea himself. What the devil had prompted him to ask her to waltz, of all things? He must enjoy being tortured. And, quite apart from that, he must now make very sure to engage his other partners for a second dance—ever since he had first been on the town he had made a point of never dancing more than once with any lady at a ball. He suppressed a sigh. How did this one woman manage to provoke him into such uncharacteristic behaviour? And why did he have to meet her this Season of all Seasons? He couldn't stop thinking about her, but it would not, could not, change the future he had mapped out.

Liberty parted her lips to reply but, before she could speak, Alex joined them, slapping Dominic on the shoulder as Hope's next partner arrived and led her on to the floor.

'Just the people I need to speak to,' said Alex. 'And both in the same place as well. Am I not the fortunate one?'

Liberty's eyebrows flicked high.

'Miss Liberty Lovejoy.' Alex bowed. 'Would you kindly do me the honour of saving the supper dance for me?'

A silent growl vibrated in Dominic's throat, not helped by the impish smile Alex directed at him.

'Why. Yes. Thank you. Both of you.' Liberty looked from one of them to the other, clearly as confused as Dominic. 'You are most kind.'

'Oh, think nothing of it,' said Alex airily. 'Livvy wanted me to ask you, so we can eat supper with her and Hugo.'

'Oh. Well...will Jane not expect—?'

She fell silent as Alex laughed. 'Lord, no. We're just friends and, besides, her stepmother has promised the supper dance to Pikeford on her behalf.' He grinned at Dominic. 'It makes you thankful we didn't end up with her as our stepmother, don't it? Thank the Lord we've got Rosalind. So, Dom...who've you bagged for supper? Livvy said I was to ask you to join us, too, but—just a hint, you understand, Brother—when Olivia said *ask* she meant *tell*.'

Dominic closed his eyes briefly, shaking his head as he suppressed a smile. Life had been dull the past few years without Alex and Olivia and their irrepressible antics to brighten his life.

'I think I might legitimately dodge that particular invitation. I'm promised to Lady Caroline and I should imagine she will wish to remain with her particular friends.'

'On your head be it, Brother. Only Olivia did say, most particularly, that she wanted us all together for supper because, believe it or not, she has missed us.'

'Oh, very well. I'll see what I can do.'

'Good man! I'll leave you two in peace.'

With a wink, Alex wandered away. Dominic had already spent too much time with Liberty that evening but, somehow, he could not tear himself away. Not yet.

'Do you not have a partner for this dance, my lord?'

'No. I do not care to dance every dance. What about you?'

'Alas, no gentleman requested my hand for this dance.' Her full lips pursed slightly, then twitched into a half-smile. 'But I *am* engaged for a waltz after supper and I am looking forward to that exceedingly.'

'In order that you may tear me off another couple of strips?'

'Avon! That is *most* ungentlemanly of you.' Her eyes sparkled, drawing him in, and it was with an effort he tore his gaze from hers, blanked his expression and cast a bored look over the dancers. 'You did admit I was sorely provoked.'

He couldn't resist another sideways glance at her, a glance that revealed twinkling eyes above pouting lips that drew his gaze like a magnet. Good grief. They were in a crowded ballroom and all he could think about was sweeping her into his arms and kissing her. His hand rubbed at the back of his neck as his inner voice of caution screamed at him to walk away. But still he lingered.

The trouble was…his interest in her wasn't confined to lust. He just enjoyed being with her, even when they were bickering. Especially when they were bickering, in fact, because she treated him like an ordinary man. Every other female—apart from his family—treated him as 'the heir'. And damned if he wasn't complicit in that…he had occupied that public position for so much of his life it had become second nature.

'As I recall,' he adopted a light, teasing tone, 'I offered you an apology without admitting fault. It is called being gallant.'

'Very well.' She sighed dramatically. 'If you are intent on making me shoulder the blame, there is nothing more I can say. But I must tell you how grateful I am that you kept your promise and are engaged to stand up with Hope.'

He read the question in her expression.

'I have not asked Verity yet, but I shall. Which reminds me—I saw her dancing with Bridlington earlier. You may not be aware, but he has a somewhat disreputable reputation—an unsuitable partner for any young innocent.'

She changed instantly from a teasing, flirting girl into a serious woman. 'Thank you for the warning. I confess I thought him rather old for her and I have noticed he seeks her out between dances, too. I shall speak to Mrs Mount.'

'Would you like me to have a word with him?'

'N-no. I do not think so. I think it is Gideon's place to do so, don't you?'

'You're probably right. But if you wish me to intervene, just let me know.'

'Thank you. I will.' They watched the dancing in silence for a few minutes. 'My lord…may I ask you something?'

'If you must.'

'Oh! You wound me. How grudging you sound.'

'I sound that way because such a request from you usually means trouble.'

She laughed. 'You barely know me and you have deduced that already? You cut me to the quick, sir.' Then she sobered. 'I realise it may be an impertinent question, but what is Westfield?'

'Westfield?'

He was happy to be a patron of the school and to help the children with their lessons and find positions for the older children in households and as apprentices but he was uncomfortable talking about it—it smacked too much of puffing off his own good deeds. He did what he did for the children, not to bolster his reputation.

'Yes. You spoke of it earlier, when we were with your sister.'

'It is an orphan asylum supported by my second cousin, Lady Stanton. I merely help her out occasionally.'

'I was intrigued by how knowledgeable you seemed about the children. And about twins.'

He shrugged, keeping his attention away from her and on the dancers. 'Much of what I said is common sense. The rest I have gleaned from Felicity… Lady Stanton, that is.' The introduction of this subject gave him the impetus he needed to tear himself away from her. 'Now, if you will excuse me, Miss Lovejoy, I ought to circulate.' He bowed. 'I expect I shall see you at supper.'

He walked away without giving her a chance to respond. He knew, from when he had first started supporting Westfield, that it elicited more questions from others than he cared to answer. Questions as to why he, a wealthy and privileged aristocrat, should concern himself with orphans and other destitute children. But to answer those inevitably led to questions about his mother and her death…and he had no wish to resurrect those memories, or to share them. With anyone. He strolled on, stopping and chatting to acquaintances on occasion, but all the time he was conscious that none of these people were really his friends. The people he wanted to be with were his family. He was looking forward to his father's arrival and that of his aunts and uncles.

He paused and scanned the ballroom, his restless gaze settling as it found Liberty. She was talking, animatedly, with her brother, who was glowering at her. Why would she not take his advice? Could she not see that the more she badgered Wendover the more likely he was to rebel?

'Keeping an eye on the luscious Liberty again?'

He gritted his teeth as Alex joined him. 'I don't know what you are talking about.'

'Come on, Dom…best to keep moving, or the wolves'll be circling again.' Alex linked his arm through Dominic's and they strolled on. 'And you know precisely what I'm talking about. I haven't seen you pay this much attention to a woman for…well, for ever, actually. What I don't understand is why you left her standing just now. I gave you privacy and you threw the opportunity away.'

'It makes no difference—I might find her attractive and enjoy her company, but you know as well as I do that she is totally unsuitable to be a future duchess.'

'Do I? How so? Her brother's an earl; you give every impression of enjoying her company.' He leaned in closer. 'And you can't tell me you don't want to—'

'Enough!' Dominic snatched his arm from Alex's. 'How about you and I meet for a sparring session at Jackson's tomorrow?'

It would give him huge satisfaction to punch that knowing smirk off his brother's face, but he could hardly plant him a facer at the Twyfords' ball.

Alex grinned. 'Not on your life, Brother. I ain't that stupid.'

'Despite appearances to the contrary!'

'Ouch! Take care! That wit of yours is sharp enough to cause real damage to a fellow.'

'Good. You deserve it.'

'Aw, come on, Dom. It's just a bit of gentle ribbing…you know I don't mean anything by it.'

Dominic scanned Alex's expression of innocence. He sighed. 'I know it's hard for you, but try to respect the fact that I am simply not in the mood for your peculiar sense of humour. Not today.'

Alex nudged him. 'We'll talk again tomorrow, then.'

He winked and strolled away, leaving Dominic to inwardly seethe. The music was drawing to a close, which meant the supper dance would be next. Battening down his exasperation, he set off to find a drink before it was time to seek out Lady Caroline Warnock—his next partner and, very possibly, his future wife.

# *Chapter Ten*

Dominic's warning about Lord Bridlington had brought Liberty's protective instincts rushing to the surface. She watched His Lordship as he sniffed around Verity—really, there was no other way to describe it—and her disquiet grew. He reminded her of nothing more than a street dog on the hunt for a casual coupling. Liberty crossed the ballroom to her sister and drew her aside.

'Lord Bridlington is very attentive, Verity. Has he put his name down for a second dance?'

Verity flushed. 'Yes. The supper dance.'

Liberty frowned at her sister's subdued tone. 'Do you like him?'

'Not…not really. But Mrs Mount told us we must never refuse a gentleman if he asks us to dance. And, if we do, we cannot then dance with *any* gentleman. And she told me I should be flattered by his attention because he is an earl and… and he would be a suitable match.'

'Well, *I* think it would be an appalling match—*if* his intentions are honourable, which I beg to doubt. I'll ask Gideon to warn him off, shall I?'

'You mean you won't go storming up to him yourself and harangue him?' There was a teasing note in Verity's tone, but Liberty recognised the kernel of truth in her question and felt her skin heat.

'No, I shall not. That,' she added, with a wink, 'is not how a lady should behave. You see… I *am* learning.'

But Gideon, when she caught up with him, was less than amenable to her suggestion that he pull rank as Verity's brother and partner her for the supper dance, ousting Bridlington.

'Don't see there's anything I can do if she's already agreed to have supper with the fellow,' he said, stretching his neck to peer over the sea of heads in the ballroom. 'I'm engaged myself for the supper dance, as it happens. To Lady Emily.' His wrapt expression as he said her name spoke volumes. 'In fact…there she is! I must go, Sis. Look, don't worry—nothing's going to happen to Verity in a crowded ballroom. I'll speak to Bridlington later.'

Liberty bit back her frustration as Gideon hurried away. Was it really too much to ask him to take an interest in his sister and to protect her?

'Libby.' A flustered-looking Hope grabbed her

arm. 'My flounce is torn.' She pivoted and indicated the damaged lace at her hem, at the back of her dress. 'Will you come and help me fix it? Only I needs must make haste because it is the supper dance next and I am promised to Lord Whiteley.'

'Of course.' Liberty couldn't mistake Hope's suppressed excitement. It seemed she was as happy with her supper partner as Gideon was, unlike poor Verity. 'Come, we'll go to the withdrawing room and pin it up. It won't take long.'

As they headed upstairs, Hope said, 'Are you quite well, Lib? You look a little out of sorts. Was it…was it something Lord Avon said?' She glanced around, then drew Liberty to one side of the landing to sit on a window seat. 'I saw you with him earlier and I cannot help but notice how you seem to…to…gravitate towards one another.' She clutched Liberty's hand. 'Oh! Would it not be exciting if he fell in love with you?'

Liberty wrenched her hand free and stood up. 'What nonsense you talk at times, Hope. No, it was nothing to do with Lord Avon. It was Gideon.'

'Oh, *Liberty*! Have you been harrying him again? Why can't you *trust* him?'

Liberty bit her tongue, hurt that Hope assumed she was interfering when all she was trying to do was to protect Verity.

'Come.' She recalled she was due to partner Alex and that Dominic might join them for supper. Perhaps she would take him up on his offer after all, if Gideon was so blind to his brotherly duty. 'I have a packet of pins in my pocket so we shall have that tear mended in a trice and you can return to your Lord Whiteley.'

They went into the room set aside for the female guests. A maid was on duty, ready to assist any ladies who needed help, but Liberty waved her away. It would be a matter of moments to pin the flounce and then they could return to the ball. They went behind a screen placed across the room to afford privacy and Hope stepped up on to a low stool while Liberty knelt behind her. She barely registered the sound of the door opening until a haughty female voice said, 'Have you seen that lumpy Lovejoy creature positively *throwing* herself at Avon?'

Liberty froze as a spiteful titter sounded from the other side of the screen. She settled back on to her heels and looked up at Hope, who was peering over the top of the screen. Seeing her sister's mouth come open, Liberty wrapped her fingers around her ankle and squeezed a warning. Hope glanced down and Liberty shook her head, putting one finger to her lips. Hope grimaced back and held three fingers aloft.

'I declare, I don't know how he remains civil to

her.' It was the same voice, one she did not recognise, but one that clearly denoted the aristocratic heritage of its owner. 'I heard that she swooned right into his arms at the Trents' rout party and, even before that, I saw her for myself in the Park, attempting to waylay him while he was driving *me* in his curricle.'

*Lady Caroline!*

Mrs Mount had identified Lady Caroline Warnock as Dominic's passenger in the Park that day and, since then, Liberty had increasingly heard her name touted as the front runner in the race to become the Marchioness of Avon. It was hard to reconcile this malicious-sounding female with the butter-wouldn't-melt-in-her-mouth young lady Liberty had seen in public.

'But there...what else is to be expected of such a family?' the hateful voice continued. 'The Earl of Wendover, indeed! The grandson of a coal merchant! Better they allowed the title to slip into abeyance than let such people be elevated above their station.'

'Did Avon mention her? I saw you talking with him.' A different voice this time.

'No, he did not. And quite rightly, too. She is far beneath his notice, although for some unfathomable reason his sister appears to be encouraging an acquaintance with the woman. No, Avon was too intent on engaging me for the supper dance.'

Caroline's smug self-satisfaction made Liberty long to slap her. A third voice joined in the conversation.

'Well, *I* saw Avon dancing with her and they talked together afterwards, too. They looked positively *intimate*.'

'Such a comment is beneath you, Elizabeth—' Caroline again, her voice sharp now '—and I suggest you do not repeat it, for it makes you appear a bad loser. I have not heard anyone whisper *your* name in connection with Lord Avon's list. But, then…a mere baronet's daughter…hardly a fitting background for a duchess, is it, Pamela?'

'Oh, no. Most unfitting, I agree.' The breathless adoration in Pamela's reply raised Liberty's hackles and presumably had the same effect on the invisible Elizabeth, for a soft *hmmph* reached the listeners' ears. 'My brother is certain you will win him, Caro. Oh, to think! A marchioness! Vincent told me he has a hundred guineas riding on you, so you'd better make sure you win.'

'Oh, I shall. I made sure to drop him a hint about poor Georgiana's shocking piano playing. I don't see *her* usurping me as favourite… and rumour has it Avon was less than impressed by Sarah and Amelia scuttling after him when Lumpy Liberty staged her swoon. But…let us not linger, or we shall miss the start of the supper dance. Did I mention that I am promised to Avon?'

The door opened and closed and they heard a muttered 'Yes. More than once' from Elizabeth before she, too, left the room.

'Well!' Hope's voice rang with indignation. 'How *dare*—?'

'Yes, yes. I agree, Hope, but let me finishing pinning your lace or we shall be late for the dance. We will complain bitterly about those arrogant madams later.'

'Very well. But you will take note that I am not the only person who noticed that you and Avon seemed somewhat…friendly.'

There was little she could say to that, so Liberty finished the repair and they hurried down to the ballroom, reaching the door just as the first strains of the dance sounded. Both of their partners were standing with Mrs Mount. Lord Whiteley's face showed nothing but relief at the sight of Hope. Alex's showed…nothing at all as their eyes met and Liberty's courage wavered as she walked forward to take his hand. No doubt here was another one who disapproved of her and the thought of sharing supper with that spiteful cat, Caroline, set her stomach churning. How would she resist retaliating if Caroline was as nasty to her face as she had been in the withdrawing room?

To her surprise, however, Alex was the perfect gentleman and at no point did his inoffensive conversation cause Liberty even the slightest discomfort. Once the dance was over, he escorted her into the second supper room where he had arranged to meet Olivia and Hugo. It was one of the smallest tables, set for six, and they were the first to sit down, shortly followed by Olivia and Hugo.

'Well!' Olivia's attention was fixed on the doorway as footmen served the dishes for a hot supper. 'I know you asked Dominic to join us, Alex, for he told me so himself. And he promised he would do so. Where can he be?' She spooned up some white soup from the bowl set in front of her. 'This is delicious! Oh! Look! *There* they are…and…is that not one of your sisters, Liberty?'

Liberty looked up at the doorway to see Dominic walk into the room with Verity on one arm and Caroline—sporting a sour expression quite unlike her usual ladylike mien—on the other. Dominic looked…impassive. But the slight compression of his lips told her he was angry. Verity looked… Liberty pushed back her chair, ready to rush to her distressed sister's aid, but a strong hand closed around her wrist, preventing her from rising.

'Don't draw attention,' Alex muttered. 'You'll find out soon enough.'

Dominic paused by a footman and murmured something, indicating their table with a nod of his head. The footman hurried away, and Dominic guided Verity and Caroline to their table. He seated Verity first, next to Liberty, and then a pursed-lipped Caroline next to Hugo. The footman brought another chair, which he placed between Verity and Caroline, and another man arrived with porcelain and silverware to set a place for Dominic. No one uttered a word until the servants were out of earshot, but Liberty could see Verity's hands gripped tightly in her lap and her chest rose and fell as though she were out of breath.

'What happened?'

Liberty's question was directed at Dominic. He saw her grope for Verity's hands and cover them, folding her fingers around them.

'Bridlington became a little over-enthusiastic,' he replied. 'Fortunately, Caroline and I happened to see what he was about and I…er…persuaded him to think again.'

Alex gestured at Dominic's hand—he saw a smear of blood on his knuckle and slipped his hand beneath the table, out of sight.

'Lord Avon was quite the hero,' said Caroline. 'Goodness knows what the outcome might have been for your dear sister, Miss Lovejoy, had he not intervened.'

She smiled warmly at Dominic, surprising him. When they first saw Bridlington trying to manoeuvre Verity into a side room, Caroline had tried to persuade Dominic not to get involved, more concerned about her own and Dominic's reputations than about what was happening to Verity. Maybe he should excuse her immediate reaction. After all, most gently born ladies would surely prefer to avoid any sort of altercation.

'I confess the entire event has shaken my nerves alarmingly.' She reached for her glass with a visibly trembling hand. 'I dare say I do not stem from such robust stock as the Lovejoys.'

Liberty's eyes glinted dangerously and her mouth opened.

'I am sure no one was unaffected, Lady Caroline,' Dominic interjected, quick to forestall Liberty. 'But now I suggest we all settle down and enjoy this delicious supper and forget all about it. Lord Bridlington has left the ball now so there is no need to dwell upon what happened.'

'But I want to know—'

'You do know, Miss Lovejoy. I have told you.'

'I should like to know as well,' said Olivia. 'Did you *punch* him, Dom? We've all seen the blood on your hand, so you needn't bother to hide it.' She leaned across the table. 'Are you *sure* you are all right, Miss Lovejoy?'

'I am all right now, thank you. I am exceedingly grateful to your brother, however.' Verity smiled at him. 'He is right…can we please forget this and enjoy our supper?'

Olivia's intervention had given Liberty time to subside, but Dominic could tell her blood was still simmering and he had no doubt he would be questioned thoroughly during their waltz. His pulse kicked at the thought of holding her even as he again mentally slated himself for taking the risk of dancing with her twice.

'Indeed. I suggest we forget all about that unfortunate occurrence.' Caroline raised her spoon to her mouth, and swallowed. 'This white soup really is excellent, do you not agree?'

'Excellent indeed. How fortunate it is not *lumpy*, Lady Caroline,' said Liberty in a kindly manner. 'That, I am persuaded, would quite spoil your enjoyment.'

Dominic frowned and he saw Olivia shoot Liberty a questioning look, but Caroline seemed not to notice Liberty's overtly sweet tone.

'Indeed it would, Miss Lovejoy.'

Her smile was all graciousness. Did she have any clue that Liberty's smile wasn't genuine? It didn't take Dominic long to realise that she did not. It was increasingly clear that none of Liberty's comments or opinions mattered to Caroline because she quite clearly viewed Liberty—and Verity, too, although she barely joined the conversation—as utterly beneath her notice. She was polite and respectful—even delightful—in her dealings with Dominic, Alex, Olivia and Hugo, however.

It took the duration of that one supper for Dominic to change his mind about his list. A beautiful singing voice was no compensation for such arrogance. And how, he wondered, would someone such as Caroline respond to the spouses of his father, uncle and aunt? Rosalind, his stepmother, might be a duchess now, but her father was a simple soldier and her grandfather a silversmith. Thea, Uncle Vernon's wife, was the daughter of a glassmaker, and Zach, Aunt Cecily's husband—who refused to allow anyone to call him uncle—had a Romany mother. Dominic would never risk introducing discord into his beloved family.

He was still hesitant about Georgiana and her fear of horses, which left him with Lady Sybilla Gratton.

As they finished their supper, Gideon appeared behind Liberty and Verity.

'I thought you said Verity was having supper with Bridlington, Liberty?' he said, accusingly.

'I've been searching everywhere for them… Mrs Mount didn't seem to know where they were and neither did Hope and now, after worrying the life out of me, I find she's been with you the whole time!'

Liberty's cheeks flushed. 'If you had done your duty as I asked, you would have known precisely where she was.'

Verity jumped to her feet. 'You are being unfair, Gideon.' She grasped his arm, and lowered her voice. 'I was due to have supper with him, but…but…'

She cast an anxious look around the table, then put her lips to her brother's ear. As she whispered, Gideon's face leached of colour and his gaze sought Dominic's as one hand came to rest on Liberty's shoulder.

'I am sorry, Sis. I shouldn't have sounded off at you… I was worried when I couldn't find them. And I am grateful to you, Avon. You can be sure I'll have something to say to Bridlington next time our paths cross.' He put his arm around Verity and hugged her. 'Are you all right? Do you want to go home? I'll take you, if you do.'

'No.' Verity raised her chin and Dominic recognised the family resemblance with Liberty in that defiant gesture. 'I shall not allow that… that…*scoundrel*…to spoil my enjoyment of my first-ever ball.'

Alert to the nuances of Liberty's expression, Dominic saw her pride at her sister's strength and then, as her gaze met and held that of her twin, love shone from her eyes. Then a tut and a sigh sounded from behind him and he sensed movement. Caroline, her lips thinly disapproving, was preparing to leave the table. He stood up and pulled her chair back.

'Allow me.'

'Thank you, my lord.'

She smiled at him and held out her hand. Dominic helped her to rise and then she placed her hand on his sleeve, clearly expecting his escort back to the ballroom. He breathed a sigh of relief when he returned her to her mother and then sought out Hope, his next partner. But throughout the dance he was distracted, watching Liberty, who was dancing with Redbridge—that incorrigible tattletale—and laughing up at him.

'You are dancing with Liberty next, I believe, my lord?'

The question jerked his attention away from Liberty and back to Hope, who was studying him with something like speculation in her eyes. Drat the girl.

'I am. I apologise for neglecting you, Miss Lovejoy. Seeing your sister with Lord Redbridge reminded me of a matter I must discuss with him, but that is no excuse for ignoring my partner.'

He set himself to entertaining Hope and, by the end of the dance, he thought his distraction a success. They reached Mrs Mount at the same time as Redbridge and Liberty, who was beaming all over her face. Hadn't anyone ever told her it was unladylike to exhibit an excess of emotion? He could not tear his gaze from her as he wondered who had conjured up such a ridiculous rule. And, more importantly, why?

He bit down his irritation at Redbridge for encouraging Liberty and then had to bite it back even harder when he noticed Hope looking from him to Liberty and back again. He didn't try to interpret her expression, he just concentrated on blanking his own.

It was a relief when it was time for the next dance and he could lead Liberty on to the dance floor.

'Why did you ask me to waltz?'

Liberty gazed up at Dominic, her eyes smiling although her lips were serious. Dominic's fingers flexed on her waist, holding her more securely as they entered their first turn. The truthful answer was that he did not know. The words had slipped from his lips before his brain could stop them. But he didn't regret his impulse—she felt so right in his arms. If only… He quashed that wish before it could fully form. There was no *if only*. Not for him. He knew his duty to the Dukedom. To his father. To his mother.

As ever, the thought of his mother conjured forth that feeling of never quite being good enough. If she had lived, what would she think of the man he had become? *Would* she, finally, be proud? His chest tightened as he recalled the last time he had seen his mother—the only time in his eight years he could remember any spontaneous gesture of affection from her. It was her custom to walk around the lake every day when she was at home at the Abbey and, that day, Dominic had asked if he might go with her. Rather than the brusque refusal he expected, she had smiled at him and patted his cheek.

'Mr Brockley will be waiting for you, Dominic, but—if you are good and pay attention in your lessons—maybe we can go out again later.'

Later had never come. He had never seen his mother again and the memory of that last encounter had, over the years, helped to fuel his determination to fulfil his destiny.

He wrenched his thoughts out of the past—Liberty awaited his answer…why *had* he asked her to waltz? He gazed into her midnight-blue eyes, breathed in the scent of roses…now not solely his mother's preserve, but that of Liberty Lovejoy as well. Mother wouldn't approve of Liberty, that was for sure. But it was only one waltz.

'Why not?' he countered.

'Well, now. Let me see. Maybe because this is the cautious Lord Avon who is intent on selecting the perfect bride to complete his perfect life and who appears to conduct his entire life with the sole purpose of protecting his reputation?'

He strove to keep his expression blank at her succinct summation of his life.

'So cautious, in fact,' she continued, 'that I have heard it whispered that he never dances twice with the same young lady. And yet this is our second dance this evening.'

He hid his surprise. 'You will note, however, that I have engaged several young ladies to dance with me twice this evening.'

Their gazes fused, her blue eyes knowing. 'I *also* noted that the other engagements followed mine as you sought to divert attention from your uncharacteristic slip.'

'Slip?'

'You masked it well, my lord, but I saw the shock in your eyes in the split second after you asked me to waltz. Were I a more generous person, I would have refused that impulsive offer, but I could not resist accepting, if only to see how you would manage your mistake.'

'It was no mistake. I did and I *do* want to waltz with you, Liberty Lovejoy.'

He heard her quick intake of breath and, without volition, his hand tightened on hers and his other hand slid further around her waist, drawing her closer. Caution clamoured through his brain, but he ignored it.

'You...' Her voice sounded breathless. 'You are unused to acting on impulse, I would guess.'

'A man in my position cannot afford to act on impulse.'

She stayed silent and a quick glance down revealed a wrinkled forehead.

'You are puzzled?'

Her head snapped up. 'No. Not puzzled. Sad.'

*'Sad?'*

He felt her shrug. 'It must be an uncomfortable existence, to be forever on your guard, wary of how you appear to others.'

Her words came close to his earlier thoughts about ridiculous rules, but they were a fact of life. His life, in any case. 'That is the world we live in. That is what it means to be part of the *haut ton*. But, to return to your original question, I asked you to waltz because it is a chance to talk uninterrupted. With no risk of being overheard.'

Her eyebrows arched. 'You wanted the opportunity to talk to me without being overheard? Why, Lord Avon...' she batted her eyelashes at him '...what can you possibly have to say to me that ought not to be overheard?' She tilted her head, her lips closer to his ear. 'Will I be shocked?'

Her breath on his skin raised the hairs at his nape. He was playing with fire. His common sense warned him to keep his distance. But something deep inside him—something older, baser, more primeval—now challenged the innate caution that had been part of his character for as long as he could remember…challenged it square on, with raised fists and a desire to knock it out. But, he reasoned, as long as he managed to keep that challenger under control, there was no reason why he could not indulge in a little flirtation.

'It depends, Miss Lovejoy, on how easily you are shocked.'

His voice sounded husky. Deep. And he felt Liberty's reaction. He *had* intended to shock her and it seemed he was successful.

She cleared her throat. 'Tell me what happened with Verity and Lord Bridlington.'

Dominic bit back a smile. For all her boldness a moment ago, that change of subject revealed much about Liberty's true character, even though she might flirt a little and take risks.

'You know what happened. I told you.'

'You punched him? Did he hit you back?'

'No. He knew he was in the wrong. He was caught before any damage was done and he will accept he has lost.'

She frowned. 'Should I be worried? Will he target Verity again?'

'I doubt it. He is an opportunist. He viewed Verity as easy prey with no father to protect her and a brother who appeared not to care less. He knows differently now. He will turn his attention to someone less well protected, especially after Gideon speaks to him, as he promised he will.'

She shivered. 'I did not realise there are such men in the *ton*, masquerading as gentlemen.'

'I am afraid there are such men in all walks of life.'

'I am so grateful you saw him and stopped him.'

'It was my pleasure.'

Her smile did strange things to him. It was the tremble of her lip—it was not artifice, he was certain—and it was the hint of vulnerability in her eyes, the deep breath she often took before replying to a comment, as if steeling herself. The truth hit him like a lightning strike. She acted and spoke boldly, but it was not boldness but bravery. She found the courage from somewhere to stand up for those she loved and for what she believed in.

He didn't want to admire her. Wasn't the ever-present lust enough for him to fight against? It felt as though his well-ordered, meticulously planned life was spinning out of control. He clenched his jaw, set her at the correct distance from him and concentrated on the steps of the waltz even as the scent of roses wove magic through his veins.

## *Chapter Eleven*

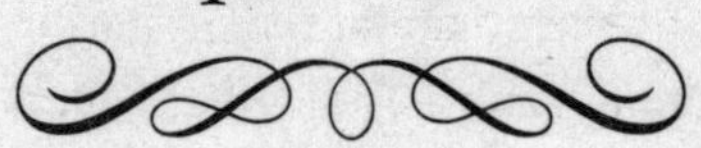

The following afternoon Liberty was about to set out on the short walk to Grosvenor Square when Gideon descended the staircase. She took a minute to admire him—he was so handsome and he looked a proper gentleman in his blue superfine coat, cream breeches and polished Hessians. She frowned. She had grown accustomed to him staying out until dawn and then sleeping most of the day away. Since their arrival in London it seemed that the only times she'd seen him this early in the day he had been unshaven and wearing a dressing robe and slippers. But last night he had escorted his sisters home and, it would appear, gone straight to bed.

'You look very smart, Gideon.'

A faint flag of colour washed over his cheeks. 'I intend to call on Lady Twyford, to pay my respects and to thank her for last night's entertainment.'

'Ah.' Of course. Gideon had spent much of his time in a group of young men surrounding Lady Emily Crighton, Lord Twyford's eldest daughter. And joined her for supper. 'Please extend my gratitude as well—it was kind of them to invite us.'

'Well, I have no doubt the invitations will roll in apace, now you've established yourself as part of the Beauchamps' inner circle.'

Stung by the implication she was a social climber, Liberty finished pulling on her second glove before she trusted herself to answer him.

'I hope you know me better than to think I would pretend friendship with someone simply for advancement.'

She held her twin's gaze, hating that he might think that of her. Particularly when her sole reason for approaching Jane last night had been to inveigle an introduction to Alex and the reason for *that* was standing in front of her looking positively angelic.

Gideon looked away first.

'No. Of course you would not. And I'm sorry, again, for not listening when you warned me about Bridlington. I'll be sure to speak to him when I next see him, but I trust Avon when he said Verity isn't in any danger now. But enough of that. Where are you off to? And where are the others? You're not…' His eyes narrowed. 'Tell me you are not going out *alone*?'

That was exactly what she had intended. It was such a short walk to Beauchamp House—just around the corner, really—that she hadn't even considered the impropriety until Gideon asked his question. Dominic's words whispered through her brain: *If you bring disgrace upon yourself, it is your sisters who will suffer.*

She put her nose in the air. 'Of course I am not going out alone, Gideon. I was on the brink of sending for one of the maids to accompany me but, as you are here now, you may escort me yourself.'

Gideon scowled. 'I ain't going *shopping* with you, if that's where you're off to. I told you. I'm calling on E— Lady Twyford.'

'Well, for your information, I am not going shopping. I have been invited to Beauchamp House to meet Lady Olivia's children.' Liberty snaked her arm around Gideon's and headed for the door, towing him with her. 'It is barely out of your way at all.'

'Very well.'

They were soon strolling in the direction of Grosvenor Square.

'Gideon.' It was rare lately that she had the chance to speak to him privately. She could not pass up the opportunity and, for once, he was not suffering the consequences of either overindulgence or lack of sleep. 'I *have* been worried about you.'

'I know. You've made that very clear.'

'That actress...'

He halted and frowned down at her. 'What,' he said, menacingly, 'do you know about her?'

'I am not a fool! I know you haven't been haunting the Sans Pareil for the quality of the performances.'

He growled, deep in his throat, then continued to walk. 'I cannot believe I am having this conversation with my sister. Listen, Liberty—you must stop thinking you can dictate where I go or what I do.'

'I am not trying to dictate to you. I—I just want you—all of you—to be safe. And happy.'

Gideon slipped his arm around her waist and gave her a quick squeeze. 'Lib. Listen to me. It wasn't your fault they died.'

Her heart clenched. 'I—I know.'

'And it doesn't mean it is your responsibility to protect all of us. I am a grown man and I can look after myself.'

'I know that, too.'

He raised his brows. 'Do you? Look...yes, I visit the theatre, but...it is just a bit of fun. I am at no risk. You say you are not a fool. Well, neither am I—I am a peer now and I'm aware of my obligations. And before you complain again about me frittering my fortune away, believe me when I tell you I can afford a few losses at the gaming tables.'

If only she could fully believe him. It seemed the habit of protecting her family, especially her beloved twin, would not be satisfied *that* easily. Wisely, she did not say so.

Gideon sighed and slanted a smile at her, his blue eyes glinting. 'I *also* admit it will not help Hope and Verity to find decent husbands if I continue to set the gossips' tongues alight. So, I shall henceforth be the soul of discretion—I shall still have fun and enjoy myself, but I shall do so well away from the public gaze.'

They had arrived at Beauchamp House and the door opened before Gideon could knock, giving Liberty no chance to reply. A haughty-looking butler peered out, looking down his long nose at her.

'Miss Lovejoy. Lady Olivia is expecting me.'

The butler's gaze slid to Gideon, perused him from head to toe, then stood back and bowed.

'Please come in, Miss Lovejoy; my Lord Wendover.'

'Oh, I'm not coming in—just wanted to see my sister safely delivered. I'll see you at dinner, Lib.'

Liberty watched Gideon walk away, whistling a jaunty tune, leaving Liberty to enter alone. She paused on the threshold, remembering the last time she had called at this house, and a smile tugged at her lips as she recalled her efforts to dodge the footman.

'Ahem.'

The butler raised one brow and Liberty wiped any hint of amusement from her features before entering the hall.

'Lady Olivia is expecting you, Miss Lovejoy. Please follow me.'

He led the way up the magnificent marble staircase to a parlour on the first floor—a cosy and informal room and not nearly as grand as the room into which Dominic had shown her. Olivia was sitting on a sofa, her legs tucked up under her, reading. She looked up, smiled and set her book aside.

'I am so pleased to see you, Liberty. Thank you for coming. Grantham, please inform Mrs Himley that my guest has arrived and she may send up refreshments. Now—' as the butler left the room '—come and sit by me... I asked Ruth to bring the twins down after we have drunk our tea—lively two-year-olds and cups of hot liquid are a poor combination.'

Liberty did as she was bid.

'I'm sorry to receive you in here,' Olivia went on, 'but the servants are working so hard to prepare the house for Papa's arrival that I could not in all conscience receive you in the salon, not when the twins will be joining us.' She grinned. 'They have the ability to reduce any room to utter chaos without even trying. Grantham was mortified when he discovered I intended to receive a guest in the family parlour, but I made sure you would not object.'

'Of course I don't object. Is Grantham your father's butler?'

'He is. He arrived in London yesterday.'

'I am rather pleased he was not here when I called—' Liberty snapped her mouth shut as her cheeks burned.

Olivia tilted her head. 'When you called…? You have been here before?'

'No. Yes. Oh, heavens…my wretched tongue! I…'

But hadn't Dominic told her Olivia had always been protective of Alex? Surely she would understand? She told Olivia of the reason for her visit to Beauchamp House and how she had mistaken Dominic for Alex. Olivia's eyes danced with merriment.

'What fun! That takes me back to my debut year—I tied myself in tangles trying to protect Alex from the consequences of his actions…but we both survived and I met my beloved Hugo, and all turned out for the best. In the end. But… forgive me, but Wendover does not seem near as wild or as…*self-destructive*…as Alex used to be. I noticed nothing out of the way in his behaviour last night. Indeed, he appeared the perfect gentleman.'

'I believe… I *hope*…that may be because he has developed a *tendre* for a certain young lady. It appears there is nothing as likely to persuade a man to behave himself as the presence of watchful parents.'

Olivia sighed. 'Oh, how I wish Alex would develop a fancy for a nice girl. I fear he will never wed—his temperament is too unpredictable.' She caught Liberty's eye and smiled ruefully. 'You and I seem very alike. As do our families. Ought I to apologise for our family squabbling last night? It's odd. Here I am, married for four years and the mother of twins, yet as soon as I am with Dominic and Alex the years seem to drop away and we slip back into the same old relationship. With me as their little sister,' she added in a disgusted tone. 'I keep meaning to resist, but it seems impossible—that role is so natural to me, it happens quite without any intent on my part.' Olivia sent Liberty a rueful smile. 'I don't know! Brothers! They spend half their life tormenting and teasing you—pretending they are so very superior simply because they are male—and the rest of the time they appear hell-bent on ruining their lives. You cannot help but try to protect them from their own folly.'

Liberty frowned. 'But…surely… Lord Avon… he, at least, is all that is proper and gentlemanly. *He* cannot give you cause for concern.'

A maid came in at that moment, with a tea tray and cakes. The butler had opened the door for her and he lingered, waiting until the maid had poured the tea and handed Olivia and Liberty their cups.

'Thank you, Betty,' said Olivia. The maid flashed a smile, then hurried towards the waiting butler and the still-open door.

'The poor things don't know what's hit them since Grantham arrived—heaven forfend Papa should find a speck of dust or a picture unaligned when he arrives.' Olivia gurgled a laugh.

'H-he sounds quite intimidating,' said Liberty.

'Oh, pooh. He gives himself airs and graces, but underneath it all he's an old softy.'

Liberty stared at Olivia, open-mouthed. Olivia returned her quizzical look, then burst out laughing. 'I meant Grantham, silly! Not Papa! Not that he's intimidating either…well, he might appear so at times, but he is not. Not really. Grantham could give any duke lessons on how to be pompous and unbending.'

Silence reigned as they sipped their tea and nibbled at slices of moist fruit cake.

'Speaking of Lord Avon—' Liberty could contain her curiosity no longer '—I was intrigued by your conversation about Westfield last night. For a bachelor, your brother appears strangely knowledgeable about twins and children in general, but when I asked him about it, he seemed to…well, to withdraw somehow.'

'Oh, Dom is never one to puff off his good deeds. Or anything about his life, in actual fact. He is quite private. But Westfield—he's been a patron for…ooh, seven years now—since he was nineteen. It is a school and orphan asylum in Islington.'

'That seems a strange thing for such a young man to get involved with.'

'Maybe to outsiders,' said Olivia, 'but not when you know Dominic. Lady Stanton, who is one of our cousins—second or third, or some such—was already a patron, even before she married, and when she told Dominic about it he decided to help. He knows how hard it was to lose Mother and *we* still had Papa. He said at the time he could not bear to imagine how much worse it would be if your family was poor and you lost both parents. He wanted to help give those children a future other than crime and begging.'

'I remember how hard it was to lose both *our* parents and I was nineteen.'

Liberty tried, and failed, to imagine how

dreadful it must be for a very young child to suddenly find itself all alone in the world. Her respect for Dominic increased—he did not have to help those children, but he chose to.

'Westfield is not just for orphans, but for abandoned children, too. There are more of those than you would care to know about. Why, just a few days ago he recognised a beggar woman on the street with a child that wasn't hers and rescued it. My Hugo was with him, or I'd never have known about it, of course. Hugo is taking me to visit Westfield soon—he went there with Dominic and he told me it is hopelessly overcrowded. He thought we might set up an establishment in Sussex, near to where we live, to take some of the children.'

'That is a kind thought.'

'I'm ashamed to admit I've never been there before,' Olivia said. 'That makes me rather thought*less*, doesn't it?' She chewed at her lip, staring down at her hands in her lap. 'I've never considered getting involved myself, even though I know how hard it is to lose a parent. And I had every advantage in life, because of who Papa is, and we had my aunt and my uncle, too.'

'What was your mother like?'

'I don't remember her very well. All I remember is rejection and impatience. I was only five, of course, when she died—I've no doubt I *was* a constant nuisance—but try as I might I can never remember approval or affection. I will never know if that would have changed as I grew up… never know if she would finally approve of me and be proud of me.' She raised her eyes and Liberty was concerned to see tears sheening them. On impulse, she took Olivia's hand and squeezed. Olivia emitted a sound, half-laugh, half-sniff. 'Hark at me, getting all maudlin. But at least now you understand why I am so determined to be a good mother to my twins.'

'I am sure you could never be a bad mother, Olivia. You have proved how much you care and all children need is to know they are loved.'

'They know how much their papa and I dote on them, but I am still curious about them being twins and interested in how, if at all, it might make them different from other children. Will you tell me about your childhood? Were you and your brother always close? Was your relationship with him different to your relationship with your sisters?'

They chatted for several minutes about twins in particular and brothers and sisters in general—although Liberty didn't feel she offered Olivia any special insight into being a twin. She and Gideon had naturally bonded more as children, but she believed that was due more to the age difference between them and their younger sisters than simply because they happened to be born at the same time. It was hard to accept the bond she had believed unbreakable had frayed so badly, although there was more hope in her heart after their talk on the way to Beauchamp House. The time flew by, until the door opened and a nursemaid entered, ushering two infants into the room. They were followed by a footman carrying a large wooden ship which he set down on the rug in front of the fireplace. The children stood stock still upon spying Liberty, their eyes huge, thumbs jammed into their mouths.

'Ruth,' said Olivia to the nursemaid, her silver eyes brimming with laughter, 'this pair can't possibly be Julius and Daisy—I do believe you have switched them for imposters. *They* are never this quiet.' She held out her arms then. 'Come to Mama, sweeties, and meet Mama's friend.'

Before too long, Julius, still somewhat shy, was perched comfortably on Liberty's knee, patting and stroking her hair and face, while Olivia had joined her daughter on the floor to play with a splendid ark and a collection of carved wooden animals.

Julius was so soft and huggable. Liberty's arms closed around the little boy and that familiar hollow ached in her chest. She no longer doubted that she was ready to find love again, but the only man she had ever come close to having feelings for was Dominic. And he was so far out of her reach it was futile to even daydream about it.

'Liberty? *Liberty!*'

She was jerked out of her thoughts by Olivia's persistent calling of her name. Then Julius stiffened in her lap before wriggling free of her arms and sliding down to the floor.

'Well, young Julius,' drawled a deep, familiar voice, 'I see you have started young with the ladies.'

Heat scorched Liberty's cheeks as she realised Dominic must have been watching them for some minutes before being noticed. She quickly tidied her hair. Her heart, from being an aching void, bloomed with joy as his mouth curved in an irresistible smile and mischief twinkled in his eyes and she struggled to keep her feelings hidden—she could not bear it if he realised how she was beginning to care for him. How utterly mortifying that would be. She smiled a cool greeting as the twins rushed to him and he gathered them both up and kissed their cheeks soundly, blowing air against their skin to make loud noises and sending them into fits of giggles.

With blinding clarity she saw he was two different men. There was the public Lord Avon, with his proper behaviour and his correct manners—the Lord Avon who was familiar to the *haut ton* and who had attended to Lady Caroline at supper last night—and then there was the Dominic who emerged when his family were around him. His family…and her. Liberty Lovejoy. Because somehow, without even trying, Liberty had been admitted into the inner circle of people with whom Dominic felt able to relax and to reveal more of the real man inside.

But did that simply mean her opinion was unimportant to him?

A lump swelled in her throat as she watched him with Olivia's children. He would make a wonderful father…and he was a man who *cared.* How many nineteen-year-old wealthy and privileged young men would bother themselves with the plight of orphans? Not Gideon, even now he was almost five-and-twenty. Dominic was clearly a man who trod his own path, regardless of what his peers expected of a man in his position.

He was so much more than she had first believed, when all she had seen was a wealthy but shallow aristocrat who knew and cared nothing for the plight of others. Not only did he take practical steps to help those less fortunate, but his selflessness was not in order to enhance his own reputation. He was well-known in society, and often talked about, but Liberty had not heard the slightest hint of his charity work.

Her thoughts whirled with what she had learned…was learning…about him. Olivia's revelations about her childhood and the mother who had never given her the unconditional love she craved prompted Liberty to wonder about Dominic and his relationship with that same mother.

'Dominic!' Olivia regained her feet and shook out her skirts. 'You are early! We agreed four o'clock, did we not, and it is only just gone three.'

'I wanted to spend a little uninterrupted time with my niece and nephew while I have the chance.'

He hugged them both into his chest again before setting them down on the floor and strolling further into the room.

'Good afternoon, Miss Lovejoy.' He bowed. 'I do hope you will not object to my disturbing your time with Livvy? I can always go up to the nursery with the twins if I am *de trop* and you wish to gossip unhindered.'

'Now, Dom, you know very well we would not gossip in front of the children…not that we do gossip, of course,' Olivia added hastily.

'Of course,' Dominic agreed smoothly as the twins tugged at him to play with their toys. He sighed. 'Very well, scamps, but allow me to remove my coat first—Brailsford will never forgive me if I soil my coat *before* I display my elegance in the Park.'

'Dominic! Miss Lovejoy is my guest. You cannot cavort before her in shirt sleeves!'

Liberty found herself the object of a penetrating look from Dominic. A look that set off a delicious fluttering deep in her abdomen.

'Will I offend your sensibilities, Miss Lovejoy?' He arched one brow. 'I know it is not quite the done thing, but surely we may relax a few of the conventions after our recent…er…slightly *un*conventional encounters?'

'You need not be coy, Dominic—Liberty has told me how she called here to beard Papa in his den and mistook you for Alex.' Olivia giggled as she sat next to Liberty on the sofa and nudged her. 'You should be honoured—he only ever teases people he likes and they're mostly family. Oh! I know! You can be our honorary sister. I always wanted a sister!'

## *Chapter Twelve*

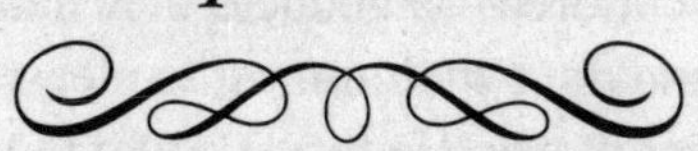

Dominic tried to ignore the tension swirling in his gut. This had seemed a good idea at the time—an opportunity to spend a little time with Julius and Daisy before Father and Stepmother arrived, when his half-sister and half-brother, Christabel and Sebastian, would also demand his attention. Besides, he adored spending time with the little monkeys.

That Liberty Lovejoy would be here was entirely incidental. Wasn't it? She tempted him like no other woman of his acquaintance and—if he was wise, which he clearly wasn't—he should do all he could to avoid her. Yet here he was, concentrating on steadying his breathing as the subtle note of her perfume weaved through his senses. That picture of her with young Julius on her lap—her pensive, wistful expression—was now seared into his brain. His heart had twitched with longing as he took in the sight and, try as he might to replace her image with any of the ladies on that original shortlist, he simply could not imagine any of them dandling a child on their knee and allowing it to fiddle with their hair.

Mother, certainly, would never have tolerated such behaviour. She had been goddess-like to her three children—a goddess they had all worshipped and done their utmost to please, forever seeking her praise. He thrust down those memories and the weight of duty, responsibility and expectation they evoked.

'Olivia.'

'Dominic?'

'By my calculations I have now spoken to Miss Lovejoy twice since entering this room, including asking her a number of direct questions, and she has yet to reply to any of them because you have rushed in to speak for her.'

He welcomed the familiar spark in his sister's eyes. 'Well, that is entirely your fault, Brother dear, for asking her such awkward questions in the first place! *I* am Liberty's hostess and it is my duty to protect her from feeling uncomfortable. You forget, she is not used to your teasing ways, Dom.'

'Good Lord, you haven't changed, Livvy! Four years wed and you are still the fiery brat you always were.'

Olivia's cheekbones sported two bright flags

of colour and he regretted the words as soon as they were spoken. What was he? Sixteen years old again? Of course Olivia was still the same spirited girl and he prayed she always would be—she would not be the little sister he loved and cherished if marriage and motherhood changed her too much.

'Liv… I'm sorry! We do seem to slip back into that same old relationship when we get together, don't we?'

The colour in her cheeks faded and she grinned. 'I was saying much the same thing before the twins came down, wasn't I, Liberty?'

'You were indeed, Olivia.' Liberty's response was calm, with just the right touch of light amusement. 'And in answer to your query about your jacket, sir, please do so. I pledge myself to remain utterly unoffended by such an action.'

Dominic saw that their little spat had given Liberty a chance to collect herself. When she first became aware of him, a soft pink blush had washed across her skin and her velvety-blue eyes had widened and darkened as her lush lips parted. Her unguarded reaction had lasted a bare second, but her joyful expression had drawn a similar happy response from him. Then her expression had shuttered and it was apparent that the woman he had first met, whose feelings shone in her expressions, had changed in the time he had known her. Her features were no longer a window into her soul. He could not blame her—society and the *ton* were enough to make even the toughest-skinned person wary—but, damn it, he hated that he could no longer read her every thought.

Olivia's words resounded through his head. *An honorary sister*, indeed. Nothing could be further from the way he felt about Liberty Lovejoy. But he could, and must, view her as a family friend, such as Jane Colebrooke was—although he had never lusted after Jane in his entire life. He could cope with thinking of Liberty as a friend…just. But in no way could he view her as his sister.

He shrugged out of his jacket and joined the twins on the rug. He was soon lost in their game, pairing up the animals and marching them up the ramp into the ark, the faint murmur of conversation fading into the background, until he realised Liberty was standing up, clearly preparing to take her leave. He jumped to his feet and collected his jacket from the chair where he had laid it.

'Did a maid accompany you, Miss Lovejoy?'

*She probably came alone. I wouldn't put it past her.*

'No. My brother escorted me, sir. I wonder if a maid might walk with me back to Green Street, Olivia?'

She caught Dominic's eye and raised one challenging brow as if to say, *See? I can behave like a lady when I choose to.*

He bit back a grin. 'There's no need to bother one of the maids—might I offer to drive you home?' He batted away the inner warning that he was, again, playing with fire. He was merely being practical. Being a gentleman. 'I ordered my curricle brought round for four but, unless Olivia has changed the habits of a lifetime, I cannot see her being dressed and ready to go by then as it is already three minutes to the hour. Unless, of course, you no longer wish to drive in the Park this afternoon, Liv?'

'Heavens! Is that the time? Oh, I have enjoyed our time together this afternoon, Liberty…do say you will come again.

'And of course I still want to go to the Park, Dom. How else am I to properly meet your young ladies without calling upon them…and that would never do, would it?'

'No. It would not.'

A shudder racked Dominic at the very idea. As soon as any member of his family showed marked attention to any one of the names that were thought to be on his shortlist, the news would be on every gossipmonger's lips and he would soon find himself in a corner and honour-bound to make an offer. At least any attention he paid to Liberty was unlikely to be misconstrued, firstly because of her friendship with Olivia but, more importantly, because no one in the *ton* would imagine for one moment that such an unsuitable female would ever be included on his list.

'Well, Miss Lovejoy? Are you happy to accept my offer of escort?'

'Indeed I am, my lord. Thank you.'

Olivia said nothing but, at the gleam in her eyes as she looked from Dominic to Liberty and back again, a warning trickled down his spine. His sister was no fool—he must work even harder at masking his growing feelings for Liberty. As Olivia, Ruth and the twins headed upstairs after saying goodbye to Liberty, Dominic walked with her to the front door where Grantham waited.

'Your curricle arrived two minutes ago, my lord.' The butler opened the door.

'Thank you, Grantham.'

'They are a beautiful pair.' Liberty surprised Dominic by heading straight to the horses, being held by his groom, Ted. She looked them over with clear appreciation, then removed her glove and held her hand to each horse's nose in turn to allow them to snuffle at her palm and take in her scent. 'Very well matched. What are their names?'

'Thank you. Beau and Buck—they are a pleasure to drive. Very responsive.' He was proud of his bays, which he had purchased last year. 'Alex bred and trained them. Do you drive, Miss Lovejoy?'

She smiled up at him, and his heart soared. 'I have never driven anything other than our old cob at home. But I have a lovely riding mare.' Then she frowned. 'At least, she *is* lovely, but she is also now quite old. We left her behind in Sussex.'

With one accord they returned to the curricle. Dominic took Liberty's hand to help her into the vehicle, his fingers closing around hers. She hadn't replaced her glove and Dominic had not yet drawn his on and, as he registered the warmth of her smooth, soft skin his breath seized and he had to stifle the urge to haul her into his arms. He swallowed and released her hand as soon as she was in the curricle. He pulled on his gloves, willing his heartbeat and his body under control as he climbed up next to her.

Liberty nudged into him with her shoulder—the slightest of movements, but his heart lurched again at that contact. He looked down into her innocent expression. One golden brow arched.

'Do not forget to order your groom to jump up behind,' she whispered. Her lips curved into a delicious, teasing smile. 'You have your reputation to protect.'

His throat ached with suppressed longing, but he refused to yield to his base desires. Duty was what mattered, not physical needs. He smiled back. 'With what you already know of me, Berty, you cannot possibly imagine I would overlook such a crucial matter.'

'Berty?' She sounded outraged, but her eyes twinkled.

'Liberty is such a mouthful.' His loins instantly reacted to his unintentional double entendre.

'What is wrong with Libby?' She stared up at him, innocently, clearly having missed the meaning. 'Or Lib? That is what my family call me sometimes.'

'Oh, I couldn't possibly,' Dominic murmured. 'They are far too easily confused with Livvy and Liv, and I most definitely do *not* think of you as another sister, despite what Olivia said.'

Her cheeks bloomed pink. The curricle dipped as Ted climbed up behind and Dominic flicked the reins. They set off on the short drive to Green Street.

'Maybe I should be relieved that we cannot now talk without being overheard.'

Another teasing smile filled him with the urge to simply touch her mouth. With one fingertip. To test whether her lips were as soft and luscious as they looked….to trace their fullness…to slip his finger into that hot, moist… Blood flooded his groin and different urges took him in their hold. He wrenched his gaze from her mouth to her eyes, full of teasing laughter, battling to keep his expression blank.

'A good groom knows when to turn a deaf ear,' he said. 'Is that not right, Ted?'

'Beg pardon, milord? Were you speakin' to me? I didn' quite catch what you said.'

Liberty laughed, a delightful gurgling sound of pleasure. 'Oh, that is famous! Lord Avon, you, sir, are such a contradiction—the perfect lord whose servants are as well trained as his horses.'

'I prefer to describe my staff as loyal rather than well trained.'

'Loyal, indeed. What else, I wonder, have your servants failed to notice over the years, for fear of sullying your reputation?'

Their eyes met. And held. And the naked look of...*longing* in those velvety-blue eyes matched exactly what was in his heart. His voice when he answered her was husky.

'I wish I could lay claim to a wild, exciting parallel existence to this life but, alas, what you see before you is the whole.'

'What? No hidden depths? You disappoint me, sir.'

And the thought of disappointing her wrenched at him. He cleared his throat and, this time, his words emerged light and airy. Nonchalant. Exactly as they should sound.

'Nary a one, I'm afraid.'

Liberty fell silent. A sideways glance revealed a blush on her cheeks and her golden eyebrows drawn into a frown. Had she, like him, recognised the dangerous territory into which they had strayed? He drove around the corner into Green Street and the relief that flooded him took him by surprise. He had intended a light flirtation. He enjoyed Liberty's company, but this…this flirtatious repartee… It was dangerous. *Here* were the depths his life had so far lacked and his inner voice of caution was screaming at him to take care and not to venture so far that he could not return to the shallows.

He offered a change of subject and her relief was palpable. 'I am pleased you and Olivia seem destined to be friends.'

'I like her very much. I… I have not had many friends my own age. Gideon and the girls were always enough.'

That comment alone explained much about Liberty—she had devoted her life to her family. Was that why she fretted so about Gideon? The huge change in their lives must be as unsettling for her as it was for her brother. Their lives would never be the same again.

He reined Beau and Buck to a halt outside the Lovejoys' house. 'Here we are.'

Ted ran to the horses' heads and Dominic leapt to the pavement to hand Liberty down. She placed her hand—gloved this time—into his. Without volition, his fingers closed around hers, pressing. Another blush coloured her cheeks and Dominic cursed himself for a weak-minded fool. What the hell was he playing at? Whenever he was in Liberty Lovejoy's presence he seemed to lose all vestige of self-control.

The second she reached the ground he released her hand as though it were red-hot. He knocked on the door and, as soon as it opened, he bowed.

'Thank you for driving me home, my lord.'

'It was my pleasure, Miss Lovejoy.'

And he meant it. He really did. It had been—it had always been—a pleasure to spend time in her company. But he must take care to avoid such tête-à-têtes in future. It was simply too dangerous and it would be Liberty's reputation that suffered. Not his.

Liberty removed her pelisse and bonnet and handed them to Ethel, her thoughts in turmoil, matching the bubbling confusion in her belly. Did it mean anything that Dominic had come early to Beauchamp House, knowing she would be there? Or was her presence neither here nor there and he had told the absolute truth—that the only reason he called earlier than expected was to spend time with the twins? Was her imagination running away with her—envisaging a happy ever after where there could never be one, simply because she had discovered that he was the man who stirred her blood like no other—even Bernard? Because she had found that, in addition to all his other attributes, Lord Avon was also a kind and charitable gentleman?

Why, then, had he insisted on driving her home? Had he been flirting with her, or was she naïve in thinking there was a special warmth in his voice when he spoke to her? He had called her Berty and the memory kindled a glow inside her. He found her attractive, she knew, but was his behaviour with her mere practised flirtation from a gentleman or did his feelings go deeper? He enjoyed her company, and he was relaxed and informal with her in a way she never saw him behave with any of the ladies on his shortlist, but did *any* of that amount to anything other than wishful thinking on her part?

She could not decide. But, increasingly, she knew what she would like the answer to be.

'Mrs Mount is in the drawing room, miss,' said Ethel.

Liberty headed upstairs to the drawing room where she found Mrs Mount having a quiet doze in a chair by the fire. She awoke with a start as Liberty entered the room.

'Where are Hope and Verity?'

'They are riding in the Park. With Lord Wendover.'

*'Gideon?'* Liberty sat in the opposite chair. 'Do my ears deceive me? Do you mean to tell me he came back home after calling on Lady Twyford?'

She had been certain that was the last any of them would see of her brother until dinner that evening.

'Yes. He returned in a rush to inform us he had hired two horses from the livery stables and that your sisters were to get changed and be ready to ride out with him. He was most insistent. Verity believes he had arranged to meet up with Lady Emily in the Park and Hope and Verity will provide him with the perfect excuse to ride with her.'

'Oh, that is wonderful news. Lady Emily would be a splendid match—'

'Stop!' Mrs Mount leaned forward. 'I beg your pardon, my dear, but please do not get carried away. Gideon only met Lady Emily last night and he is still young.'

Liberty sighed. 'You are right. I cannot help but be happy she is distracting him from that horrid actress, though.'

Mrs Mount relaxed back with a relieved sigh. 'Now. What about you, my dear? You must count yourself fortunate that Lady Olivia has taken a shine to you.'

'Fortunate? How so?'

'So there will be no repercussions from your… um…*unusual* encounters with Lord Avon, of course. He could scarcely cut his sister's friend—he is far too much the gentleman—and, to think, he not only danced with you last night, but with Hope and Verity, too! I always prayed they might catch his eye.'

She beamed with satisfaction and Liberty bit her tongue against telling her the real reason Dominic had danced with her sisters.

'Well, I do not see what is so very special about His Lordship,' she muttered, even though she knew exactly what was so very special about Dominic. But she would be mortified if anyone had the slightest suspicion of her growing feelings for him.

'And that attitude, miss, will get you nowhere in society.'

A blush heated Liberty's cheeks at Mrs Mount's reprimand. She had been hired to help Liberty and her sisters learn how to behave as well-brought-up young ladies should and Liberty was aware of the flaw in her own personality that prompted her to rebel against such strict mores.

'Whether you approve or not, Liberty, the heir to a dukedom will always command respect and be fêted and courted by those lower in precedence.' Mrs Mount's voice softened. 'Now, tell me all about your visit—did you meet the twins?'

'Oh, they are delightful! Olivia is besotted with them, but I cannot think I have helped her understand how raising twins is different to raising other children. She is so determined to be the perfect mother to them.'

'Well, I hope for their sake she is a better mother than her own proved to be.'

'Olivia's mother? Why?' Olivia's confidences about her childhood had piqued Liberty's interest. 'What was she like? Did you know her well?'

'The first Duchess? Why, yes, my dear. We were close in age and we made our debut together. She was three years older than Cheriton, you know. Oh, she was as selfish as they come and utterly arrogant, especially after becoming a duchess. She had not a thought for anyone or anything beyond her own selfish pleasures. Poor Cheriton. He married young...far too young...and all *she* wanted was the glamour and acclaim of the title. She had no interest in those poor children—she spent as much time as possible in London after Olivia was born. She could not bear to be "buried in the depths of the countryside" as she used to put it.' Mrs Mount huffed a laugh. 'Ironic, really, when you consider that's where she ended up—buried at Cheriton Abbey.'

'What happened?' Liberty could not help her curiosity. 'Did she die in childbirth?' That tragic fate befell so many women it seemed a reasonable assumption. Then a shiver chased across her skin as she recalled her parents and Bernard. 'Did she fall ill?'

'No, my dear.' Mrs Mount lowered her voice. 'She was *murdered*.'

'Murdered?' That was the last thing she expected to hear. A duchess, murdered? 'But… how?'

'No one knows, my dear. They say it was probably a passing vagrant. And, much as it pains me to speak ill of the dead, it was probably a blessing for those poor children and their father. Their aunt, Lady Cecily, raised them after that and it's a wonder they have all turned out as well as they have. Well, apart from Lord Alexander…he was ever a wild youth, but it does seem he has settled at long last.

'Now, tell me all about today, my dear. Has the Duke arrived yet?'

'Not yet—only Lady Olivia and her family are in residence at the moment but the staff are all bustling about preparing the house, so the Duke and Duchess and their children must be expected soon. And Lord Avon called while I was there.' She hadn't meant to mention him, but his name slipped past her lips quite without intention. 'He had arranged to drive Olivia in the Park, but came early to spend some time with the twins.'

'The Park?' Mrs Mount clapped her hands

together. 'How wonderful… I do hope he will acknowledge your sisters! He is sure to do so after dancing with them last night. Oh, I do hope Gideon has chosen their mounts wisely, to show them off to best advantage!'

'Mrs Mount!'

'Yes, my dear?'

'I do not believe you. You criticise me for getting carried away with the possibilities for Gideon and yet you insist on imagining castles in the clouds when it comes to Hope and Verity's prospects.'

'It does not hurt to have ambition, my dear Liberty. Who knows what might happen should a man like Avon lose his heart? And your sisters are exceptionally pretty.'

Liberty ground her teeth in frustration. 'He drove me home this afternoon. Lord Avon, that is. In his curricle.'

And, again, she hadn't meant to say such a thing, but the words, and his name, were battering the inside of her head, desperate to be spoken. She held her breath, awaiting Mrs Mount's response.

'*Avon* drove you home? Good gracious…such condescension! Although you are, of course, his sister's friend so no doubt he felt under some obligation. But, still, what a feather in your cap, my dear—to be singled out and driven by such a notable whip.' Then her eyes narrowed and a slow smile stretched her lips. 'Especially after such a sought-after gentleman singled you out last night, to dance. Twice! And you had supper together!' Mrs Mount's voice shrilled with excitement. 'Oh!' She lowered her voice into a conspiratorial whisper. 'Has he *said* anything to you, my dear? Has he passed any hints?'

Exasperated, because she really wished she could say yes, Liberty said, 'No. He has said nothing. And I had supper with his brother, not him. As you quite rightly said, ma'am, I am his sister's friend and both Avon and Lord Alex were merely acting the gentleman. You told me yourself about Avon's list and Lord Alexander mentioned it last night…it appears to be common knowledge and Avon did not deny its existence.

'In fact, that is precisely the reason he is driving Olivia in the Park as we speak, because she insisted she wants to meet the ladies concerned before he makes his decision.'

A surge of energy sent Liberty to her feet. She crossed to the window, which overlooked the street, and peered out.

Who in their right mind would have a list of candidates for a wife? What about the heart? What of love? That emotion clearly had no place in Dominic's plans. She thought of the time he had compared her to Olivia…that protective care each of them held for their family. That was love…a different sort of love, maybe, but Dominic clearly did not completely dismiss the emotion. Could such a clinical choice of partner ever lead to happiness? It hadn't for his father, so it seemed.

She returned to her chair. 'You said Olivia's father married too young, Mrs Mount. Why did he do so? Did he fall in love?'

'Oh, no, my dear. Many more marriages back then were arranged affairs, you know. He was only eighteen and he married to please his ailing father. Margaret was three years his senior, but she was the daughter of a marquess—very suitable in that respect. She was one of the most selfish creatures I have ever met, although she put on a good show for Cheriton and, at eighteen, I dare say he did not know enough about human nature to see the danger signs.' She shook her head. 'She had affairs. Many affairs. And not always discreetly. She even played him false with his own cousin, although I'm not sure he ever knew about that.'

She sounded an awful woman. Poor Dominic, to have such a mother.

'What about the present Duchess? Olivia seems fond of her.'

'I do not know her well, but they say it was a love match and that the Duke is very happy, even though she was only a soldier's daughter. They wed five years ago now.' She sighed. 'Now *that* was a year for romance—first the Duke, then his brother Vernon and lastly their sister, Cecily. All in the same year, all love matches and all with unexpected and, some would say, unsuitable partners.' She studied Liberty, who felt a blush heat her skin. 'I wonder…?'

Liberty leapt to her feet again. She could not allow Mrs Mount to speculate. That way lay heartache, she knew, because if someone else began to think the unthinkable she just knew that her hopes would mushroom out of control. And she could not bear that. Lord Avon had his shortlist and her name was not on it. She did not possess the qualities he looked for in a bride and to hope he might change his criteria for a woman he only met for the first time less than a fortnight ago was stretching believability a little too far, even for her.

'Please excuse me, Mrs Mount. I must consult with Mrs Taylor on dinner tonight.'

She fled the room before she could be tempted to stay and hear what Mrs Mount was going to say.

# *Chapter Thirteen*

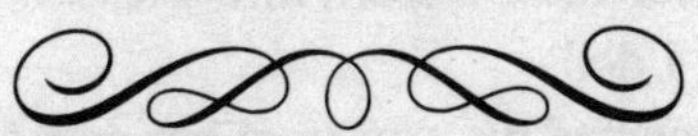

Bond Street, as usual, was busy with members of the *ton* shopping, Liberty, her sisters and Mrs Mount among them. Liberty's heart was not really engaged in finding the perfect hat to go with Hope's new walking dress, but she'd realised that staying at home brooding over Dominic would be even worse than being forced to exclaim at each and every hat Hope tried on, only for her to then discard it as being not *precisely* what she wanted.

As they exited the third milliner's shop, however, her attention was grabbed by a high-pitched yelp and, half-hidden in a doorway, she caught sight of a burly man, wearing a bloodied apron, who had a squirming dog tight by the scruff of his neck as he raised his other arm. The thin stick in his hand swished audibly through the air and landed on the dog's back with a resounding crack. A scream split the air, and a bloodied welt appeared in the dog's pale golden fur.

Rage surged though Liberty. She raced to the man's side, grabbing his arm as he raised it once more.

'Stop that, you rogue!'

The man paused and eyed her with astonishment. 'Get your hands off me,' he growled. 'The dog's a thief and I'll learn him a lesson if it's the last thing I do.'

He wrenched his arm from her grip and lifted it again. The dog cringed, fear in its eyes.

'Liberty! Come away. Please.' Mrs Mount took Liberty's arm and tugged her from the doorway, away from the man and the cowering dog. 'Don't get involved,' she hissed. 'People are watching.'

The whistle of the stick cut through the air once more and the dog's scream this time was even more desperate. Gorge rose to clog Liberty's throat. She snatched her arm from Mrs Mount and rounded again on the brute. He was tall and wide, his face showing no emotion as he prepared to hit the dog again. She couldn't bear it. She didn't care who saw her. She thrust herself between man and dog and shoved at his chest with all her strength.

'Stop!' Fear and rage in equal measures sent her voice soaring a couple of octaves. 'You *will not* beat that poor animal!'

'An' 'oo are you to tell me what I may and may not do? That's my livelihood, that is.'

He gestured to the ground, to a half-mangled joint of meat. 'I chased that mangy runt from my shop an' now I've got 'im bang to rights. He won't be nabbin' meat off anyone again. Not when I've finished with 'im.'

He shoved Liberty aside and she stumbled back, her shoulder and arm colliding painfully with the hard edge of the door recess. The man raised his arm again and she pushed her hands against the brickwork and propelled herself forward, again putting her body between the two in a desperate effort to spare the dog.

'I wonder what's going on over there?'

Hugo paused outside the doorway to Angelo's Fencing Academy and drew Dominic's attention to a crowd gathering further along the street. Dominic shrugged.

'Some altercation or other, it looks like. Nothing that need—'

He stopped speaking as he recognised Hope and Verity clutching one another on the periphery of the crowd. He didn't know, not for certain, but something told him Liberty was in there, somewhere. In the thick of it.

'I'll join you directly,' he called over his shoulder as he set off at a run towards the crowd. He hadn't even covered half the distance when he realised Hugo was by his side.

'You don't get to have *all* the fun, Dom,' he panted, with a grin.

Dominic shouldered through the crowd in time to see a huge brute of a fellow shove Liberty against a wall and raise a stick high. He took in the scene in an instant—the pain and shock on Liberty's face as she collided with the brickwork and the cowering, bloodied dog, its neck held fast by a huge hand. He recognised her utter determination as she thrust herself away from the wall. Rage boiled and he leapt forward even as Liberty pushed herself between the dog and that stick. He thrust his arm over Liberty's shoulder and grabbed the stick just as it began a downward trajectory.

The brute struggled, trying desperately to free the stick from Dominic's grip, as he glared down at Liberty and the dog she shielded. He hadn't even spared a glance at Dominic, he was so intent on his target. He didn't even appear to realise that, if he continued, he would hit Liberty.

'Leggo!' Spittle flew from his lips as he roared his rage.

Seeing the other man's uncontrolled fury just made Dominic more determined to control his own temper.

'I will take that.' The man's gaze snapped to Dominic. 'Or is it your intention to hit a lady in broad daylight, in front of witnesses?'

The man paled and gulped, and his grip on the stick loosened. Dominic took it from him and handed it to Hugo, standing to one side of him. Then he stepped in front of the bastard who had dared to threaten Liberty and he bunched his lapels in his fists. 'Don't you *ever*...' he spoke softly, '...let me see you again. Or the pain that dog suffered will be nothing to what I inflict upon you. Do you understand?'

The man's mouth twisted. 'It *stole* from me, m'lord. A man has to make a living.'

He felt a hand tug at his arm.

'Leave this to me, Miss Lovejoy.'

She took no notice, though. Almost before the words had left his lips she was nudging him aside so she could confront the brute.

'You are a despicable specimen of a human being.' She glared up at him. 'But even disgusting types like you need to make a living. Here.' She cast a handful of coins at his feet. 'The meat is paid for. Now, give me the dog.'

Dominic released his lapels and the man, with a snarl, thrust the pitiful dog at Liberty, scrabbled for the coins and then disappeared into the slowly dispersing crowd. In the absence of any means of holding the dog, Liberty grabbed its scruff, crooning to it in a low voice. Dominic placed a hand on her shoulder.

'He's gone, Miss Lovejoy. You can leave it now.'

She looked up at him, her eyes swimming. 'Look at him. The poor creature. He is skin and bone. I *cannot* leave him to fend for himself.'

'But what do you mean to do with it? It is filthy and no doubt riddled with fleas.'

'It really is not your concern, is it, my lord?' She regained her feet, but had to remain half-bent in order to keep hold of the animal, twisting her head to look up at him. 'I am grateful for your help in seeing off that scoundrel, but if I choose to keep this sweet little dog then I shall. I do need some way of securing him, though.'

She gazed around, then her eyes lit up.

'Be pleased to hold him a minute, sir, if you will.' She thrust the dog at Dominic, who had little choice but to comply. Next thing, she had removed her bonnet and was pulling at a ribbon that was threaded through her lustrous hair. 'This will do nicely, I believe.' She smiled happily as she thrust it at Dominic. 'Would you be so good as to tie it around his neck while I put my bonnet back on?'

Dominic registered the sound of a muffled snort and he relieved his feelings by glaring at his brother-in-law. But he did tie the blue ribbon around the dog's neck. It left a very short length with which to lead the dog, however. Liberty frowned as she studied the dog.

'Liberty.' Her chaperon, Mrs Mount, took Liberty by the elbow. 'We *cannot* take that filthy creature home with us.'

'Of course we can, my dear ma'am. Why ever not? Once he is bathed and his coat brushed, he will be quite respectable and he really does have the sweetest expression, do you not agree?'

'My lord?' Mrs Mount gazed at Dominic beseechingly.

Dominic looked down at the dog, who returned his look with a curl of his lip and an ingratiating grin. Then he looked at Liberty, taking in her outward bluster of confidence, but that same hint of vulnerability in her eyes that unmanned him every time he saw it.

'I cannot see what harm it will do.' Liberty's smile was his reward. 'Allow me to hail a hackney—that will make it easier to get the animal home. Hold him, will you, Hugo?' He thrust the short length of ribbon at his brother-in-law, who grinned and stuck his hands behind his back.

'*I* shall hail a cab,' he said. 'You're doing such a fine job there, Dom. I should hate to let the little ru—*darling* slip!'

After they had deposited the Lovejoy sisters and their chaperon at their home, Dominic and Hugo elected to walk together back to Beauchamp House. Dominic was soon aware of Hugo's amused scrutiny.

'Something on your mind, Hugo?'

'Just wonderin' where the lovely Liberty fits into your future plans, Dom.'

'Nowhere.'

Hugo shrugged, strolling on without further comment, swinging his cane.

'I admire the way she takes a stand for what is right,' Dominic said eventually, goaded by his brother-in-law's continuing silence and his mildly sceptical expression.

'Rushing in where angels fear to tread?'

'Not at all! She reminds me of Olivia, as it happens.'

Hugo cocked an eyebrow and his lips curved. 'Quite.'

'Are you calling your wife a fool?'

'Far from it—but you have to admit she used to act first and worry about the consequences afterwards. She has…er…mellowed somewhat in that regard. Since the twins. But she has *always* had her family's backs and still does.'

'That is what I admire about Miss Lovejoy.'

'But that, my dear Dominic, was a stray dog.'

'It is to her credit she did not ignore the suffering of a fellow creature, as so many others do.'

'Something like you and your orphans?'

Dominic's stomach clenched in warning. Oh, Hugo was a sly one…he could see exactly where this conversation was leading. He knew his brother-in-law well enough to know he would not continue to badger Dominic once he had replied to that initial question about Liberty, not like Olivia or Alexander might—questions that would inevitably lead to an argument. Hugo was far more subtle, skirting around the same subject until a less cautious man might let too much information slip. Well, he'd have no luck here.

'*Nothing* like that.'

Hugo smiled and Dominic promised himself he'd make him suffer next time they sparred at Jackson's.

They reached Beauchamp House and Dominic accepted Hugo's invitation to come in to visit Olivia. He very soon wished he hadn't, although at least Olivia didn't plague him about Liberty Lovejoy. No. *She* was far more interested in his blasted list...and how he wished he had never written the damned thing! Or at least had taken more care that nobody but he ever set eyes on it.

'Have you thought about Miss Whitlow? Why is she not on your list?'

'Unsuitable. Her father's a reckless gambler.'

'And only a viscount,' Hugo pointed out.

'Lady Elisa Critchlow? Oh! I know! Lady Frederica Sutton.'

'No and no. You're like a dog with a bone, Livvy,' Dominic growled. 'Why can't you accept this is my business and my decision?'

'Talkin' of dogs—'

'Hu-u-u-u-go…'

Hugo opened his eyes wide at Dominic's growled warning. 'I merely thought the tale might distract my wife and stop her throwing an endless succession of names at you. It was, after all, merely a diverting interlude of little importance.' He arched his brows. 'Was it not?'

'You know it was.' But Hugo had a point… it *would* divert Olivia from the subject of his damned list. 'Your friend Miss Lovejoy rescued a dog that was being beaten. It was nothing. Over almost before it began.'

'With your intervention,' said Hugo.

'I shall ask Liberty to tell me all about it,' said Olivia, somewhat absently. 'Now, Dominic. What about Miss Fothergill?' She frowned, tapping one finger to her lips, then sat bolt upright. 'Of course! Jane Colebrooke! She would be perfect! So sweet-natured!'

'Good God, no! It would be like marrying my sister! And that thought, at this moment in time, fills me with abject horror. Olivia…if you do *not* stop pestering me I shall never call on you again. Or are you *trying* to drive me away?'

Olivia leapt up from the sofa to perch on the arm of Dominic's chair. She ruffled his hair and he jerked his head away. What did she think he was? A small boy to be humoured? He was the eldest, dammit. *He* had always been the sensible one; the one they listened to. Her arm slid behind his neck and she hugged him to her.

'I'm sorry. I don't mean to plague you. But I'm worried, Dom. I can't picture any of those women in among us. The rest of the family, I mean. I know Papa is a duke, but the thought of how some of them might behave with Aunt Thea, or with Zach, sends shivers right through me.' Her voice betrayed the strength of her feelings. 'We Beauchamps always stick together—I couldn't *bear* the thought that anyone might drive a wedge between us.'

'You're being overdramatic, Liv.'

But his anger dissipated at her words—he knew how much the family meant to Olivia. And to him, too. But that would not stop him doing his duty as he saw it and as he had promised Mother. *Make me proud, my Son.* The memories, as ever, weighted him down.

Duty. Expectation. Responsibility.

Except recently they had also brought doubts creeping into his thoughts. Undermining his determination. And he shied away from examining those doubts too closely, for fear of what they might reveal.

'You know me better than to think I would marry anyone likely to upset any member of the family. That is the reason I am taking my decision so seriously.'

'But what is so wrong with marrying for love? We did. Uncle Vernon and Aunt Cecily did. Even *Papa* did.'

'Father only married for love because the succession was already secure through his marriage to our mother.'

Olivia pouted. 'I suppose I cannot argue with that, but I still think you are making a mistake. When do you think you will decide?'

'Soon.' His spirits dipped as he said the words: 'I shall speak to Father when he arrives and, as long as he has no objection to her family, that will be it.'

His life sorted. It was what he wanted. It was what he had always planned.

'Romeo!'

A sleek head emerged from behind the floor-length curtain that, a moment ago, was being shaken with vigour, accompanied by ferocious growls. Liberty marched across the room and took her new pet by the collar. It was the day after she had rescued him and already she doubted her wisdom in keeping him. Not that she would admit that to the rest of the family, or to Mrs Mount, who were all extremely vocal in their condemnation of both her actions yesterday and her stubbornness in bringing him home. It had taken her two hours to bathe him and, by the time she had finished, the kitchen was in uproar and Mrs Taylor was prostrate on a chair in the corner, her apron over her face. It did little to muffle her shrieks. They had dined on cold meat, bread and cheese last night.

The name, Romeo, had popped into her head when Gideon asked what the dog's name was and the resulting hilarity from her entire family had been enough to stop Liberty changing her mind. Even though the name, she silently agreed, did not suit him in the slightest. He was a rascal. Up to every kind of mischief, having already chewed a rug, one of Gideon's slippers and now attacking the curtains.

Romeo gazed up at her, his brown eyes innocent and full of adoration, his head, with its two permanently upright ears, cocked to one side and his tail, tightly curled over his back, waggling his entire bottom. Liberty's heart melted. She dropped to her knees and hugged his thin body close. And then, without warning, she was crying into his soft golden coat; sobbing, her arms tightening around him as he wriggled, trying to reach her face and lick the tears from her cheeks.

'I must be cursed, Romeo. Bernard died and now there's Dominic—so far out of my reach he might as well be a prince.'

She hugged the dog closer, as the agony of unrequited love clawed at her. Twice she had loved and twice lost. And now she felt she was losing Gideon as well.

'I miss him, Romeo. I thought nothing could weaken the bond we shared, but now I don't know how to mend it. I *hate* London.' She'd been content before they came here. Numb, but content. 'I wish we'd never come here.'

'Liberty?'

She froze and desperately gulped back her sorrow as Gideon came into the room and sat on the floor next to her. He handed her his handkerchief and put his arms around her, pulling her close.

'Don't cry, Sis. You *never* cry.' She hid her face against his chest and hot tears flowed anew. 'I heard what you said. This is my fault.'

She shook her head, but he took no notice. 'Please don't cry. I know I've been selfish. I'm so sorry—I never thought how it must bring it all back to you, being in London again. Look.' He tilted her face up, his expression serious. 'I don't deny all this went to my head at first, but I will behave better. I promise. Our bond is not broken. It will never break, but it *will* change. It is inevitable. You do see that, don't you?'

Liberty nodded, then dried her face on his handkerchief.

'And I'll say no more about the dog. I promise.

I can always buy new slippers and I'll make sure the others know he's welcome to stay.'

'Th-thank you.'

She bit her lip against the confession that her tears were not entirely about Gideon and not at all about the arguments over Romeo. It was no use admitting the real cause, because no one could help her and her family's pity would be far more painful than enduring her heartbreak alone.

Gideon handed Liberty a sealed note. 'Lady Olivia has sent a message—her footman is waiting for your reply.'

'Thank you.'

Liberty broke the seal.

'Olivia has asked if I would care to join her to promenade in the Park this afternoon,' she told Gideon.

'Shall you go?'

'Yes.'

Her spirits lifted even as anticipation and hopelessness warred in her mind—Dominic was likely to be in the Park at that hour, too, but he would no doubt be discreetly courting one, or more, of his contenders. Anticipation won that battle. Any glimpse, any contact, was better than none. And she did enjoy Olivia's company—she would help keep Liberty from chasing impossible dreams.

'I'll escort you there if you like,' said Gideon.

'You are not riding today?' Liberty asked as

she headed for the small writing desk to reply to Olivia.

'Not today.'

'Then I accept. Thank you.' Liberty penned a quick acceptance to Olivia, agreeing to meet her in the Park at four o'clock.

'Maybe we could ride in the Park together one afternoon soon?'

Liberty laughed. 'Only if you can hire me a better beast than the ones Hope and Verity ended up with. They told me all about it.'

'I'll see what I can do,' Gideon said. 'They *were* a poor couple of plodders…bad enough for our sisters, but hardly suited to a rider of your ability.' Gideon held out his hand. 'I'll take that to Lady Olivia's man for you.'

Pleasure at his compliment warmed Liberty as she handed over the folded note. 'Thank you.'

An hour later, Liberty walked to the Park with Gideon and met Olivia, as arranged, just inside the gates.

'I thought you might have brought your new dog,' Olivia said with a smile as they strolled among the crowds. 'Hugo told me all about it and how you rescued him from that cruel brute.'

Liberty gazed around. Some ladies did indeed have dogs on leads, or in their carriages.

'I am not certain Romeo is quite respectable enough for promenading in the Park,' she said.

'Romeo? Is that his name? Oh, I cannot wait to meet him. And don't worry whether he's respectable enough. You have every right to walk your dog here. It doesn't matter what anyone else thinks.'

*Spoken like a true duke's daughter.*

'Maybe I shall.'

A few paces further on they met Dominic, Lady Sybilla on his arm. Liberty's heart sank and jealousy clawed her. She curtsied, Dominic bowed and Olivia and Sybilla inclined their heads graciously.

'Such a pleasant afternoon for a walk,' said Sybilla.

'Indeed,' Olivia responded.

'Mama and I had the intention of driving around the carriageway, but Lord Avon persuaded me to walk with him instead and Mama gave her permission. Is Lord Hugo not accompanying you this afternoon, Lady Olivia?'

'As you see, he is not,' Olivia replied gravely. 'He is otherwise engaged, I am afraid.'

'That is regrettable.' A slight smile touched Lady Sybilla's lips. 'However, one cannot expect one's husband to dance attendance upon one *all* of the time, can one?'

Liberty risked a glance at Dominic. His face

was impassive, but his silver eyes betrayed a hint of resignation.

'No, indeed,' Olivia agreed.

'We ought perhaps to keep moving, Lady Sybilla,' said Dominic. 'It would not do to catch a chill.'

'Good heavens, no.' She tinkled a laugh. 'That would indeed be unfortunate this early in the Season.' She inclined her head again. 'Good afternoon to you both, Lady Olivia; Miss Lovejoy.'

'Oh, dear.' Olivia tucked her arm through Liberty's as they strolled away. 'Although my brother is nothing but discreet, I do fear he is now angling towards Sybilla Gratton as first choice.'

Dominic's list was the very last thing Liberty wished to dwell on, but at the same time the subject drew her back like a magnet.

'I thought his preference was for Lady Caroline?'

'Her attitude after that business between your sister and Bridlington at the Twyfords' ball changed his mind, I believe.'

'I see.' Liberty was glad Dominic had seen through Caroline, but she knew very little about Lady Sybilla other than she was the eldest daughter of the Duke of Wragby and she always appeared perfectly poised and calm. In other words, perfect for Dominic's bride. 'You do not approve?'

'I do not. She is like a…like a statue carved out of ice.' Olivia huffed in disgust. 'I have never seen a natural expression on her face nor heard an unconsidered word leave her lips. Not that I have known her long, for her family were late coming up to town, but still… Poor Dominic will be frozen out of bed by that one.' She gasped and clapped her hand over her mouth. 'Oops. I apologise. I should not talk to you like that. I keep forgetting you are unmarried.'

Liberty couldn't help but laugh. 'I am not so easily shocked, Olivia. But you cannot deny she meets all of your brother's requirements. She's the daughter of a duke and her upbringing, manners and behaviour are impeccable.'

'She is…oh, I don't know! She is so false, somehow. I wonder if she even knows what joy is? How will she ever make him happy?'

'I don't believe his own happiness features very highly on your brother's list of requirements.'

'But it *should*. Oh, Liberty… I don't how I shall do it but, somehow, I must find a way to persuade him to think again, even though I know very well he will not listen to me.' Olivia swished her closed parasol in a gesture of frustration. 'Not one of them is right for him, but he is so stubborn and he will not listen to sense…he just accuses me of meddling! But all I want is for him to be happy, as I am with my Hugo. But it is like Alex says…once Dominic has set his mind on a course of action he is the very devil to divert from it.'

'But…' Liberty ignored her inner voice that shrieked at her to change the subject. 'But…what if he, say, met someone and fell in love?'

'Hah! You don't know my brother and his…his…*blinkered*ness! He believes the wife of a future duke should be chosen with the head, not the heart. He will marry for the sake of the Dukedom, not for himself.'

'Could your father not talk to him, if you ask him to?'

'I doubt Papa will interfere,' said Olivia gloomily. 'His whole life, Dominic has done his utmost to be the perfect son and the perfect heir—constantly aware of his responsibility as Papa's heir. If Papa was to say *Don't marry Lady X, marry Lady Y*, Dominic would do just that to please Papa. *That's* not choosing with his heart. And Papa knows he would do it, too. So he won't risk interfering. Oh…how I wish Aunt Cecily were here. *She* might talk some sense into Dom, but she and Zach aren't coming for another three weeks at least. It'll be too late by then.

'No. I don't know how I shall contrive it, but I must try. *Someone* has to do *something*.' She lapsed into a brooding silence before adding, 'Oh, and talking of Dominic… Hugo and I are going to visit Westfield tomorrow. Would you care to join us?'

'I would love to—as long as your brother will not object to my accompanying you?'

'Why should he? Hugo is happy for you to accompany us and I don't suppose Dominic will even be there. He'll be too busy courting his blasted list of perfect brides.'

# *Chapter Fourteen*

The following afternoon, Dominic entered the schoolroom at Westfield where Mrs Whittaker was supervising the children at their lessons. He pulled up a low chair next to Tommy, who he knew struggled with his reading. Westfield prided itself on teaching both letters and numbers to the children in its care—not to make scholars of them, but to prepare them to become useful members of society, able to earn their living. And that was where Dominic and Felicity were invaluable, in helping to place the older children in positions with tradesmen or in households where they had the opportunity to better themselves with hard work. But Dominic also loved to spend time helping the individual children when he could—and, just at this moment, it was exactly what he needed to take his mind off his dilemma.

The past few days had been thoroughly dispiriting. He had spent time with all five ladies from his original list and the only thing he was certain of was that he was less sure of his ultimate decision now than he had been a week ago. But speculation in society was rife and he would look a dithering fool if he did not proceed when the talk was of nothing else. And yet he still hesitated over making that final, irreversible decision.

*Make me proud, my Son. You were born to be the Duke...never disgrace your position in society...the eyes of the world will be on you. Judging you. Never let them see weakness.*

His mother's strictures when he was a boy. The demands he had striven to obey as a boy, desperate for her love and approval…the same demands that had driven him to follow his duty all his life, ever conscious of his responsibility to his heritage, his mother's memory and to the family name.

But, also, the gentleman in him rebelled against insulting the ladies on his list with the implication that not one of them was up to his standards. He was eager to set up his nursery—that was the one bright, hopeful thing in this mess—and he knew he'd be in a worse position if he delayed until later in the year, or even until next Season. The same names would be on any list he drew up, only now they would be aware of his reluctance. And the name he longed to include—Liberty Lovejoy—would still not be on his list. Her maternal grandfather would still be a coal merchant.

*You are the Marquess of Avon. You will be Duke of Cheriton one day, and your son and your son's son. That is your destiny. Do not allow the weakness of base desires to contaminate the bloodline—it is your duty to keep it pure.*

His father would arrive in town within a fortnight. By then, the decision *would* be made. That had been his plan from the beginning of the Season when he had been keen to get on with his selection and to start his own family. But now he simply felt numb as his well-ordered plans appeared to fragment around him.

He pushed his worries aside and pointed to the word *apple* written on the slate.

'Try again,' he said.

Tommy scowled down at the slate. He'd not long been at Westfield, having been referred by the magistrates' court after being arrested as a pickpocket…his first offence.

'Sound out each letter…you know the sounds they make, Tommy. Come on. You can do this. I have faith in you.'

He barely registered the sound of the door opening until he heard Peter Whittaker—who owned and ran Westfield with his wife, Jane—say, 'And this is the schoolroom.'

Dominic glanced around, then shot to his feet

as he saw Liberty, her eyes huge and riveted on him. He felt the colour build in his face and he gritted his teeth as he struggled to control his suddenly erratic breathing and to keep the smile in his heart from reaching his lips.

'Good afternoon, Miss Lovejoy.' He bowed. 'It is a pleasure to see you again.'

He nodded at Hugo and Olivia—whom he had expected—and who followed Liberty into the room.

'I invited Liberty to come with us.' Olivia smiled happily. 'I knew you would not object and she is very interested in Westfield.'

*Is she indeed?*

He was somewhat gratified to see Liberty's blush. At least it wasn't just him who felt awkward. But he also caught a glint of surprise in her eyes…she hadn't expected him to be here? Or was her surprise that he was helping teach the children?

'Why should I object?'

Olivia crossed the room to him. 'Well, you are so very close-chested about this sort of thing, Dom, you know you are. Does Lady Sybilla know of your connection with Westfield?'

Beyond Olivia, he could see Hugo questioning Peter as Liberty listened intently.

'Why would I mention it to Lady Sybilla?' How did Olivia know Sybilla had been his favourite until his current state of indecision? He'd taken such care not to single out any one lady more than another. 'Or to anyone else, come to that?'

'Why indeed? Your Lady Sybilla has about as much compassion in her as that statue of Venus in the British Museum—I cannot see her ever sharing your interest in the welfare of these poor children, Dom.'

Dominic bit back his frustration.

'Shouldn't you go and listen to Mr Whittaker, Livvy? I thought Hugo brought you here to find out about Westfield, didn't he? Not to plague me about that dam—dratted list.'

'Of course he did, silly! I didn't even know you would be here. I'll see you later.'

With a quick smile, she returned to the others, where Peter was explaining the workings of the school and what they hoped to achieve for their children. Dominic returned his attention to Tommy and his reading.

Finally, realising Tommy's concentration was drifting, Dominic stood up and realised, with a start of surprise, that although Peter's voice had long since fallen silent and he had assumed the entire group had left the schoolroom, Liberty was still there, crouching by the side of another, younger, lad, and helping him with *his* reading. His heart lurched as she smiled up at him.

'Little Ronnie here is doing very well, Lord Avon, but I think he is growing a little weary. Would you mind…?'

She reached out to him and he took her dainty hand in his. He helped her to rise, stifling the urge to press his lips to her palm, and released it the second she gained her feet.

'Thank you. I am grateful you are here, for my legs had grown quite stiff with crouching down like that and I feared a most inelegant lurch to my feet.'

Her smile twinkled in her eyes.

'I was unaware you were still in the room.'

'Mr Whittaker offered Hugo and Olivia a tour of the place, but I preferred to remain here, with the children.' She hesitated. Then touched his arm. 'This is admirable…that both you and Lady Stanton have been involved in this place for so long. I…' She paused before continuing, 'It's not what I would ever have expected of…'

'Of a man like me?' He didn't wait for her reply. A glance at the room showed the children paying more attention to them than to their lessons. 'Come. Let us leave Mrs Whittaker to teach in peace. We are disrupting her lesson.' He sent a smile across the room to Peter's wife, then ushered Liberty out into a passage and towards the entrance hall, where the afternoon sun sent beams of coloured light through the stained-glass windows either side of the front door. 'We can wait here for the others—or we can go and find them if you prefer?'

'No.' She stared at him, a light of calculation in those beautiful midnight-blue eyes of hers. Her throat rippled as she swallowed. 'There is something I should like to say to you.'

So serious. A shiver of disquiet rippled across the skin of his back.

'I… I…'

He moved closer, breathing in her scent. Roses—they no longer exclusively recalled his childhood and his mother but, increasingly, brought the image of Liberty Lovejoy into his thoughts.

'It is not like you to be hesitant, Berty. I thought you were unafraid of any subject, or any man.'

She sucked in a breath. 'It is about your list.'

He felt his forehead bunch. 'What about it?'

'I…' She paused. Gold-flecked midnight-blue eyes searched his and then her lips set in a determined line. 'I am worried about the…the…singlemindedness of your plan.'

'My plan is actually none of your concern.' He heard the finality in his tone, sensed the barrier rise up between them. 'Do you not believe me capable of making the right decision?'

'I just feel… I am worried…' A frustrated

growl rattled in her throat. 'Surely by sticking so rigidly to this list of yours, you are limiting your choice of bride?'

'But that is the idea. It is all about finding the perfect bride.'

She frowned at him. A puzzled frown, not angry. 'But why not just choose the lady you like best?'

He set his jaw, feeling his own frown deepen. 'What do you mean?'

Liberty sighed, a gust of exasperation. 'Exactly what I say. Who—do—you—like—best?'

He tensed. 'That is neither here nor there. Personal taste doesn't come into it.'

She didn't understand. How could she possibly understand? This was his destiny. His duty. He was the Duke's heir.

'But…it is madness! The lady you choose… Dominic…you will be bound to her. For ever. Surely you want to be happy?'

'That is not how our world works. Many people marry for convenience.'

'Olivia and Hugo did not. Nor did the rest of your family, from what Olivia has said.'

A suspicion seized him. 'Did my sister put you up to this?'

'No! No, of course not. Although I do know she is worried about you, too.'

'No one needs to worry about me. My life is under control. *My* control.'

*Then why haven't you decided yet? Why do you still hunger after what you cannot have?*

He thrust down that inner voice.

'And in answer to your question, the rest of my family are not in my shoes. *I* am my father's heir. He married my mother for the future of the Dukedom, to keep it secure for the generations to come. It is my destiny…my *duty*…to do the same. Happiness does not come into it.'

'But that is so sad. It sounds a lonely life to me.'

He shrugged and could see his indifference infuriated her. But it really did not matter to him—any one of those ladies on his list would do.

'What do you actually want from this marriage, Dominic?'

'Me?' He paused, pondering her question. 'I want to do my duty. To do what is right for the title and for my father. And I am ready to start a family. I want my children to grow up close in age to Olivia's twins and to my father's second family and my little cousins.'

'So you will choose duty over happiness?'

'There is no reason for me to be unhappy once I make my choice.'

'Dominic…' his name on her lips and the hand she rested on his chest as she gazed up at him sent his silly heart tumbling '...please...at least consider other young ladies in addition to your shortlist.'

'Like you?' His voice rasped. The unfairness of that question shocked him, but that did not stop the rest of it from spilling out. 'Or maybe you still harbour hopes for your sisters?'

She snatched her hand away and stepped back, hurt in her eyes. 'That is not what I thought for one moment. I know only too well that neither I nor my sisters match your requirements. Dominic... I am speaking to you now as your *friend*. At least, I hope we are friends?'

He raised his hand to the back of his neck and rubbed. He craved more than friendship with this woman. But it could never be. And he should have known better than to accuse her of self-interest. He had seen her passion for protecting those she cared about, from her brother to a stray dog. And she cared for *him*, too. She felt that same connection between them that he was trying so hard to resist.

Of course she would want to protect him from making what she saw as a mistake. He should expect no less.

'I apologise. That accusation was unjustified. Yes, we are friends and I value it.'

'Then, as your friend, *please* think again about your choice of bride. I don't believe any of those on your shortlist will make you a comfortable wife.'

'Comfortable?' He huffed a laugh. 'I do not seek a comfortable wife, Liberty. I seek a suitable wife. There is a world of difference.'

'And there is a world of difference between a suitable match on paper and the reality of marriage to that same person.' She laid her hand upon his sleeve. 'Please reconsider. There is nowhere as lonely as a poor marriage. Make certain you have at least something in common with your bride.'

'We'll have the most important thing in common,' he growled. 'Breeding.'

She shook her head and sighed. 'I can say no more.'

A door opened at the far end of the hall and Hugo and Olivia emerged.

'Do you go to the Attwoods' ball tonight?' Liberty asked Dominic as the others joined them.

The evening was mild for April. Afterwards, Liberty used that as an excuse for what happened at the Attwoods' ball. If it had been cool, she would never have ventured alone on to the terrace instead of going to supper. There were a few others out there, taking the air, but she did not approach them, preferring her own company. One by one, they returned inside, but she had no wish to indulge in more polite conversation. She sighed, propped her hands on the stone balustrade and gazed up at the stars. Somewhere, up there, Bernard was watching her, wishing her well. She was sure of it even though, with every year that passed, his memory faded—his features more indistinct; his voice more silent; his touch… She shivered, pushing that memory away. But that old guilt persisted. That nagging feeling she might have saved them, if only she had done more.

His scent alerted her to his presence and she turned. His features were in shadow as he stood close. Almost too close.

'I neglected to ask you earlier. How is that dog?'

'Romeo? He is—'

She fell silent as he erupted into laughter. 'Romeo? You could not give that mongrel a more inappropriate name if you tried!'

Still shaky after her memories of Bernard, she shoved at his chest. 'Do *not* mock me!' She pushed past him, heading for the French window and the ballroom beyond. As she reached for the handle, Dominic grabbed her wrist, bringing her to an abrupt halt.

'Don't go!'

She would not look at him. 'Why not?'

He tugged her to the side, away from the window and out of the patch of light that spilled on to the terrace and into the shadow of the house wall.

He turned her to face him and, his free hand on her shoulder, he backed her against the wall. The bricks were hard and cool through the silk of her gown, but she was anything but cold as her stomach flipped and heat spiralled through her. He towered above her—dark, strong, masculine—the trace of his spicy cologne mingling with the scent of wine and brandy on his breath. He moved closer, his body against hers, all that hard, solid muscle...all that strength...all that power... Her breathing hitched and her lips parted as she desperately sucked in a new breath.

His head bent towards her as his hands slid lower to settle on her hips. It was too dark to decipher his expression, but his tattered breathing punctuated the silence of the night air and his thudding heartbeat vibrated through her.

'Liberty...'

Warm breath feathered across her face and the ache in his voice tore into her heart. She reached up to touch his mouth...those fascinating, sensual lips she had fantasised about kissing. Her forefinger traced his bottom lip and she craved...oh, she craved... Her fingers splayed and her hand slipped up and around his cheek, learning the shape of that sculpted cheekbone, tracing the curve of his ear and pushing into the thick softness of his midnight-dark hair.

With a tortured groan, he slid his hands around

her, hauling her away from the harsh unyielding bricks at her back, crushing her against his sculptured heat, his hands cupping her bottom, lifting. His lips captured hers, demanding as his tongue plunged into her mouth. Helpless to resist, she returned thrust for thrust, relishing every moment of that stormy kiss. Her arms wrapped around him, clinging, as that initial passionate desperation eased, as the movement of their lips slowed and gentled, as their murmurs of appreciation mingled in the night air…until the sound of the musicians resuming play in the ballroom ended their kiss.

Dominic's tight embrace eased, his hands gliding soothingly up her back as she regained her balance. He rested his forehead against hers, his chest heaving even as Liberty, too, struggled to catch her breath. Eventually, he raised his head and she caught the glitter of his silver-grey eyes as their gazes met. And held.

Frustration tangled her stomach into knots. Nothing had changed. Nothing *could* change. Not unless *Dominic* changed and turned away from what he had grown up to believe was his duty. And, unless that miracle happened, Liberty could never be more to him than…

'Just friends?'

'Friends.' His eyes bored into hers, sending

waves of longing crashing through her. 'It is all we can ever be.'

Regret coloured his tone, but also resolve. Could she accept his decision, even though it broke her heart?

'I… I should not have kissed you.' His fingers brushed her cheek. 'It was self-indulgent and I am sorry.'

'I am also at fault.' The blame was equally theirs. They were both grown-ups. He had not forced her. 'We shall forget it happened.'

She gathered every vestige of strength she could find and stepped aside, away from his warmth and his strength. She turned from him and returned to the ballroom.

She had survived worse, although it would be hell watching him with another woman. Especially when she fully believed he was heading towards disaster. Without volition, her eyes swept the ballroom until she had seen each one of his shortlist, but her worried gaze lingered on Lady Sybilla. Olivia believed she was now his preferred option—*option! How cold that sounds*—and of all of them, she was the one Liberty knew the least about. Oh, she knew the public guise, but of the woman beneath that ice-cool exterior she knew nothing. Did Dominic know any more than she did, or had he, too, only ever seen what the lady chose to reveal?

There was little she could do other than hope he came to his senses in time, but if she wanted to protect herself…her heart…she should not risk being alone with him again.

*Heavens!* The entire surface of her body heated at the memory of that kiss and her stomach swirled with unspent restless energy. How had she become entangled in the web of desire so quickly? So fiercely? And now, if she allowed herself to, she could easily succumb to misery, knowing there could be no happy ending. But she would not indulge herself. She had known him but a few weeks. Passion would fade. It couldn't be anything more…meaningful.

It couldn't be love.

Could it?

With Bernard there had been a slow, sweet build to love and desire over the years they had known one another. There had never been that sudden violence of passion that had held her in its thrall on the terrace.

It *couldn't* be love.

'Miss Lovejoy.' Lord Silverdale, an attractive man in his middle thirties, bowed before her. 'If you lack a partner, may I request the pleasure of this dance?'

The distraction welcome, she accepted, smiling up at the Earl. As he led her into the set, she caught sight of Dominic, with Lady Sarah as his partner. Their gazes fused and a shiver chased across her skin, desire pulsing at her core. She tore her eyes from his and directed her attention to Lord Silverdale, pushing all thought of Dominic from her mind.

Afterwards, she stayed close to Olivia and Hugo when possible and occupied herself by watching Gideon as he danced attendance on Lady Emily Crighton, and her sisters, both happy, both contented, partnered by a succession of good-looking, handsome and eligible bachelors.

'You are not still worried about your brother, are you?' Olivia asked later.

'No. He and I…we had a talk—' she would never admit to Olivia that Gideon had found her weeping '—and he has allayed my fears.'

Olivia's silvery gaze swept the room, settling on Dominic and Alex, deep in conversation. 'I wish I could say the same about my brothers. I fear Alex will never change and Dominic is still determined to select his bride before Father arrives.'

Liberty did not want to talk, or even think, about Dominic and his future wife and she soon took her leave of Olivia and wandered around the perimeter of the ballroom, trying not to catch any gentleman's eye. She really was not in the mood for dancing. She spied an empty chair in an alcove and settled gratefully into in, partially shielded from the floor by a floral arrangement on a pedestal. She relaxed, closing her eyes, trying to dismiss that kiss from her mind and her heart and yet reliving every second of it, and relishing it. Her heart sang—he had kissed her as though he meant it—and it ached, because that kiss could never lead to what she now admitted she wanted above all else.

Him. And her. Together.

'Why are you hiding away?' Her eyes flew open at Dominic's question. 'Are you unwell?' He stood two paces away, worry creasing his brow. He lowered his voice, but came no nearer. 'Are you upset about what happened?'

Her throat ached. This was torment. Did she have the strength to see him, talk to him, to pretend that kiss had not pierced her heart?

'I am not upset, merely enjoying a little peace.'

'I cannot leave you sitting in here all alone—who knows what manner of undesirable men might corner you?' His smile slipped, becoming crooked, and she longed to soothe it. To soothe him. 'Will you allow me to escort you to Mrs Mount or to Olivia?'

Dominic held out his hand and, as she placed her hand in his, he murmured, 'Are you certain nothing is troubling you, Berty?'

The strength of his fingers as they closed

around hers, and his use of her private nickname, stirred all sorts of warm feelings deep inside. They were still friends and, if she could expect nothing more from him, she would settle for that.

As she rose to her feet, she said, 'I am certain.'

# Chapter Fifteen

Liberty stepped towards Dominic, her hand still enclosed in his, her midnight-blue gaze open and honest. The silky fabric of her blue gown clung to her curves, her décolletage enticingly framed by her low, lace-trimmed neckline. Her honey-blonde hair was piled on her head, leaving tendrils to frame her face and brush her bare shoulders.

His hands twitched with the longing to stroke. To caress.

His back was to the ballroom, blocking her from view and, without volition, his forefinger trailed down her arm, from the lace that trimmed her short sleeve to the edge of her elbow-length glove. Her skin was warm satin and his eyes charted the shiver that followed in the wake of his touch.

He was playing with fire. Again. He clenched his jaw and locked his feelings inside, placing her hand on his sleeve as he turned to face the room and escort her to Mrs Mount.

'I am engaged with Lady Sybilla for the next,' he said. 'But I hope to see you in the Park tomorrow afternoon.'

Her face lit and her soft gasp whispered past his ears, but the glow in her blue eyes quickly dimmed. Her tawny brows gathered in a frown.

'Why?' Her whisper was fierce.

'Why what?'

'You kiss me. You say we can never be more than friends. Yet still you stroked my arm and now you "hope to see me in the Park". What is it you want from me, Dominic?'

He wanted *her*, that was the truth. And she was right to rebuke him. He was being unfair and he would take greater care from now on. But tomorrow...he was almost tempted to tell her the reason he mentioned the Park and to reveal the secret Alex had told him earlier. But it was not his secret to tell. And although he would be wise to stay away, he could not wait to see her face. Was it so wrong to indulge himself?

He told her none of that. 'I am sorry.'

He bowed, leaving Liberty with Mrs Mount, swallowing past the emotion that thickened his throat as he walked away. He had struggled to keep away from her after that kiss, knowing that all he wanted was to kiss her again. And again.

But he must protect her reputation and so he had kept his distance. Until Alex had let slip that it was Gideon and Liberty's birthday the next day and that Gideon and her sisters had planned a surprise for Liberty. In the Park.

And because Dominic would never have the right to give Liberty a gift of any kind, he could not resist the chance to see, and to share in, her joy and excitement when Gideon revealed his present to her.

He did his utmost to push Liberty from his thoughts as he danced with Lady Sybilla, but it proved impossible. Sybilla was utter perfection in her looks: a beautiful brunette with burnished locks and porcelain skin. Her serene expression rarely altered and her behaviour was correct in every way: she never displayed a vulgar excess of emotion; she agreed amenably with every opinion he uttered; she, quite properly, revealed little knowledge about any subject under discussion. Dominic had spent enough time with her in the past week or so to know she was polite to servants, but never overly familiar, and that she never appeared to look down on anyone she might deem beneath her because of their more lowly birth. In short, she was the perfect bride. She was exactly the lady he had set out to find at the start of the Season.

And he was already bored. She was simply *too*

perfect. Try as he might, he couldn't imagine her having fun, teasing him, cuddling a child, rescuing a dog, crouching beside a child to help it read until her legs were so stiff she couldn't rise without help. The entire time he danced with Sybilla, it was Liberty's face he saw in his mind's eye. Liberty's lips he could still taste. His head ached with the constant inner battles that plagued his thoughts and, lately, kept him awake at night.

*What would it matter if you changed your mind? Why not follow your heart? Others have and the world did not end.*

*But what of my promise to Mother? And how can I abandon my duty to the succession and to the family name?*

He had spent his boyhood trying to live up to his mother's expectations…trying to be good enough…determined to be worthy of that approval he had glimpsed just before she died. And still he chased that image of duty and responsibility that was part of the expectations of society as well as his own expectations of himself.

Still he strove to conform.

He escorted Sybilla back to her mother, the Duchess of Wragby, the arguments still raging inside his head, which was starting to throb.

'Well, Avon?' The Duchess looked him up and down with approval. 'Do you have news of your father's arrival in town?'

'Indeed, Your Grace. He and my stepmother arrive next week.'

*Time is running out.*

That thought had clawed at him for days now. The time was coming when he must announce his decision and his future would be set in stone. His stomach clenched with nerves. He had always been decisive, but now he dithered, unable to take that final, irrecoverable step. And his indecision, he knew, was because, in his heart of hearts, he simply didn't care *who* he wed, unless it was Liberty.

And as soon as any such thought arose, an image of a coal merchant would materialise in his head…a man such as Liberty's grandfather.

*'Never allow your base desires to contaminate the bloodline, my Son. Keep it pure. Make me proud.'*

Not one whisper of his inner turmoil was allowed to surface, however. His behaviour was as correct as it had ever been. No one would suspect the whirlwind of indecision that plagued his thoughts. If Lady Sybilla was the perfect lady, *he* had always taken care to present himself to the world as the perfect gentleman.

He had only ever allowed himself to relax that perfection when he was safe among his family.

*And with Liberty.*

He shrugged that thought away. If he was a

different man beneath the gentlemanly exterior, then Sybilla, too, might be different.

*But different how? In a good way or a bad way?*

He could stand no more. He felt as though he rode a runaway steed, the reins slipping through his useless fingers. He bowed abruptly to the Duchess and Sybilla. 'If you will excuse me, ladies?'

Not by a flicker did either lady reveal any disappointment in his departure. He really could not read either of them. He was sick of puzzling over his dilemma. He would speak to Alex and Gideon and check on the arrangements for tomorrow, then go to his club and banish that blasted list from his mind for a few hours.

The following afternoon Dominic met Gideon and Alex as arranged, at three o'clock by the Park gates. Gideon looked as giddy as a schoolboy, his blue eyes dancing with excitement, as he sat on his black gelding, holding a pretty chestnut mare by her reins. This was his surprise… Bella. A new horse for Liberty's birthday—one with outstanding conformation and, Alex had assured him, perfect manners. And Alex should know, because he had bred and trained Bella, using one of his stable lads to help accustom her to the side-saddle.

Alex was astride his huge grey, standing up in his stirrups, scanning the crowds for their first sight of Liberty. Hope and Verity had pledged to be in the Park by three and to bring Liberty with them.

'I do hope she doesn't suspect anything,' Gideon said for the umpteenth time.

Dominic was on foot. He wished he felt half as lively as Gideon, but his head still thumped from his late night at White's, when he had imbibed rather too freely of the brandy, and another restless night. He massaged his temples and closed his eyes briefly.

'I see her.' Alex lowered himself into his saddle. 'She's with your sisters, but they've got that dog with them.'

'I heard Liberty say she planned to walk it in the Park today,' said Gideon, 'and I *told* Hope on no account were they to bring him along. Why do sisters *never* listen?'

'I'll go and meet them,' said Dominic. 'I can steer them towards a less crowded spot, in case Bella should start to fidget.'

Gideon glanced at the mare. 'She seems calm enough—I just hope she doesn't object to dogs.'

'Indeed,' said Alex, with a wink. 'Or you'll be left holding Romeo, Dom. That won't do your image as a suave man about town any good at all.'

Dominic didn't dignify that remark with a

reply. He set off through the throng of walkers and, before too long, he came across Liberty, Hope and Verity. Romeo, tongue lolling, was prancing by Liberty's side, exhibiting a showy action that would not be out of place on one of Alex's specially bred high-stepping carriage horses. His upright ears were even more highly pricked than ever, and his tail curled tightly over his back.

Dominic bowed, taking in Liberty's blushing cheeks and the hint of self-consciousness in her eyes. Her periwinkle-blue walking dress fitted her like a glove, moulding to her breasts, and the memory of their fullness softly pressing against his chest last night sent the blood surging to his groin.

He conjured up Sybilla's serene half-smile and his lust subsided.

'Good afternoon, ladies. May I wish you a happy birthday, Miss Lovejoy?'

'Good afternoon, sir, and thank you.' Liberty's lips curved in a smile as all three ladies curtsied, but her smile was strained.

'Good afternoon, Lord Avon,' Hope and Verity chorused.

Hope caught his eye, raising her brows, a question in her blue eyes, and Dominic gave her a brief nod. Yes. Gideon *was* at the Park with Liberty's gift.

'And Romeo…' Dominic continued smoothly,

eyeing the hound, who eyed him back, a definite hint of arrogance in his stance. 'Well, he appears to have fully recovered from his ordeal. Anyone would think he was born to parade in the Park at the promenade hour.'

'We did try to persuade Liberty to leave him at home, my lord,' said Hope, 'but she would not listen.'

'Well, as it is your sister's birthday, I think she might be allowed a little indulgence.' He patted Romeo, who tolerated it. Gone was the cringing, fawning animal of only a few days ago. 'May I walk with you a short way, ladies?'

'We would be honoured, my lord.' Liberty was all graciousness, but, as they fell into step, she whispered, 'Your sister suggested I should walk Romeo here, but is it *really* acceptable?'

Her disquiet was unmistakable.

'Are you actually *asking* my advice? Is this the Liberty Lovejoy I… I first met on my father's doorstep?' He maintained his teasing tone, but flinched at the words he had so nearly uttered. *The Liberty Lovejoy I know and love.* It might be trite and a cliché, but those words had come from somewhere.

From the heart.

*Nonsense. Friends. She agreed with me. It's lust on my part. That's all.*

'I am sure it could not be anything *other* than

acceptable now *I* have lent you countenance by walking with you,' he said, using his haughtiest tone.

He was rewarded with a gurgled laugh and a light slap on the arm.

It was a relief to see Gideon and Alex riding towards them. Dominic clasped Liberty's elbow and drew her to a halt. She looked at him, an enquiring frown hovering. He nodded to the carriageway ahead. Her eyes widened and her mouth fell open. Dominic removed Romeo's lead from her slack hold and nudged her forward.

Gideon slid from his horse's back and waited, a huge grin on his face, as Liberty walked towards him.

'Lib, meet Bella. Happy birthday.' He handed her the lead rein.

As Dominic watched Liberty's joy and excitement a previously unknown emotion raked his insides. It took him a moment to realise he was jealous of Gideon. *He* wanted to give her things. *He* wanted to be the recipient of that joyous smile and that unrestrained hug. For the first time in his life he cursed that he was a duke's son. The heir. He longed to break free of the shackles and expectations of society.

He concentrated on keeping all trace of emotion from his face until, with relief, he spied his cousin and friend, Felicity Stanton, driving her pony pair, Nutmeg and Spice, at a spanking trot towards him. He thrust Romeo's lead at Verity and flagged Felicity to stop, which she did with a flourish.

'Dominic! How lovely to see you… I was at Westfield this morning and Peter told me all about your visit yesterday. And what splendid news, that Lord Hugo and Olivia are going to become patrons. Do you know any more of their plans?'

'Take me up and I will tell you all I know,' he said.

Gideon, Liberty and her sisters were all preoccupied examining Bella. They wouldn't even notice Dominic had gone. He caught Alex's eye, raised his hand in salute and then climbed in next to Felicity.

His destiny was ordained and it did not include Liberty Lovejoy, the granddaughter of a coal merchant. The time until his father arrived would pass quickly and as long as he kept reminding himself that he and Liberty were only friends all would be well.

He filled those days with activity: visits to Westfield, where he again helped the older children with their lessons; boxing and fencing sessions; visits to his clubs, where he partook in several lively political debates; and daily rides in

Hyde Park, where he had yet to see Liberty out on Bella. He both longed for and dreaded seeing her, knowing his resolve would not be strong enough to refrain from riding by her side, even if the most he could hope for would be polite chit-chat.

Friends.

The evenings were trickier, but he was proud of his demeanour. He remained totally in control and even Olivia and Alexander had stopped badgering him about his damned list, although Olivia couldn't quite disguise her anxiety whenever she thought he wasn't looking.

No one, he was certain, would suspect the knot that had taken up residence in his guts and that inexorably tightened with each day that passed.

He danced with every lady on his shortlist and a few more besides, keeping up a flow of frivolous conversation. If Liberty were present, he danced with her, too, his stomach muscles rigid with the effort required to maintain his mask of light friendship. Not by a word or a look did either of them refer to that kiss.

In short, he presented the same Lord Avon to the *ton* that he had presented for the past nine years, since he first came to town at seventeen years of age.

On the day of Father's arrival it brought him no relief to realise that this strange charade was near its end and so he awarded himself one last indulgence. Olivia and Hugo were to ride in the Park with Liberty. Dominic made sure to join them.

The days since their kiss had provided a salutary lesson for Liberty.

Dominic had proved time after time that their kiss meant nothing to him even though that same kiss haunted her dreams. He was the same suave, sophisticated gentleman he had always been. Any observer would claim he behaved no differently to her, but she knew there was a faint but discernible detachment in the way he acted around her. He avoided any situation where they might speak privately and, when they danced, he no longer teased her, but merely kept up the same light, inconsequential conversation he maintained with all his partners.

She ought to be pleased at his caution, but she missed him and she missed their friendship and his teasing. Her heart sank whenever she saw him with one of the ladies on his list, especially Sybilla following Olivia's suspicion that she was now Dominic's choice.

On the day Olivia's father was due to arrive in town, she and Hugo arranged to meet Liberty for a ride in the Park. Gideon rode with Liberty and waited with her by the Park gate until Hugo and Olivia arrived. Liberty tried to ignore the silly way her heart leapt at the sight of Dominic accompanying them, telling herself his presence meant nothing. She marshalled her courage and smiled serenely as he greeted her, but no sooner had they started to walk their horses along the carriageway than they appeared to fall naturally into two pairs: Hugo and Olivia, followed by Dominic and Liberty.

'I hope you do not object to my joining you this afternoon?' Dominic said, after they had exchanged comments on the weather—which was dry but still unseasonably cold.

He grinned at her. Totally relaxed and utterly gorgeous. No hint of self-consciousness over that kiss. No tinge of regret either. It was as though it had never happened.

'Why should I?' She was pleased with the light nonchalance of her reply.

'I have been wondering how you were getting on with Bella. Do you like her?'

Liberty smoothed one gloved hand along Bella's silken mane. 'Oh, yes. She is perfect. It was a lovely surprise.' She narrowed her eyes at him. 'I collect you knew all about it at the Attwoods' ball, when you said you hoped to see me in the Park the following day?'

'I did—and now you see why I could not tell you the reason for my question. You were a tad irritated with me at the time, as I recall.'

She *had* been irritated and still was—but by his ability to sweep the memory of that kiss…of her…away. She must have tensed because Bella threw her head up and danced sideways. Liberty forced her hands to relax on the rein and settled her with a hand to her neck and a soothing word. Dominic watched her and she caught a glint of admiration in his silver gaze.

She didn't want his admiration. It made everything so much harder to bear.

'You are well aware, my Lord Avon, that was not the only reason for my irritation,' she snapped.

Her mood only appeared to amuse him and a teasing smile stretched his lips.

'Ah. So you *were* upset because I kissed you.'

His remark riled her still further, until she realised he was being deliberately provocative and that she was rising to it. She reined in her temper and aimed for a similar kind of teasing banter.

'I was not. It was merely a kiss.' She stuck her nose in the air, but kept her tone light. 'It was hardly my first! It was your subsequent behaviour that I found so objectionable, sir.'

'*Sir* is it now? You *are* in a huff with me!' He laughed. 'Very well. I apologise for taking advantage of you by stroking your naked arm.' His choice of words set her pulse racing. 'But, really,

Berty…what do you expect of a red-blooded man when you present him with such temptation in a secluded alcove? If you will take my advice, you will remain close to your chaperon in future and not run the risk of leading random gentlemen astray.'

'Why, thank you so much for those words of wisdom, Lord Avon. Truly…' she placed her hand over her heart and fluttered her eyelashes at him '…I do not know how we weak females would manage without such penetrating male insight to guide us. Perhaps I should clothe myself in a nun's habit for future balls, if one expanse of bare skin can have such an undesirable effect on so-called gentlemen.'

She saw the effort it took him to bite back his grin. 'Now, now, Berty. I have told you before, sarcasm does not suit you.'

'And pontificating about the blinking obvious does not suit you, Dominic.'

*'Touché,'* he murmured.

They drifted into an amicable silence as they rode on, but the question that had plagued her for days bubbled in her brain, foiling her efforts to ignore it. She had to know the worst. She had to prepare herself.

'I have something I wish to ask you.'

His features blanked, a hint of wariness in his eyes.

'Go on.'

'Have you made your choice?'

He would know what she meant, no need to elaborate further. She burned to know *who* and *when*, so she could be ready to stand by and smile benignly even though she was still convinced he was heading for a cold and miserable future.

His eyebrows met in a dark slash. 'I have.'

Her heart tumbled and nausea rose to choke her. She swallowed hard. 'Is the young lady aware of her good fortune?'

His lips firmed and a muscle leapt in his cheek.

'Not as yet. You are the first to know.' He paused, the groove between his eyebrows deepening. 'I shall ask Lady Sybilla to be my wife,' he said eventually.

Her throat thickened. She had asked and now she knew. Olivia had been right. Sybilla was exquisitely polite to Liberty if ever their paths met, but she had never caught the slightest glimpse of the real woman beneath that emotionless façade. And now Liberty would be forced to smile and congratulate the happy couple.

*How will he be happy with Sybilla? He'll end up lonely and embittered...he needs a woman with warmth and kindness to bring joy into his life, not an ice maiden.*

Sybilla was cold enough to freeze a stream of lava in mid-flow.

'And when shall you offer for her?'

His silver gaze roamed restlessly around the Park.

'Father arrived today and the family will all dine at Beauchamp House tonight. I shall inform them of my decision then.'

'So you will tell your family before you speak to Lady Sybilla?'

'Of course.' His chest swelled as he inhaled. He switched his gaze to Liberty. Then the air left his lungs in a rush. 'You know very well this is a practical arrangement. I want my family's blessing before I make any commitment. Once I make my offer there will be no going back.'

She knew that. Knew that his gentleman's honour, let alone his obsession with *duty*, would never allow him to behave otherwise. And her heart ached for him. From everything she had learned from Mrs Mount and from Olivia, the members of his extended family were all happily married—every one of them a love match. But even with those examples, Dominic still steered resolutely on his chosen course.

'And if your father gives his approval?' She knew it was his father's approval that was crucial. The rest of the family were important, but the Duke's opinion was the one that mattered.

'Then I shall call on the Duke of Wragby in the morning.'

She had pushed him far enough. There was a finality in his tone that warned her to stop. She swallowed again and concentrated on maintaining her posture in the saddle even though she longed to slump in defeat.

'I wish you well.'

'Thank you.'

They rode on in silence.

# *Chapter Sixteen*

Dominic felt no relief at announcing his decision. What he didn't tell Liberty was that, until the moment she asked, he had still not made his final choice—wavering from one name to the other and back again until he was in a state of utter confusion—even though he still planned to tell the rest of the family tonight. Her question had pushed him into the final decision, but the words in his head had felt alien and they felt even worse coming from his mouth. But he said them none the less, that promise to his mother still on his mind…his promise and her expectations…he had vowed to prove to her that he was worthy. And he also wanted to please his father; he surely deserved at least one trouble-free son.

Dominic had spent his life conforming to what was expected of a man of his birthright precisely in order to protect his father from pain and anxiety. He was not about to change now.

Besides. He glanced over at Liberty. All that 'follow your heart' nonsense was just that. Nonsense. Pure, honest-to-goodness lust was the driving force behind his craving for Liberty Lovejoy. Without volition, his gaze slid over her, lingering on her full breasts, outlined by the snug fit of her dove-grey riding habit. Everything about her sent desire racing through his bloodstream, but he could rise above that visceral response. He'd done it before, often and often.

He'd made his choice. Lady Sybilla. She was twenty-one years old—no green girl on the town for the first time. He'd met her many times, during the Season and at house parties out of season, and she had never put an elegantly shod foot out of place. She was beautiful, reserved, well-mannered, a graceful dancer and an accomplished rider and she deferred to a man's opinion just as she ought.

He frowned, sneaking another sideways look at Liberty. No one could ever accuse her of deferring to a man's opinion simply because of his sex. If she thought her opinion was right, she had absolutely no compunction in voicing it. Much like the rest of the females in his family, he mused, except, maybe, Aunt Cecily…until she met Zach and had changed from the quiet, compliant lady Dominic had always known. He frowned. Aunt Cecily, it turned out, had not been truly happy all those years when she was raising her brother's children. She'd been content, but not happy. Not fulfilled. But she had never said so.

Would Liberty end up the same? A maiden aunt, quashing her own desires and deferring to her brother and sisters? He shook those thoughts away. It was her decision…there was nothing to stop her marrying if she chose to, even though the thought of her with another man sent anger spiking through his veins.

'Why do you care about my choice? Or when I intend to make my offer?'

He thrust down the voice that reminded him that she had kissed him. Passionately. Of course she cared. Probably more than she should and more than he deserved.

'You are my friend. I *care* about you… I want you to be happy.'

'I shall be happy.' His reply came by rote.

She shook her head at him, then smiled. Her pearly teeth sent waves of longing crashing through him and he wrenched his gaze from hers with a silent snarl at his rampant lust.

'We *have* become serious,' she said. 'Come. Let us enjoy our time together for, once you make your announcement, I make no doubt you will be far too busy with your betrothed to spend time riding in the Park with me.' Was it his imagination, or did her voice hitch, just a little? 'The ride is less crowded here,' she continued gaily. 'Let us canter.'

She didn't wait for his reply, but set off and, after a moment's hesitation, Dominic sent Vulcan in her wake.

Beauchamp House was alight with chatter and laughter when Dominic arrived at six that evening. He entered the salon and paused, unnoticed for a few moments, just taking in his family…the smiles on their faces as they caught up with one another's news. The children, too, were there, together with their nursemaids who would whisk them away once dinner was announced. His two-year-old half-brother, Sebastian, was the first to see him.

*'Dominic!'*

He scurried across the room, closely pursued by his older sister, Christabel. Dominic swung Sebastian up and around, the boy's dress flaring out, his chubby legs kicking in delight as he giggled. Dominic planted a kiss on his cheek, then settled him under one arm as he scooped up Christabel with the other. Her arms wound around his neck and she pressed her hot cheek against his.

'I love you, Dominic. You're my *bestest* brother.'

'I love you, too, sweetie-pie!' Dominic hugged her close for a minute, then groaned theatrically and staggered. 'Help! Help me! I… I… I can't hold these monsters any longer!'

The conversation had paused as everyone watched the byplay then, accompanied by more laughter, Father strode forward and plucked Christabel from Dominic's arms.

'I *told* you not to eat so much, Christy—you've reduced your big brother to a quivering wreck.'

He cradled her in one arm and freed his other to tickle her. She shrieked and squirmed.

'Papa! No! Mama! Help!'

Dominic's stepmother, Rosalind, came up with a smile. As he kissed her in greeting, she said, 'I might have known you would reduce our ordered gathering to chaos as soon as you arrived, Dominic. It is good to see you, though.' She turned to Father. 'Let me take her, Leo, or Penny will complain they're too excited to sleep.'

'Yes, Your Grace.' Leo handed his daughter over to Rosalind and gave her a mock salute.

Dominic's adopted sister, Susie—now thirteen and growing up into a serious, studious girl—came over to take charge of Sebastian and order reigned once more.

'How are you, my Son?' Father's silver gaze—so like Dominic's—scanned him. 'Are these rumours I've heard true?'

Trust Father to know what was going on in advance and to have no compunction in raising the matter. He always seemed to be two steps ahead of everyone else.

Dominic forced a nonchalant shrug. 'There are always rumours. Have you taken to listening to gossip now, Father?'

*Tell him! Get it over with!*

'Ah, well. I dare say I have it wrong.'

His tone suggested otherwise, but Father merely slung his arm across Dominic's shoulders and they joined the rest of the family. Dominic sought out Olivia, Hugo and Alex one by one and sent each of them a look of warning. This was his business—it was not their place to pre-empt him. Not that Alex was likely to, as he rarely voluntarily spoke to Father, but Olivia… she was a very different matter. She returned his look with an innocent lift of her eyebrows, but Dominic thought she would stay silent, not least because she had made it clear she did not approve of any of the ladies on his shortlist.

He stood to one side of the room, drinking, and he watched his family, paying particular attention to Rosalind and Olivia as they interacted with their children and their husbands, trying to picture Sybilla in that role. Then he tried to imagine her fitting in with his family as they chattered together, laughing and teasing. But he could not imagine her behaving with such informality, even in a family setting. Liberty, though…

He thrust her image away, clenching his jaw. Perhaps one of the others would be a better choice? After all, nobody knew he had selected Sybilla. Apart from Liberty and she would not tell anyone. He tried to put any one of those ladies into this scenario, but the only face that surfaced in his imagination was Liberty Lovejoy's.

'Things on your mind, Dom?'

'No.'

'Have you made your choice yet? Have you been picturing her here in the bosom of our family?'

It was too close to the truth. Dominic drained his wine glass. 'Don't be ridiculous.'

Alex leaned closer. 'Father knows. Look at him. He's waiting for you to broach the subject.'

'He told you that, did he?' Irritation with Alex prompted him to add, 'Or did you somehow let it slip during one of your cosy father-and-son chats?'

One corner of Alex's mouth lifted in a half-smile that roused Dominic's guilt. He was normally careful not to enflame his brother's hostility towards their father.

'Unworthy, Brother. You should know by now the Duke doesn't need to be told things…he just knows.'

Again, Dominic was conscious of his father's gaze on him even though he carefully avoided looking in his direction. He signalled to William, who crossed the room to fill his glass again. As soon as the footman was out of earshot, Alex turned serious.

'Dom. Listen to me. Don't tie yourself to any of 'em. Not yet. Any fool can see your heart isn't in it—'

'The heart is irrelevant, Alexander. I make decisions with my head. With logic and planning.'

'You're a damned stubborn fool once you get an idea in that head of yours, that's for certain,' Alex growled. 'Tell me, once and for all. Are you going to tell Father tonight or not?'

Dominic's clenched jaw ached as he battled with his answer. Yes? Or no? One simple word. That's all it needed.

'No,' he said finally and the relief when his decision emerged washed over him like a tidal wave, sweeping all tension and friction from him. 'No. I will not tell him tonight. There is no hurry.'

Alex grinned and slapped Dominic on the back. 'Best news I've heard in an age. There'll be a lot of anxious punters at White's, wondering what the verdict will be, mind.' He leaned in again and lowered his voice. 'I know you won't take my advice, but I shall say what I think nevertheless. Scrap that list and think again.' He walked away before Dominic could reply.

How easy it was for Alex to say that and to believe it.

He was not the heir.

*He* didn't have the weight of expectation on his shoulders.

*He* was not bound by duty.

Dominic's chest ached and his throat constricted. He had never felt so alone, even though his family were all around him. He rubbed at his chest and the action brought Liberty bouncing into his head. How many times had he noticed her doing the exact same thing? He scowled down into his glass. How many times would he continue to allow her to invade his head and upset his carefully laid plans? No matter how many times he caught himself wishing to share a joke with her, or to point out a beautiful flower or an interesting cloud formation in the sky, nothing could change the fact that the granddaughter of a coal merchant was unsuited to the position of Marchioness of Avon, let alone the future Duchess of Cheriton.

The children were shortly packed off to the nursery and dinner was served. Throughout the meal, even as the conversation ebbed and flowed, Dominic was conscious of his father's eyes resting on him from time to time, a crease between his dark brows. He didn't doubt his father knew all about the list...the question was, would he speak to Dominic about it or would he wait for Dominic to approach him? Somehow, Dominic thought he would wait. The relief he had felt had been temporary. Tension still wound his gut, robbing him of his appetite. He picked at his food.

'Are you quite well, Dominic?' Rosalind spoke softly. 'You are hardly eating a thing and you are very quiet. And drinking more than usual. Is...is something troubling you? Your father has noticed...he looks concerned.'

'I am perfectly well, thank you. I made the mistake of eating at my club earlier—I must have eaten more than I intended for I am simply not hungry now.'

The excuse slid readily from his tongue, but her face was still etched with worry. He raised his wine glass in a toast.

'Good health.'

Sarcasm laced his words and Rosalind, after another long, level look, turned her attention from him. He thrust away the guilt that stabbed at him—it was unfair to take his mood out on his stepmother, but he didn't want to talk. Not about anything. He just wanted this damned Season to be over with...for all decisions to be made and irreversible. Surely, then, he would stop this nonsensical yearning after a woman he could never have?

*If that's how you feel, why not make the announcement now? This minute? The decision would be made then.*

He stared blindly at his plate, unaccustomed rage battering at his chest. It was the pain from his jaw—again clenched so tightly his teeth hurt, too—that pulled him back from the brink. He concentrated on breathing steadily until he was back in control. He would not be goaded into a hasty announcement, not even by his own inner voice. He slipped on the cloak of urbanity that he wore in public and joined the conversation, but he was rattled by his uncharacteristic gibe at Rosalind. His father's frown revealed it had not gone unnoticed, but he had not mentioned it.

Yet.

But Dominic was sure it would come and he was in no fit state to verbally spar with the man who had never lost a match yet.

*I cannot cope with much more of this.*

He craved solitude. As soon as it was polite, Dominic made his excuses to leave Beauchamp House and Alex, to no one's surprise but to Dominic's exasperation, elected to leave with him. Dominic wanted to be alone to think through his future. Yet again. Did he need to rethink his strategy? He couldn't deny his doubts about choosing a wife from his shortlist all stemmed from his feelings for Liberty. But that didn't make her any more suitable. He could not get away from that. So, in that case, wasn't one shortlist much like another?

'Come on, Dom. A few hands of whist will shake you out of the doldrums.'

They had reached the corner of his road and Dominic glanced towards his house, further along, on the opposite side. A flash of pale skin by the area steps caught his attention and all his senses went on to high alert. He halted.

'Thanks, Alex, but not tonight.' He clapped his brother's shoulder. 'You go on. I'm for my bed. I've a session booked at Angelo's in the morning.'

And after he'd honed his fencing skills with Henry, he might very well call in next door to Jackson's—maybe a sparring session would work off some of his bottled-up energy. Or—and his grip tightened on his ebony cane—maybe whoever was lurking near his front door might provide him with that opportunity right now.

'Oh, well.' Alex shrugged. 'I'll be off then—I arranged to meet Nev and Gid once I'd done the family duty bit. G'night, Dom!'

'Goodnight, Alex.'

Dominic watched his brother saunter away before he crossed the road and strolled along the pavement towards his house, swinging his cane nonchalantly. If it was a thief lying in wait for an unwary passer-by, he would get more than he bargained for. Dominic was in just the mood for some physical action. Something to work out his frustrations.

As he drew level with the steps that led down to the basement kitchens, a movement flickered in the corner of his eye. He gripped his cane, unsheathing the sword in one smooth movement. Then the scent reached him, curling through his senses, bringing with it a sense of peace…and a desperate longing.

Roses.

Liberty gasped as a steel blade flashed in the light from the nearby street lamp.

'It's me,' she hissed.

His face was in shadow, but she saw from the way he squared his shoulders that he was annoyed.

*Of course he's annoyed! What am I doing, lying in wait for him like this?*

But she had to try, one last time, to save him from himself. If she failed…well, if she failed she would at least know she had left no stone unturned and, once she returned to Eversham, she would probably never see him again. The melancholy thought weighed heavy on her, her heart aching with loneliness. She rubbed at her chest.

'What the devil are you *doing*?' He growled the question. 'Do you *want* to cause a scandal?'

He still stood on the pavement. She still stood on the steps, her face at the level of his groin. She felt her skin heat as she remembered the things Bernard had told her a man and a woman could do together. Things with mouths and…

She swallowed. Such shocking thoughts—she would never be a lady. Dominic was right not to even consider her. Although Bernard had not taken her innocence, they *had* kissed and been intimate—hardly the behaviour suitable for a society lady—and she was familiar with a man's anatomy and what it could do. She had seen and recognised Dominic's physical reaction to her more than once—and she'd felt his arousal that time they kissed. He wanted her as a man wants a woman.

And she… God help her…wanted him. She could not deny it. She was five-and-twenty now… would probably never marry…and Dominic haunted her dreams.

And though she knew she could never have him, she still wanted him to be happy. She couldn't bear to think of him unhappy. She had failed to save one man she loved, Bernard, and now she was here to try to save Dominic from this huge mistake. She wasn't entirely sure what lay in his heart, but she was damned certain it was not Lady Sybilla Gratton. So she would try, one last time, to open his eyes and his heart to the truth…to show him the difference between what he wanted and what he needed.

'Of course not.' She kept her voice to a whisper as she answered him, conscious that any member of his staff could see them if they happened to look out of the window behind her. 'But I cannot stand by and watch you make a mistake you will live to regret.'

'How can you possibly know I would regret it? And, besides, how does it concern you?'

'You asked me that this afternoon. My answer is the same. You are my friend. I want you to be happy.'

'And you think my choosing a suitable wife will make me *un*happy?' His head snapped round and he stared along the street. 'You cannot stay there. How did you get here?'

'I walked.'

'Walked? Alone? Good God, Berty…anything could have happened. You know it's unsafe for a lady to walk alone, especially at night.'

She might as well admit the worst, because he would see for himself soon enough. She sucked in a shaky breath and stepped back, away from the wall. Dominic craned his neck over the railings. She heard his spluttered laugh and, offended, she rammed Gideon's best beaver hat back on her head. It slid down to rest atop her ears, the brim half-covering her eyes.

'There is a reason females do not wear trousers.' He was using his superior voice and it set Liberty's hackles rising. 'They are entirely the wrong shape for them. At least...*you* are entirely the wrong shape.'

She didn't think she looked that dreadful... although, admittedly, her hips and legs *were* curvier than Gideon's and the pantaloons *were* stretched somewhat more thinly than they were designed for. She *hmmph*ed quietly even as she registered the change in Dominic's voice. It had turned, somehow, caressing. He couldn't hold on to all that anger, she knew he couldn't. She stared up at him.

'Did you tell them?'

He shook his head. 'No.'

The knot in her stomach loosened, just a little. She wasn't too late. If only—

'I want to talk to you. Please.'

'But I know what you are going to say and it will make no difference. Besides, we cannot stand here much longer without attracting all sorts of the wrong attention.'

'Please?'

He tipped his head back and stared up at the house. 'Stay there and keep quiet.'

He disappeared from her sight and she heard the sound of a key in a lock followed by the murmur of masculine voices and the quiet sound of a door closing. She waited...and she had just begun to think he had abandoned her there as a joke or a punishment when the door opened, spilling light on to the pavement.

'Be quick.'

Liberty ran up the remaining steps and in through the front door as quickly as she could. Contrary to what Dominic thought, she really did have no desire to be seen dressed in men's clothing and loitering outside his door. It had taken all her courage to come here, but she had come nevertheless—scurrying through the streets with her head down—because she simply couldn't bear the thought of the future that awaited him. She'd come prepared for a lengthy wait—not knowing what time he might arrive home—and had almost cried with relief when she had seen him turn the corner into his street.

Dominic ushered her into a very masculine, but comfortable sitting room. A fire blazed in the hearth. A cold repast was laid out on a side table next to a silver salver with two glasses and a full decanter. The door closed behind Liberty with a soft click and she wheeled around to face Dominic.

# *Chapter Seventeen*

Liberty's heart tumbled in her chest, her breathing quickened and her pulse leapt, heat flushing her skin.

*Dear heavens, he is gorgeous. If only...*

She batted away that errant thought. There were no 'if onlys'. She clung tight to that knowledge. She would not fool herself…she loved Dominic. And she knew he…what? He liked her, certainly. They were friends. They enjoyed one another's company, they made one another laugh. But she also knew that caring for him…loving him…meant wanting what was best for him. And that was *not* to burden him with a wife who was so far removed from his ideal that she might as well be a duck.

This was not about persuading him to throw away the principles he held dear and to marry her regardless. It was about persuading him he deserved to find a suitable lady for his wife who would make him *happy*.

'Do take off that preposterous hat, Berty,' Dominic drawled as he crossed to the table and poured two glasses of wine.

She removed it with relief. Her ears were already sore from the brim chafing them. Dominic handed her the glass and gestured to the fire, bracketed by a pair of green-leather wing-back chairs. Liberty sat and sipped her wine.

'Let me have it, then, Berty.'

Dominic moved to stand in front of her, his glass in one long-fingered hand. His reflection in the gilt-framed mirror above the mantelpiece revealed a muscle bunching in his jaw as he clenched it. The firelight played across his skin, making it glow and highlighting the dark hairs that dusted the back of his hand. There was strength and beauty in that hand and she itched to just reach out and touch it.

'Best we get this out of the way. I'm tired and I need my bed.'

His bored tone didn't fool Liberty for one second. He was as tense as she'd ever seen him. She mulled over how to start.

'You do realise how preposterous your behaviour is?' he drawled. 'And what would happen if someone caught us in here? Like this?'

She jumped to her feet at that. 'You know that

is not why I have come.' She couldn't bear him to even suspect she might try to entrap him. 'I would never behave in such a low, sneaky, despicable way.'

A mirthless smile stretched his lips. 'I do know it. You are doing what you always do…risking yourself for those you…those you *care* for. You are a good, kind-hearted woman, Liberty Lovejoy, but you must allow other people to tread their own path, even if you believe they are making a monumental mistake.' He raised his glass in a mock salute and downed it in one again, before eyeing his empty glass in disgust. 'I need something stronger than this.' He wheeled away and went to a side table, returning with two glasses in one hand and a bottle in the other. 'Brandy?'

Her wine glass was empty. She nodded and watched him pour amber liquid into the glasses, her eyes following him as he bent to set the bottle down on the hearth, took Liberty's empty glass from her hand and passed her the new one. She sipped. It was good brandy—the fiery spirit slipped down a treat. She'd occasionally enjoyed a glass in the evening with Bernard. They'd shared a glass the night before she left for London. It had been the last time she ever saw him.

Without warning, her eyes brimmed. She should never have gone to London. She should never have left Gideon… Mama… Papa… The guilt scoured her.

'Liberty?' The gentleness of Dominic's tone was nearly her undoing, but she blinked furiously and swallowed back her tears before facing him again, chin up.

'I am sorry. It is nothing…a memory caught me unawares, that is all.'

'Your intended?'

She nodded, rubbing at the lonely ache in her chest as she stared into the flames. What was she doing here? *Could* she ever persuade Dominic to think again?

'How do you know about Bernard…my intended?'

'Was that his name? Gideon told Alex who told Olivia. I just happened to be present.' Dominic steered Liberty back to her chair. He sat opposite and fixed her with an unwavering silver gaze. 'Will you tell me about him?'

And she did. How they had grown up as neighbours, always knowing they were destined to be married.

'You were childhood sweethearts, then?'

'Yes.'

'And no other man will ever usurp the sainted Bernard in your affections?'

She frowned. 'That is how Gideon always refers to Bernard. It's not true. He was no saint and I never set him up on a pedestal to worship.'

'I meant no disrespect. To either of you.'

Liberty pushed her fingers through her hair and stood up. 'I am too hot.' She unwound her roughly tied neckcloth and then began to shrug out of Gideon's coat. 'Do you mind if I take this off?'

'Be my guest.'

He pushed himself out of his chair and came behind her to help, for which she was grateful. She'd had enough of a struggle getting the tailored coat on in the first place. Removing it was even more difficult. As Dominic grasped the collar his fingers brushed Liberty's neck and she gasped as tingles radiated through her body. Her arms free, she then felt him lift one lock of hair, just behind her ear. His breathing in her ear was erratic, almost harsh. Their reflections in the mirror above the mantelpiece showed his attention transfixed by that tendril as he allowed it to slip through his fingers to drape over her shoulder.

She stepped away. 'Thank you. No wonder you gentlemen need valets.'

She sat down again, avoiding eye contact, conscious of that visceral attraction between them, careful not to tempt fate. Liberty Lovejoy was still Liberty Lovejoy. Not a suitable future duchess.

Dominic placed the coat on a wooden chair

near the door and then flung himself into the other fireside chair.

'So...when did you get betrothed to the s—to Bernard?'

'Two days before I left for London to make my debut. He urged me to go...to take advantage of my godmother's offer to sponsor me.' She swallowed. 'He fell ill two weeks after I left...'

In a halting voice, she told Dominic about the message that had reached her...the worst day of her life...that terrible dash back to Sussex, urging the post boys to go ever faster.

'The worst thing,' she said, at the end of her tale, 'is the guilt that I was not there. At least I saw my parents again and helped to nurse them. But not Bernard... I never said goodbye and I can barely picture his face any more.'

'There is no portrait?'

'No. He promised to have a miniature painted for me, but he never did.'

Again her throat ached with the memory, but the sorrow was distant now...almost as though it had happened to another person. Slowly, the thought surfaced that she had never felt for Bernard what she now felt for Dominic. She had loved him, but it had been a quieter love... steadier. Passion had kindled, when he had kissed her, and touched her...but it had been a slow burn. It had never been this all-encompassing fire that consumed her whenever she thought of Dominic. Whenever she was near him.

'I suppose I am fortunate that there is a portrait of my mother at the Abbey.' Dominic was staring into the fire, the orange flames reflected in his eyes. 'And I still had my father and my aunt and uncle. You suffered a dreadful blow, losing your parents at the same time, too. It must have been so hard for all of you.'

There was no answer to that other than *Yes*. Liberty sipped her brandy as she, too, contemplated the flames.

'How old were you when your mother died?'

'Eight. And she didn't just die. She was *murdered*.'

His bitterness shouldn't shock her, but it did. He sounded so…angry. 'Did they ever find out who did it?'

'No. Alex found her body. He was only seven. He didn't speak for a year and he was never quite the same afterwards.'

'Oh, poor little boy. That must have been dreadful for him…for all of you. And for your father, too, to lose his wife that way.'

His eyes glittered. 'The memories of that time are hazy now…as though a veil covers the details. I just remember feeling…disbelief, I suppose. I was upset but, looking back, I doubt I fully understood I would never see her again.' He sank his head into his hands, elbows propped on his knees. 'As a family, we never talk about it. We were too young when it happened and I suppose we all just got used to not discussing it. The past is the past and we move forward into the future.'

'And is that how you feel inside? That it's all in the past? That it cannot affect you…any of you…now?'

'Yes. No.' He scrubbed his hands through his hair. 'I don't know.'

Liberty said nothing, waiting for him to go on—sensing his battle between wanting to unburden himself and family loyalty.

'I do know it affected Father for a long time.' His words came quietly. 'He had refused to allow her to go to London. He told her she must spend more time with us. Her children. And a week later she was dead. I know he felt guilty for failing to protect her.'

She knew that feeling…the guilt of failing to protect. Dominic stared down at the rug.

'We were never enough for her.' His voice was raw. 'She used to say she was proud of "her boys"—particularly me, as I was the heir—but they were just words to her. They had no meaning—there was never any pleasing her. And poor Olivia never got *any* maternal attention or affection from her.

'My memories are those of a child—at the time

I overheard things that made little sense, but as I got older I understood. Probably more than I cared to.' He huffed a mirthless laugh. 'I know she married Father for his wealth and for the prestige of being a duchess. She was never happy at the Abbey—she craved the excitement of London and the adulation of her admirers even though we all tried hard to behave well and to be worthy of her attention and her approval.

'But we knew no different—she was our mother, and we worshipped her, constantly seeking approval. Now…when I look back… I compare Cecily and how she loved us all and I can see that all we ever got from Mother was coldness and rejection.'

The pain in his voice wrenched at Liberty's heartstrings, and she ached for those children.

'She wanted to be adored by us all, but she gave nothing…apart from one time…' Dominic faltered, then he cleared his throat and dashed one hand across his eyes. His voice hardened. 'She gave us nothing in return. Certainly not love.'

Liberty stared at him. 'But…you…'

He met her gaze, his eyes glittering. 'But…? I…?'

His tone mocked. She tried to gather her thoughts, frowning. It made no sense.

'I do not understand. Why are you so set on

fulfilling a promise to your mother if she was as cold as you say? Surely you owe her nothing?'

'I don't…' He emptied his glass and set it down. He leaned forward, his head bowed, his eyes screwed shut. His elbow propped on the armrest and his splayed hand covered his face, all four fingertips pressed to his forehead, his thumb digging into his cheek. 'I don't know…' he said, his voice muffled. Aching. 'Just before she died, I hoped she might…' He shook his head. 'I suppose I still want to prove I am worthy of her and to make her proud of me.'

Liberty longed to take him in her arms and soothe away his pain.

'You were eight years old, Dominic. You should not feel bound by such an oath.'

His head jerked up. 'I shouldn't be talking to you like this. Besides, there's my father to think of. He suffered, too, and Alex… Alex… Well, I don't understand, but Alex and Father will never be close. I am his heir… I cannot let him down.' His voice broke. '*He* did not shirk his duty. I want to make him proud.'

'Oh, Dominic.' Liberty went to him, sank on to her knees on the floor and cradled his face in her hands. 'I have not met your father, but how could he not be proud of you? And the rest of your family love you—that is obvious. Do you really think they wish you to be unhappy?'

He jerked his head from between her hands at that, lowering the hand that shielded his eyes. For the flash of a second, Liberty saw his vulnerability before his silvery eyes shuttered.

'Why should I be unhappy? My marriage will be no different to hundreds of others—it is the norm in our world.'

'It is not the norm in your family, from what I have been told. What is your stepmother like? Does she make your father happy?'

Dominic's eyes warmed. 'Oh, yes. She is perfect for him. We all love her.'

'And can you picture Lady Sybilla in the bosom of your family? Will she fit in?'

His gaze slid from hers. 'Why should she not?'

Liberty's hands were on his knees. Her thighs and belly pressed against his shins. A knot of emotion lodged in her throat as she struggled to find the arguments to get through to him…the words that would help him to see what a huge mistake he was about to make.

'Can you not see, though?' She slid her hands up his thighs, the muscles rock hard beneath her fingers. She captured his gaze. 'If you marry a woman like Lady Sybilla, you are asking for history to repeat itself.' Her hands moved further, up his flat belly to his chest, his silk waistcoat smooth and warm to her touch. His eyes darkened and a thrill spiralled through her. 'Is that truly what you want? Look around you, Dominic. Look at your father and your stepmother, your uncles and aunts, Olivia and Hugo. They all have love matches and are happy and content.' Olivia had told Liberty all about the Beauchamps. 'Is that not what you want for yourself?' She reached his neck and curved her fingers around his jaw, his dark stubble scratching her skin.

'Dominic…is that not what you want for *your* children?'

All her altruistic notions fled as she gazed deep into those silvery-grey eyes that were no longer cold mirrors, but deep, white-hot furnaces that blazed, sending bolts of pure energy and need sizzling through her. He needed a woman with warmth and curves and love to bring happiness to his life. He needed—if only he could see it—Liberty Lovejoy. But could she persuade him before it was too late?

She pressed closer and his knees parted as his hands gripped her sides and lifted, pulling her almost roughly to him. For what seemed an eternity their eyes locked and held as blood rampaged through her veins like a river in flood and the heat of desire pooled between her thighs. She fancied a question formed deep in his silvery gaze—and she knew her answer.

With a sigh of pleasure, she slipped her fingers into the heavy silk of his hair and she pressed her mouth to his.

Neither the frantic attempts by his controlling inner voice nor the stridency of the warning bells that reverberated inside his head could stop him. The groan vibrated deep, deep inside Dominic's chest as he wrapped his arms around Liberty Lovejoy and gloried in the caress of her mouth. He had no strength to fight the strongest impulse he had ever known: the impulse to take, to enjoy, to wallow. To simply *feel* and not to plan…or to control…or to consider any implications. His mind might clamour all it liked for him to resist, but his body would not…could not…obey. This was what he had craved since the day he'd met her. The dam of his self-control had burst and this was what he wanted.

Right here. Right now. Regardless.

His hands plunged into her hair, shaking it loose, the heavy tresses spilling down her back as her soft body moulded to his. Her breasts—glorious, abundant, wonderful—pressed between them. Her scent curled around him, through him, drugging him…roses…no longer a smell to awaken regret and failure, but a smell to conjure forth hope and possibility. With another heart-felt groan, one hand at the small of her back, the other between her shoulder blades, he slithered from the chair, holding her carefully until they were on their knees on the rug before the fire, caressing her sweet mouth that tasted of honey. His tongue traced the soft fullness of her lips and, as they parted, swept inside, his lips sliding over hers, kissing her with a hunger that set his entire being on fire. Gently, he eased her back and he half-covered her—exactly where he had fantasised having her ever since the day she had burst into his life.

He explored her mouth at first with dreamy intimacy—lingering, savouring every moment… a kiss for his tired soul to melt into. He shifted to ease the fullness in his groin and angled his head, deepening the kiss, his tongue thrusting now with more urgency, his fingers curling into her silken tresses, holding her head still as he plundered her mouth. Her hands skimmed his back restlessly as a low moan sounded in her throat and her body arched beneath him. He forced his mouth from hers, raising himself on one elbow to look his fill, his heart pounding in his chest.

Heavy lids half-covered slumberous midnight-blue eyes. Her sweet-scented skin was flushed and her lips…oh, her lips, were softly sheening and succulent. Her breasts rose and fell with every fragmented breath, the sound intensely, intoxicatingly feminine.

'Dominic...'

Her voice low and husky, she reached for him again, her fingers insistent as they clutched at his shoulders. He brushed her hair back from her temple and took her lips again in a slow, intoxicating kiss that made his senses swim and every nerve ending pulse with life. Every thought that tried to intrude was ruthlessly quashed.

She was all that mattered. All he wanted. She...*this*...was what he needed.

Her arms wound around his neck and her fingers tangled again in his hair. His fingertips skimmed down the side of her face to her neck and lingered over the sensitive skin by her ear as a delicate shudder racked her. He deepened the kiss, plunging his tongue again and again, and she responded—each sensual stroke ensnaring him deeper in her spell. He stroked her neck, inside the open collar of the shirt she wore, tracing the delicate skin over her collarbone, then moving lower, seeking...he bit back a groan as his hand closed possessively around her breast, only the fine fabric of her chemise between his hand and the heat of her skin, her nipple a hard bud against his palm.

He dragged his mouth from hers and nuzzled her neck, searching for her pulse, laving it as it hammered beneath his tongue. His own heart pounded, sending hot blood surging through his veins, around his body, flooding his groin.

How long had he dreamed of her breasts? Conscious thought played no part in him tugging both shirt and chemise free from her waistband. He pushed both garments high, then reared back to gaze his fill at her beautiful, full breasts, the nipples and areoles a dusky pink. Each firm globe more than filled his hands. She shivered, a low moan escaping her lips as he teased her nipples into hard peaks, rubbing and tugging.

Her hands were on his jacket, pushing it open. On the buttons of his waistcoat. Again he reared back and shrugged out of both garments. She watched him, her eyes glinting.

'Your shirt,' she whispered. 'I want to see.'

He didn't think he could get any harder, but he did as he pulled his shirt over his head and saw her reaction. She reached up, and stroked her hands up his belly and across his chest, then down each arm to his hands.

'Help me.'

She sat up, took hold of her shirt and began to pull. He needed no further encouragement and the feeling of those wonderful breasts as they brushed against his chest was torture. He dipped his head and she gasped as he paid homage to them, licking, sucking and nipping to his heart's content while she explored his arms and torso—

seemingly fascinated with the dark hair that covered his chest. He didn't know who initiated it, but before long they were on their feet, ripping off the rest of their clothes.

He stilled, feasting his eyes on all that glorious, naked flesh and gently, reverently, he cupped her upper arms, willing his body to be patient even as slender fingers wrapped around his length, squeezing and stroking. He removed her hand and pulled her towards him, kissing her long and deep as her body softened, moulding into his, and she moaned her pleasure.

He wanted nothing more than to lay her full length on the floor and to plunge his aching arousal into her heat, but he wouldn't rush this. He would make it good for her. So he laid her down and followed her. He took his time, worshipping her with his touch and his mouth, listening to her sighs and her gasps of pleasure, learning her, feeling her body arch beneath him, her nails digging into his shoulders, the impatient tilt of her hips, her husky 'Dominic…please…'

And when her fingers clutched harder and her head moved restlessly from side to side, when she was hot and wet and ready for him, he moved between her open thighs, positioned his throbbing shaft at her entrance, reached again for the pearl hidden in her secret folds and he pressed.

She screamed his name as she reached her zenith and, as her body shuddered with ecstasy, he thrust inside her. It took only a few thrusts for him to reach fulfilment, but he was happy. Her pleasure was his pleasure, her ecstasy, his ecstasy.

He gathered her close and settled down with her in his arms.

# *Chapter Eighteen*

She felt so right in his arms, nestled into his chest, her hair tickling his chin.

But…

Those warnings he had successfully kept at bay came clamouring into his brain. The head-banging, gut-churning reasons why he could not even dream of marrying Liberty Lovejoy, even though his soul cried out for her. Even though he had, tentatively, begun to believe dreams might come true.

*'Make me proud, my Son.'*

His mother's words…uttered in that cold, demanding voice…the one all three of her children had striven to obey, desperate to win words of praise and approval. A taunting reminder of the past. Those insidious words—sneaking around his head, prying into the corners where hope had dared to germinate, marshalling his embryonic dreams together and, mockingly, dismissing them as the unworthy fantasies of a child.

*'Never forget your duty—you were born to be the Duke. Never disgrace your position in society—the eyes of the world will be on you. Judging you. Never let them see weakness. You are not the same as other men, driven by base desires. You are the Marquess of Avon. You will be Duke of Cheriton one day, and your son, and your son's son, and countless generations to follow will also fulfil that role. Do not allow your weakness to contaminate the bloodline—it is your destiny to keep it pure. Choose your wife with care and with pride and, above all, with your intelligence.'*

Nausea and a deep, throbbing dread filled him. He tightened his embrace and breathed in her sweet, subtle essence—mixed now with the scent of their lovemaking. Honour whispered he must offer for Liberty. His heart craved nothing more than to spend his life with her. But duty and cold hard reasoning dictated otherwise.

He scrambled to his feet and grabbed his clothes, pulling them on hastily and haphazardly, the battle between heart and mind filling his head.

'Dominic...?'

Low, pained, questioning...her voice grabbed at his emotions and twisted. Hard. There was Liberty to think of...*her* feelings. Her future. And that tipped the balance of the scales in favour of his honour and his heart.

'I'm sorry. That shouldn't have happened… would never have happened had you not…had I not…' He was gabbling…his words sounded cold. Heartless.

*'Never forget your duty, my Son.'*

The scales tilted the opposite way. But he could not abandon Liberty. Not now.

'I will apply for a special licence in the morning. Get dressed. I will escort you home.'

'What?'

He looked at her then—sitting before the fire, the flames bronzing her skin, highlighting the honey and gold of her hair, her brother's shirt clutched to her breasts, her midnight-blue eyes with those glinting gold flecks, huge… searching…uncertain.

What more could he say? He could not reassure her, not properly. How could he when he barely knew which way was up? How could he, with his head churning with such conflict? Everything was in turmoil…his carefully laid plans… he barely knew what to think, let alone what to say or do. For once in his well-ordered, meticulously planned life, he was lost. The path he had followed from childhood had not only forked, it had vanished, leaving him frantically searching with no clue which way to turn.

A childhood memory surfaced of tumbling out of a tree, scrabbling at the branches, trying desperately to slow his fall. He felt the same sensation now—as though he were tumbling, ever faster, out of control.

His heart twisted in his chest at her beloved face, her doubt. The last thing he wanted was to hurt her, but he couldn't find the right words, not when he was still reeling. He needed space and time to get his thoughts straight. But he *would* make it right—explain properly—later. He just needed time to think.

He softened his voice. 'Get dressed, Liberty. I will call on you in the morning and we will put this right.'

Her eyes flashed and she bounced to her feet.

*That shouldn't have happened...would never have happened had you not...*

He hadn't needed to finish that thought… Liberty could read between those lines. What he meant was: it would never have happened had she not defied all the rules of proper behaviour and come here clandestinely, and then compounded her offence by drawing him out about his mother and resurrecting all those painful memories for him.

Humiliation burned through her as she tugged

Gideon's shirt over her head and pulled on his pantaloons, wriggling to fit them past her hips.

'A licence will not be necessary, Dominic.'

Her gamble had failed. She had hoped—stupid, forlorn, immature hope—that by loving him...by showing him what he *could* have in his life...he would finally open his eyes and his heart to the truth. He did love her—he had proved that with every kiss, every caress, every touch. He had proved it every time he looked at her with his heart in his eyes.

But that was not enough. If he was only offering for her under duress—from some stuffy, ridiculous sense of honour—she could never accept, no matter how much she loved him. He might love her now, but she feared that love would never survive if he was ashamed of her. And his reaction...his words...confirmed that fear.

'I have taken your innocence. We *must* be wed.'

'You did not take my innocence.' God help her, she lied. She had been intimate with Bernard, but they had never actually made love. But the act had not hurt as she had thought it might. It had been wonderful...swept along on a tide of passion...the slightest of discomforts when he first entered her...but she had been wet, and so ready for him, longing for him. There had been no pain. 'Bernard and I...'

She had no need to finish; she read his comprehension in his eyes. And was that a tinge of relief? Her heart tore…not even in two, but into shreds. Too numerous to count.

'You need not concern yourself with me. Just promise me you will think twice before pledging yourself to Lady Sybilla.' She couldn't help herself. She couldn't bear to think of the cold, lonely life that awaited him. She went to him, touched his arm. 'Please. You deserve better than her, whatever her pedigree might say.'

'You must marry me!' His silver gaze pierced her, filling her with sudden hope. Hope that was dashed with his next words. 'What if you are with child?'

Liberty swallowed hard. 'And what if I am not? Marriage is for a lifetime and my grandfather was still a lowly coal merchant.'

*Please. Argue with me. Tell me you've reconsidered. Anything!*

Dominic passed one hand around the back of his neck, then picked up his discarded coat, shrugging into it. 'We will talk about this tomorrow. But…' he paused, and she saw his throat move as he swallowed 'if you find there are consequences you must let me know.' He avoided her gaze. 'I will see you want for nothing… I will pay you an allowance. Buy you a—'

She shoved him. He staggered back a pace,

taken unawares. Liberty followed him, thrusting her face close to his. *'I do not want your money.'*

She cast an eye around the room. Boots. She grabbed them and easily pulled them on as they were many sizes too big for her. Jacket. She snatched it from the chair, passed it wordlessly to Dominic. He held it for her while she wriggled into it. Hat. She bundled her hair into a rope, piled it on top of her head and rammed the hat down hard, relishing the pain as the brim folded her ears and trapped them. Any pain was preferable to what she felt inside.

She reached for the door. 'And I do not need your escort.'

He reached past her and held the door shut. 'I will not allow you to walk the streets alone.'

'I got here without mishap. I can get home.'

He released the pressure on the door and Liberty marched into the hall and out of the front door, crossing the street to make her way home. There were a few people about, but most were in carriages. She kept her eyes fixed firmly on the pavement in front of her and walked as quickly as she could. As she reached the corner, a movement caught her eye.

Dominic. Five paces behind her.

'Berty!'

She ignored his whisper and increased her pace to a trot, a stitch forming in her side at the unaccustomed exertion. He made no attempt to catch her up. Good. The less she had to do with that stubborn numbskull in the future, the better she would like it! Lord Arrogant could ride to hell backwards on a donkey for all she cared! He didn't deserve her!

As they turned into Green Street, however, he caught her up and grabbed her arm, forcing her to a stop.

'What are you doing? Someone might see us,' she hissed.

They were close to a street lamp and Dominic manoeuvred her so her face was in shadow. She supposed she should be grateful for that. She wasn't so enamoured of the lift of one dark eyebrow and the quirk of his lips that she could now see quite clearly, with the lamplight illuminating his features.

'They might indeed. But that doesn't matter because we *will* be married, Liberty. I will call on you tomorrow at noon and I shall request a private interview.'

She thought quickly. If he did that, there would be no doubt in her sisters' or Mrs Mount's minds that he intended to propose to her. Her heart quailed at the thought of trying to convince them she would refuse…they had all noticed how friendly the two of them were and her sisters had both, laughingly, accused her of carrying a torch for Lord Avon.

'Come at two,' she said. They had arranged to pay visits tomorrow afternoon…she could easily excuse herself.

His eyes narrowed. 'Are you up to something, Berty? Because, I warn you, I expect you to be at home. Or I shall come looking for you.'

She suppressed the shiver his softly spoken words aroused. 'I will be there.'

He tilted her chin with one long finger and for one wild moment she thought he might kiss her. But he merely said, 'Good.'

Anger sustained her as she crept indoors and upstairs. Safely back in her bedchamber, she struggled out of Gideon's coat—hearing an ominous rip in the process—then shed the remainder of his clothes and shoved them beneath her bed, out of sight. She would deal with them in the morning. She had the rest of her life to deal with them. She burrowed under the bedclothes and, finally, she gave way to her misery.

After Mrs Mount and her sisters left the house the following afternoon, Liberty paced around the small salon feeling like a caged animal. She didn't fool herself Dominic would give up easily—he would consider himself honour-bound to marry her even though it had been her decision to visit him and they had been swept away on a mutual tide of passion. Her stomach swooped and her skin tingled at the memory of his touch, his whispers, the caress of his lips...and of *him*. The spicy, musky scent of aroused male; the salty tang of his skin; the texture of his hair-roughened skin beneath her questing fingertips; the slide of skin over his hot, hard length as she stroked. His weight on her, between her thighs...her belly tightened at those memories and hot, sweet need pooled at her core.

They had both lost control, that was the honest truth, and she did not shy away from her own culpability—it was more her fault than his. *She* had gone to *him* with the genuine aim of stopping him from making a dreadful mistake. Had she truly believed he would suddenly discard his belief in his duty? A belief that had lasted a lifetime. How utterly foolish, to think that she—Liberty Lovejoy—could ever influence a man like the Marquess of Avon.

But then, once they were alone together... when he told her about his mother...oh, then her heart yearned to heal him. And she had wantonly indulged her own desire to make love with the man who haunted her dreams, knowing she might never again have the chance.

And because it was more her fault than his, she would save him from another mistake and protect him from marrying her out of a misguided sense of honour. It was a marriage she was afraid he would come to regret and she could not bear that he would grow to rue the day he met her.

If she allowed herself to, she could sink into a swamp of despair. But a thought had surfaced… the faintest glimmer of a hope. There was no doubt that Dominic would try by any means to persuade her to accept his offer today. And she could not, would not, accept.

But…if the possibility of a child were removed…what then? What if, by some miracle, Dominic *did* change his mind? What if her gamble had borne fruit and opened his mind to the possibility of another way…of a marriage for love instead of duty?

It was a fragile hope, but it was all she had to cling to. If, of course, he *did* love her. Last night, she had been convinced. Now, in the clear light of day, she was not so sure.

All she could do, for now, was to remain steadfast in her refusal of him. For both their sakes.

And pray she was not with child.

She was so lost in thought she jumped when Ethel opened the salon door to announce Lord Avon. Her heart hammered and it felt as though every muscle in her body turned to jelly. She hauled in a steadying breath and smoothed her palms down the skirt of her gown.

'Show him in, please, Ethel.'

She took advantage of the few minutes it would take him to come upstairs to check her reflection in the mirror on the wall by the door. Her cheeks were flushed, her eyes somewhat wild and there was a quiver in her lower lip she could not quell without taking it between her teeth and biting down on it. She patted her hair into place, then hurried to stand before the window, feeling more confident with the light at her back.

'Lord Avon, miss. Would you like me to stay?'

Just one look at him set her heart skipping and jumping—his tall, broad frame, his dark good looks, his crooked smile revealing his uncertainty over the action he intended to take.

Liberty switched her attention to the maid. 'No, Ethel. That will not be necessary. His Lordship will not remain above five minutes.'

As soon as they were alone, Dominic strode across the room and reached for her hands. She tucked them behind her back. He frowned, but he took the hint and stepped back.

'Liberty...look...' He swept a hand through his hair. 'I am aware I made a complete mull of it last night after...after we...well. I am sorry. Truly I am... I didn't think what I was saying before I blurted it out.'

'You voiced your immediate thoughts, Dominic. It is quite all right. I understand.'

'No. It is not all right.'

He moved closer again and his spicy cologne weaved through her senses as he cupped her shoulders. The warm, steady strength of his hands was nearly her undoing. How simple it would be to bow to the inevitable…to fold into his embrace, to lean into his solid frame and allow him to take control, to accept him and to worry about any consequences later. She blanked her expression and forced herself to remain rigidly upright.

'Accept me and I shall leave here and arrange the licence straight away. We can be wed by the end of next week.' He put his lips to her ear. 'We will be happy together.'

His breath tickled, but she gritted her teeth, determined not to squirm. Was he trying to convince himself as much as persuade her? It was not hard to believe and it made her even more determined to stick to her plan.

'No, Dominic. I will not marry you. You are only offering for me out of guilt, but there is no need. I am an adult, not some green girl who did not know what she was doing. There is no need to ruin both our lives.'

'*Both* our lives?' His grip tightened. 'What are you saying…that you do not care for me after all? Are you in the habit of giving yourself to random men you have no feelings for?'

She tore herself from his grasp and paced across the room before whirling to face him. 'I care for you too much to saddle you with a wife you are marrying out of duty.'

He visibly flinched. '*Duty?* It is duty that resulted in that damned shortlist. It is my honour that dictates I make an honest woman of you.'

She stared at him, holding his gaze without wavering, willing him to say more…to speak of what was in his heart. Did he love her? Or was last night purely about lust after all? If she accepted him like this, she might never know. But of one thing she was certain—if he did not love her and he was offering purely with his honour, then he would soon grow to resent and even hate her.

She had faced heartbreak before and survived. She would do so again.

'No. You are free to continue with your perfect, dutiful life, my lord. You are under no obligation to me.'

'And if you are with child?'

She had done the calculations. It would not be long before she knew. A matter of days only.

'If I am, we will talk again.' She moved to the door and opened it. 'I hope we may remain friends, when we meet?'

He searched her face, then nodded.

'Then I shall bid you good afternoon, Lord Avon.'

* * *

If she thought he would give up that easily, she could think again. Dominic strode up Green Street, fury at her stubbornness biting at his gut. The clip-clop of hooves behind him reminded him that he had driven his curricle to her house. He gestured at Ted to stay back and he kept walking.

*Who does she think she is? Doesn't she realise the honour I've—?*

His whirling thoughts steadied and he lopped off his diatribe before he could finish it, recognising his sheer arrogance to even think such a thing. As his thoughts slowed down so did his pace and his tumbling emotions, and his churning gut.

*Why are you so damned furious?*

He halted on the corner of the street, staring blindly at the houses opposite as he strove to untangle his thoughts from his feelings.

Why *was* he so furious? Madly, rigidly, agonisingly furious?

He had what he wanted. He'd told himself, time and again, that it was lust driving his obsession with Liberty Lovejoy. He should be rejoicing. He'd had her. She'd set him free. Free to have what he wanted—the perfect Lady Sybilla Gratton as his wife. His Marchioness. The mother of his children. The future Duchess of Cheriton.

He paced onwards, his steps slow and measured, his gaze on the pavement.

And slowly the truth emerged out of that muddle of emotions and he finally accepted it with a clear head. The idea of having Liberty Lovejoy as his wife had taken hold in his brain and it felt right. He could not dislodge that image. It grew stronger and brighter with every second, every minute that passed. He didn't only want Liberty Lovejoy, he *needed* her. In his life. Always.

On the brink of spinning around to march back to Green Street, he halted.

She had refused him. And he—the perfect, gentlemanly Marquess of Avon—had managed to both insult and infuriate the woman he loved. If he returned to her now and prostrated himself at her feet, she would no doubt laugh him out of the house. And he wouldn't blame her. He'd made an utter mess of the entire thing.

He walked on.

He would make a plan.

*I'll court her properly... I'll* make *her change her mind.*

He halted at the next corner and waited for Ted to bring up his curricle. He felt a burning need to work off his frustration. A visit to Jackson's would help.

The next few days tried his patience to the limit. A new and different Liberty Lovejoy had emerged—coolly correct in everything she did and said. She smiled graciously. She danced with precision and with elegance. She smiled at him, but with her lips closed. And she refused to rise to any provocation, merely agreeing with every word he said. She had encased her heart and her soul in an exquisitely polite but impenetrable shell and nothing he said or did could pierce it.

*If she should get with child, though, it will change everything. She won't refuse me then.*

A part of him understood he was clutching at that thought in the hope it would solve this impasse for him. But that was all he had to cling to.

# *Chapter Nineteen*

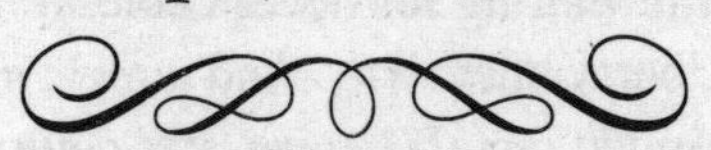

A mere six days after *that night*—the night when Liberty had gambled the highest stakes of all and lost—Lord and Lady Stanton threw a ball at their mansion in Cavendish Square. The Lovejoys, along with most of the *ton*, were invited and Liberty waited with bated breath and with a thudding heart for Dominic to make an appearance. She had a very important message for him.

At every ball since *that night* Dominic asked Liberty to dance. And, if she had a dance free, she accepted. But she avoided any hint of personal conversation, talking only of inconsequential matters and agreeing with every single one of Dominic's opinions, which grew increasingly outrageous as the days passed. He was being deliberately provocative, she knew, but she refused to lower her guard for one single second. He wanted a perfect lady? Well, she might have missed out on the strictly correct upbringing of

Lady Sybilla and her ilk, but she would show him she could be a lady when necessary.

As far as the rest of the *ton* were concerned, his behaviour was still impeccable. He partnered several perfectly eligible young ladies, including Sybilla, at every ball but the announcement everyone was waiting for never came.

And Liberty knew why. And tonight she would set his mind at rest. If he was *still* determined to marry the perfect Lady Sybilla, he could now do so with a clear conscience. This morning her prayers had been answered and tonight she would reassure His Lordship that there had been no unwanted consequences from *that night* and that he was free to continue with the life he'd mapped out from a young boy.

And she was free to continue with hers. She rubbed absently at her chest. This hollow feeling was one she must grow accustomed to…unless this final, desperate gamble of hers bore fruit. But the decision must be his. She would give him no encouragement. And if *this* gamble paid off, she would *know* he loved her, even if he never actually said those words.

She gazed around the room despondently. Olivia and Hugo were absent tonight as Olivia was suffering from a slight head cold and Liberty could garner no interest in joining Mrs Mount and the chattering chaperons. A nagging ache low in her belly was a constant reminder of her news for Dominic. How would he react? She didn't fool herself that he would suddenly throw himself at her feet and declare his undying love for her, but would he…*could* he…reconsider his plans?

She was confident she had been right to refuse Dominic's offer. Although offer wasn't the right word—it had been more of a statement.

*This is what we will do. I have decided. You will comply.*

Her heart still ached for him. Her body still craved him. But, most disconcerting of all, she missed him—just talking to him, laughing with him, teasing him.

Being teased in return.

No one but he called her Berty.

The heart of her uncertainty was that she knew he liked her and cared for her and was attracted to her. She was almost certain he loved her.

But did he love her *enough*?

And would he give himself the chance to find out, or was he so committed to his lifelong vision of his future that he would continue along that path without considering the alternative? Without considering her?

A flurry of activity at the ballroom door grabbed her attention as all activity seemed to freeze for an instant before conversations restarted, seemingly brighter and more animated than before. Liberty knew without looking what that meant. She had become accustomed to the phenomenon since Dominic's father had arrived in town—he had that effect whenever he walked into an event.

Liberty had never been introduced to the Duke, but he did not appear to be the sort of man who would welcome someone like Liberty Lovejoy as the wife of his son and heir. As Dominic had said, on *that night*, his father had not shirked *his* duty—his first wife, Dominic's mother, had been the daughter of a marquess and the granddaughter of a duke. The aristocratic heritage of the Dukedom was intact, even though the current Duchess's grandfather was a simple silversmith. And that also confirmed Liberty had been right to refuse Dominic because, unless she knew without a shadow of doubt that he loved her and, more importantly, unless *Dominic* knew and admitted it, she was convinced he would grow to regret their union and become ashamed of her.

Only love, in all its strength and glory, would give a union between them the chance to stand strong and withstand other people's opinions.

So. Had Dominic arrived with the Duke and Duchess or would Liberty have to be patient a little longer? She tiptoed up to peer towards the door. She could not see. There were too many people in the way.

'What are you up to, Sis?'

She smiled up at Gideon as he slipped his arm around her waist. 'Looking for Hope and Verity,' she lied.

Since Gideon had caught her crying he had become a calmer, nicer person. Lady Emily, too, had influenced him in a positive way although he still stayed out late with his friends. Liberty, however, no longer fretted about him quite so much and, surprisingly, the less she worried about him, the closer they had grown.

'You're a proper mother hen, aren't you, Sis? Don't worry about them—that's what Mrs Mount is for. You should be looking to your own future.' His blue eyes searched hers, suddenly serious. 'It's been five years, Liberty. It's time you began to live your life again. Bernard would want you to.'

Tears prickled at the back of her eyes. 'I know he would.'

It was the first time she had admitted to any member of her family that she might be ready to find love again. Until now it had felt as though she were laying her soul bare to be trampled over but, somehow, this time in London had helped all of the Lovejoys to change. They had grown closer as a family, although her sisters still complained bitterly when Romeo got up to mischief.

'You deserve to be happy again, Lib. And you

will be. I can feel it in my bones. I'm on my way to make sure Verity is all right. Bridlington is here. I had a word with him, but it's best to be sure. I'll see you later.'

Gideon hugged her closer before releasing her and she watched as he made his way across the room.

'Is he still causing you concern?' The deep voice sent tingles racing through her.

It was the same whenever they met.

Whenever they spoke.

Whenever they danced—the touch of his hand pure agony with the wanting of him. And, if he could, he always picked a waltz—her hand on his shoulder, his hand on her waist, the helpless longing in her heart and the aching void of loneliness in her chest. That void had begun to fill. Before. Now, it gaped wider and blacker than ever.

She stretched her lips in a cool smile and turned to Dominic.

'No. He is doing his duty as an older brother. It seems Bridlington is here tonight. He has already spoken to him and now he is checking on Verity.'

'I'm pleased to hear it.'

A swift scan of him showed he was on edge, as he had been ever since *that night*. He disguised it well, but she could read his moods where other, more casual, observers would see nothing. It was time to put him out of his misery. And time to take that chance…to destroy that last tie that bound them together, that final strand that had been keeping her fragile hopes alive. And to hope Dominic would reach into his heart and see that the power was in his hands to forge a deeper, stronger link that could join them for ever.

'Have you a dance free this evening, Liberty?'

'I am afraid I do not dance this evening, my lord.' She would go home early, with a headache as an excuse. 'But I have news for you.'

Their gazes fused, his as opaque as it ever had been, his face impassive.

'I can confirm there were no c-c-consequences.' Try as she might, she could not control the wobble in her voice. Anguish scorched every fibre of her being. 'You need delay your betrothal no longer.'

She bobbed a curtsy and turned away, but Dominic grabbed her elbow, stopping her. 'Liberty!' His voice was low. Urgent. 'We need to talk.'

She pivoted to face him. '*We* need do nothing. *You* are free now to make your choice—and you know as well as I that not one unattached lady in this room tonight would refuse an offer from you. The choice is up to you.'

She stared up into those silvery eyes, but all she could see was her own image, reflected in them.

'Not one, Dominic,' she added softly. 'Your choice.'

She tugged her arm free and hurried away through the crowd to where Mrs Mount sat with the other chaperons. She looked up at Liberty enquiringly, her look changing to one of concern.

'You were right, dear ma'am,' said Liberty. 'I should have remained at home this evening.'

She laid her hand briefly to her lower belly and Mrs Mount gave her an understanding smile. She knew Liberty's courses had begun. She would not think it odd for Liberty to leave.

'There is no need for concern,' Liberty continued. 'I shall ask Gideon to escort me home and he will be back before you know it.'

Dominic watched as Liberty was absorbed into the crowd. He should feel released. He felt the opposite—as though prison walls were closing in on him. Ever since that night—the most glorious, wonderful night of his entire life—he had been as though held in limbo. He saw an insect trapped in amber once, at the British Museum, and that is exactly how he had felt since *that night*. But he had made a complete mull of it afterwards… talking of them marrying by special licence, speaking of *consequences*. Offering her *money*.

She was rightly disgusted with him, but no more disgusted than he was with himself. What had happened to his famed manners? His powers of address? They appeared to have deserted him at the time he most desperately needed them. He had tried everything to recover their friendship as a prelude to courting Liberty Lovejoy properly. To prove to her that he loved her. Only her. And to prove he could not give a damn whether she was the daughter of a duke or the daughter of a ditch-digger. But how could he do that when she kept him at arm's length with her perfect lady image and her exquisitely correct manners? His heart yearned for the old Liberty back…the real Liberty.

Dominic snagged a glass of champagne from a passing footman, swallowed one mouthful and then stilled.

It was not only his life that had been in limbo since *that night*. His thinking, it seemed, had been suspended, too. The family had noticed—he'd seen them watching him with concern when they thought he wouldn't notice—but none of them had mentioned his list.

Except Father.

'You may feel you have backed yourself into a corner, Dom, but there is absolutely no need to make any decisions this year. It will wait. What is your hurry?'

And he could not bring himself to admit that the hurry was the fear he might lose Liberty for good. And neither could he admit he had fallen in love. Not to Father, because he would then move heaven and earth to put things right for Dominic.

But this was *his* mess. He was a grown man and it was up to him to sort it out.

He tipped the remainder of the champagne into a nearby urn of flowers—with a silent apology to Felicity—and cursed himself for even more of a fool.

He had been waiting…hoping…that circumstance would intervene and that Liberty would find herself with child and she would *have* to marry him. A coward's hope. Her words tonight had shattered that dream, but now, picking through the wreckage of the plan that had not even been a plan but a weak, vague hope that everything would turn out all right, he understood that Liberty's news was a blessing.

Now, she had provided him with the perfect way to prove he loved her. If she had been with child, she would never believe he *wanted* to marry her. She would always fear he had been, in effect, trapped into it. Now…*now* he was free to prove to her that he loved her and only her.

With renewed vigour, he turned on his heel and went to find his stepmother. He had plans to make. Proper plans this time.

## *Chapter Twenty*

It would be *the* ball of the Season. Everybody who was anybody would be there.

'But you *must* attend, Liberty. Tell her, Hope.' Verity looked from one of her sisters to the other. 'It is the first ball the Duke of Cheriton has hosted since Lady Olivia made her debut *five years ago*!'

The ball had been announced just four days before, much to the consternation of those members of the *ton* who already had evening events arranged for tomorrow night. They had bowed to the inevitable and many events had been cancelled amid speculation as to whether there might be a specific purpose to the ball...whether a *special announcement* was imminent.

And people had nudged one another and cast surreptitious looks at the Marquess of Avon as they did so, convinced that he had finally chosen his bride and that the ball was to celebrate their betrothal. But not even the most incorrigible tittle-tattles could pretend they had an inkling of his choice. His Lordship went about his daily life as inscrutably as ever and not one of the young ladies believed to feature on his shortlist gave the smallest indication that she harboured a grand secret.

Liberty had no more idea than anyone else. Dominic had continued to be friendly whenever their paths crossed and he continued to dance with her as well as with many other young ladies, including those on his shortlist. His provocative teasing had stopped, however, much to Liberty's mingled consternation and relief.

His behaviour to her was that of the consummate gentleman and hers to him was that of the perfect lady.

Not even Olivia had let any information about the ball slip, although that, Liberty was fairly sure, was because even *she* did not why the ball had been arranged with such haste. All she knew, she had told Liberty crossly, was that her stepmother was rushing around like a whirlwind—for, as the lady of the house, the ball was under her jurisdiction—and that Grantham was being impossibly officious. Her father, she added, had brought in an army of additional servants to help get the ball ready on time.

But Liberty's entire family appeared unable to accept that she was happy not to attend the ball. Ever since the Stantons' ball she had steeled herself for the announcement of Dominic's betrothal and now, having been forewarned it was likely to happen tomorrow night, she would be a fool to put herself through such a trial in such a public setting.

'You *must* attend.' Hope added her voice to Verity's. 'Think how dreadful it would be for us to miss it.'

'*You* do not have to miss it.' Liberty put her arms around Romeo—seated beside her on the sofa—and kissed his head. 'Mrs Mount and Gideon will be there. Nobody will even notice or care about my absence.'

'Lady Olivia will be offended if you do not attend,' said Hope. 'You are friends—why on earth do you not want to go to her stepmother's ball?'

*Really! Can they not see my heart is breaking?*

No sooner had that very unfair thought surfaced than it was swept aside by the reassurance that no one actually *knew* Liberty's heart was shattered or that her life was over. She hadn't felt pain like this since Bernard died. She simply could not summon the strength to stand there and smile and look happy for Dominic and the flawless Lady Sybilla and, even worse, to congratulate them and wish them happy together.

She couldn't do it.

'I have no suitable gown to wear.'

It was no lie. Liberty had worn each of her three new ball gowns at least twice and the *ball of the Season* surely warranted a new gown.

'That is no excuse!' Hope grabbed Liberty's hand, forcing her to pay attention. 'Gideon, Verity and I decided it was time to show you our appreciation for everything you have done for us and we ordered a new gown. Cinderella *shall* go to the ball!'

Despite her dejection, Liberty could not help but laugh. 'Does that make you two the Ugly Sisters?' Then she sobered. 'But the ball is tomorrow night. There is no time. I shall send a note to Olivia explaining I am indisposed. The dress will come for another night…perhaps the Derhams' ball next week?'

Hope pouted. 'I think you are being very mean, Liberty. What have you got against the Duke and Duchess?'

'Nothing!'

Other than that the Duke terrified her. She had met him just two days before, introduced by Olivia, and his silvery-grey gaze—so like his son's—had swept over her, leaving her feeling as though he knew all her deepest, darkest secrets. Including that she was in love with his son and heir and had seduced him in the hope he might see sense. She shivered at the thought the Duke might find that out.

'I simply…it will be too grand. I do not care for such huge occasions. Now, please, stop pestering me. You will be perfectly safe attending with both Gideon and Mrs Mount and once you are surrounded by all your fawning admirers you won't have a thought to spare for me.'

Liberty spent the next day at home, even eschewing a ride in the Park. She could not face the growing excitement. It was just a ball, for goodness sake. What did the reason behind it matter? The Duke would no doubt announce the betrothal between Dominic and Lady Sybilla, and then the *ton*, in all its glittering, gossiping glory, would move on to the next shiny piece of news.

Much ado about nothing.

Except it wasn't nothing. Not to her. Romeo was beside her on the sofa and she buried her face in his soft fur. He licked her ear. Although it tickled, she could not summon even a giggle. Everywhere felt so numb.

'Miss Lovejoy?'

Her head jerked up at the maid's voice. 'Yes, Ethel?'

It was early evening and, having already dined, Liberty was alone in the drawing room, waiting to see the rest of the family, all dressed in their finery, before they left for the Cheritons' ball.

The maid looked flushed and flustered.

'It's Mrs Mount, miss. She's had the megrim come on.'

'Oh, dear!' Liberty stood. 'I shall go to her at once. Ask Mrs Taylor to prepare some willow-bark tea, if you will. That may help.'

'Yes, miss.'

When she reached Mrs Mount's bedchamber, Hope and Verity were both in attendance and Mrs Mount herself was in bed, the covers pulled up to her chin and a damp cloth draped across her forehead.

'My dear Mrs Mount.' Liberty went to her bedside, ushering her sisters out of the way. 'You must tell me if there is anything I can do to help.'

Mrs Mount moaned softly, her eyes shut. 'Nothing,' she whispered. 'I just need peace and quiet.'

'Of course.' Liberty scanned the room. The curtains were drawn, blocking out the light, and there was a glass of water on the bedside table. 'I have ordered willow-bark tea and I shall send one of the maids up to sit with you, in case you require anything. Come, girls…' she waved Hope and Verity towards the door '…let us leave poor Mrs Mount in peace.'

Once on the landing, she said, 'Why aren't you dressed for the ball? I thought the carriage was ordered for half past?'

Verity pouted. 'How can we go now? We have

no chaperon. Mrs Mount is indisposed and *you* have refused to go.'

'It's the ball of the Season,' Hope wailed, 'and we shall be the only ones not there!'

'Oh, good grief.' Liberty thought quickly, but could see no alternative. 'I… I must accompany you, I suppose. I can hardly expect Gideon to watch over you both.'

Verity flung her arms around Liberty and kissed her cheek. 'Oh, *thank* you. You are the *best* sister.'

Her heart expanded, knowing she had made her sisters happy. But what about her? She would have to face Dominic and, probably, endure his happy news. It was the last thing she wished to do. And yet…by staying away, would he not guess the reason why? She thought she had managed to hoodwink him so far, acting as though she could not care less, but he was no fool. Her absence would scream the truth more loudly than her stoical attendance.

Perhaps this was for the best. It would be but a few hours of her life. She had endured worse and coped. She would survive this.

'I suppose it will have to be the violet silk again,' she said. 'But no matter—no one will be looking my way, after all.'

'Oh! I forgot to tell you!' Hope's blue eyes

sparkled. 'You won't need your violet silk. Do you recall that new gown I told you about? It was delivered this afternoon, but Lizzie stupidly put it in my bedchamber, thinking it was mine! She will bring it to you and she can help you with your hair, for mine is already done.'

The gown was perfect. If Liberty could have chosen a gown for herself, without consideration of cost, it was just what she would have chosen—a high-waisted gown of blush-pink crepe over a satin slip, the skirt decorated with two festoons of pink rosebuds at the hem. The bodice—with scattered seed pearls and tiny rosebuds stitched to the fabric—was cut low over the shoulders, in the current fashion, with short sleeves held up by narrow satin bands. Lizzie pinned her hair on top of her head, threading a string of pearls through her locks and leaving a few curls to frame her face. Her mother's single strand of pearls was clasped around her throat and matching pearl eardrops hung from her lobes.

Her sisters' gasps when she appeared at the head of the stairs were balm to Liberty's soul. She straightened her shoulders and raised her chin as she descended to where they waited in the hall. Gideon came in the front door.

'The carriage is waiting.' He let out a low whistle as he caught sight of Liberty and he walked to meet her and kissed her hand. 'You look like a princess.'

The line of carriages waiting to deliver their occupants to Beauchamp House stretched all the way around Grosvenor Square. As they waited, the evening dry, the sky spangled with stars, Liberty remembered the very first time she had called at Beauchamp House: the heavy rain, the thunder and lightning, the footman with the umbrella. And Dominic. The very first time they met. Little did she imagine then how she would come to feel about him. Little did she imagine he would break her heart. She swallowed, forcing down the aching mass that invaded her throat.

*I will not disgrace myself. I am braver... stronger...than that.*

By the time the Lovejoys entered the front door Liberty's nerves had wound so tight she could barely hear a word said to her as she climbed the magnificent marble staircase with Gideon, Hope and Verity, and then stood in line to be greeted by their host and hostess.

The Duke was resplendent in severe black evening clothes and the Duchess looked lovely in lemon gauze over a cream underdress. As they waited their turn, a quick sweep of the surrounding area revealed no trace of any of the rest of the Beauchamps and, for that, Liberty was grateful. One step at a time. Get the formalities out of the way and she could hopefully lose herself in the crush—and it truly was a crush. As they reached the Duke—Gideon bowing and she, Hope and Verity sinking into curtsies—Liberty caught a glimpse of the crowded ballroom, down a short flight of stairs. How on earth anyone would manage to dance was beyond her although, no doubt, the elders would soon disperse to the card rooms and salons, leaving the ballroom free for the dancers and their chaperons.

She rose from her curtsy to find herself being regarded by a pair of friendly golden-brown eyes.

'We have heard a great deal about you from Olivia, Miss Lovejoy,' said the Duchess. 'Thank you for being such a good friend to her...she puts so much pressure on herself to be the perfect mother to the twins, even though we keep telling her not to be so hard on herself, is that not so, Leo?'

Gideon and the girls had moved on, waiting now at the top of the flight of steps down into the ballroom, and the following guests had not yet moved forward, leaving Liberty in limbo with the Duke and the Duchess. She sucked in a sharp breath in an attempt to quell her nerves as the

Duke's penetrating silver-grey gaze studied her unhurriedly.

'Indeed.' He smiled at Liberty, his eyes crinkling at the corners, and suddenly he did not look as intimidating. His gaze did not swerve from hers. 'It is a pleasure to meet you again, Miss Lovejoy. We are honoured that you accepted our invitation.'

Liberty managed a smile in return, even as she wondered at the strange phrasing used by the Duke. She joined Gideon and the girls at the head of the stairs.

# *Chapter Twenty-One*

'The Earl of Wendover; Miss Lovejoy; Miss Hope Lovejoy; Miss Verity Lovejoy.'

Their arrival was announced by Grantham—very erect and clearly relishing his role as Master of Ceremonies—in resonant tones. They descended the stairs into the ballroom. Liberty rested her hand on Gideon's arm as Hope and Verity followed behind, and aimed her gaze resolutely above the heads of the crowd. As they reached the foot of the stairs, Gideon slipped his arm from beneath her hand.

'I see Emily over by the window. I shall see you later.'

He melted among the crowd, lost to sight within seconds. Liberty didn't even know which window he might be heading for—there were five sets of French windows along the far wall, but she had been so determined not to catch sight of Dominic or Sybilla that neither had she seen Lady

Emily, or where she stood. She turned to Hope and Verity, but they were already surrounded by young men eager to reserve dances.

Liberty rubbed her upper chest, feeling the hollow swoop of her stomach as she did so. This had been her worst fear. Being alone, in the crowd, waiting for the axe to fall. She peered around anxiously, and froze.

Dominic. Two paces away, handsome and debonair in black evening clothes, a dark sapphire pin in his neckcloth. His gaze steady. On her. She swallowed and forced a smile. She would not evade this meeting. Her actions had been her own, the decisions her own. She had gambled of her own free will and it was not Dominic's fault that he still believed in duty over love.

'Good evening, Liberty.'

His rich voice sent shudders of helpless desire through her, as did the look of intent in his silvery gaze. He moved closer and she could smell the spicy, musky cologne he favoured. When she closed her eyes at night, it was that remembered scent that started the memories rolling through her head. She blinked, forcing her mind out of her feelings and into the practicalities of coping with this meeting without making a complete idiot of herself.

'Good evening, my lord.' Love—pure, despairing, eternal—squeezed her heart, catching at her breath. How could she bear this? But bear it she must. 'It is…it is a crush tonight, is it not? Your stepmother must be pleased with the success of her ball.'

He smiled. Tenderly. She blinked again, too accustomed to him blanking his emotions to believe her own eyes. But she was not mistaken. That tender smile was aimed directly at her. It reached his eyes, too—no opaque silver coins tonight, nor even mirrors reflecting the world back. For almost the first time since she had known him—other than *that night*—he appeared to be inviting her in. Inviting her to see the real man inside.

'I am sure she is.'

Her heart beat a little faster. That vice constricting her heart eased a fraction and hope stirred as Dominic extended one hand. As though in a dream she placed her own hand in his. His fingers closed strongly around hers, warm, comforting, safe. Tears stung her eyes and she desperately swallowed her emotions down. She could not cope with comforting. Or with safe.

Her heart began to pound. Disjointed questions ricocheted around her head. *What...? Why...? How...?* Her knees trembled and her mouth dried, and all coherent thought scattered, as out of reach as the stars in the sky.

Dominic captured her other hand, bringing their joined hands together, between them, at chest height. Then, in a gesture that stole her breath, he opened his fingers leaving his hands side by side, palm up, almost in supplication. Her own hands lay on his, palm to palm, but she was not controlled in any way. She could remove her hands. She could move away, if she chose to. But she would not…could not…move. Her mind had ceased to control her body. She stood, helpless, waiting to hear what he might say. Dreading and yet hoping…yearning…*praying.*

He smiled into her eyes.

'If you do not want this, Liberty Louisa Lovejoy…if you do not want *me*…please tell me now and we shall say no more about it.'

She could not grasp his meaning, so she picked on the familiar.

'How do you know my middle name?'

One corner of his lips quirked up in a half-smile. 'Verity told me.'

Her gaze skimmed past him, to where she had last seen her sisters. Hope and Verity, beyond Dominic's right shoulder, were watching her, wide smiles on their faces. She wrenched her attention back to Dominic.

'V-Verity? Wh-why did she tell you that?'

'I asked her.'

'Oh.' Her throat ached unbearably. She still could not allow herself to hope…to believe…

what his words meant. 'Wh-what is this? What are you doing?'

He ducked his head close to listen to her whispered question. His ear, his dark hair curling slightly over its rim, was tantalisingly close to her lips. He was so close she could see the texture of his skin, the faint shadow of his beard, even though he was freshly shaven. He raised his head again and she saw the glisten of his tongue as it moistened his visibly dry lips. She slid her palms over his and her fingertips found the pulse in his wrist. It pounded even faster than her own.

'I am about to propose to you.'

Her heart leapt. Her lungs seized. Her sisters were still watching avidly…with Gideon and… *Mrs Mount*? Liberty swallowed down a swell of tears as she processed his words. Propose? To her? But… 'What about Sybilla?' she whispered.

'Forget Sybilla,' he said roughly. 'It is you I love. You I need.' His chest expanded as he inhaled, then his words came out in a disjointed rush. 'Berty…if you can forgive me…if you can love me…if, when I ask you to marry me, your answer is yes…then stay here, by my side. But if you cannot, if your answer is still no, then we will say no more.'

He captured her gaze again. Heat swirled in his eyes and she could feel the dampness of his palms.

'My intention was to declare my love and to propose to you tonight—here, in front of everyone, so neither you nor anyone else will doubt my love for you is true. But I changed my mind.'

Liberty's heart had begun to soar. Now, she could not stifle her gasp of dismay.

'I changed my mind,' Dominic continued, 'because I will not back you into a corner in front of all these people. I will not put you in a position where you feel you *cannot* refuse me. You are in control, my darling Berty. Walk away now, if you wish, and no one will be any the wiser. But know that my heart will go with you.'

Her heart somersaulted. This private man—a man who concealed his heart and his emotions behind duty and obligation—was about to make a public declaration. To her!

The cacophony of surrounding voices was fading—a tide of sound receding. She sensed they now stood in a clearing and that the people around them were moving back, but she could not tear her gaze from his.

She slid her hands back until just their fingers overlapped and then she curled her fingers until they were linked with his. She smoothed her thumbs across his knuckles and put all of her love into her smile. 'I will not walk away, Dominic. I love you.'

His lips curved and his fingers tightened

around hers. He raised his head, clearly seeking someone over the heads of the crowd. A gong reverberated throughout the room and now the hush of the crowd could not be mistaken.

'My lords, ladies and gentleman.' Liberty recognised Grantham's voice. 'Pray silence for His Lordship, the Marquess of Avon.'

The difficult part was over. So why did his knees still shake and why was his stomach still churning? She would not walk away. She had said so. But this was still the most important moment of his life and he was desperate to get it right. Dominic swallowed past the swell of emotion that clogged his throat and clasped Liberty's hands even tighter, revelling in the knowledge that he could hold her hands whenever he chose, from this night onwards, for the rest of their lives. He could feel her suppressed emotion in the tremble of her hands and he could see it by the quiver of her lower lip.

Then their eyes met. And she smiled and it was as though the sun broke through dark clouds and everything...*everything*...was all right. His tension fragmented and a surge of energy...of hope...of joy...radiated throughout his entire body. He hauled in a deep breath and, when he spoke, there was no hesitancy in his words or in his voice.

He had prepared what he would say—the proper words and sentiments for an occasion such as this—but he ignored all his careful plans. He gazed out at the sea of faces surrounding them and he spoke from the heart.

'There has been much speculation in the past weeks about my intentions. I arrived in town with the aim of finding the perfect wife for me and for my position as my father's heir. I have to tell you…' his gaze swept the crowd '…that I was possibly even more undecided than any one of you as to whom that lady might be.

'And then this lady—Liberty Louisa Lovejoy—burst into my life like a…like a…'

He paused, and stared down at Liberty. How could he sum up what she had come to mean to him in just a few words? What words could do her justice? She smiled, her gold-flecked blue eyes urging him on. And then the exact words didn't matter. He was talking with his heart, not his head—and if they came out less than perfect, he did not care.

'She burst into my life like a whirlwind of sunshine, lighting my life with laughter, with love and with joy. And I had found my perfect partner in life. And, if she will have me, my perfect wife…my perfect Marchioness.'

It was his turn to smile, while Liberty looked serious.

'Liberty Lovejoy, I love you with every beat of my heart. I love you with every breath I take. You already have possession of my heart. Will you now do me the great honour of accepting my hand as well? Will you marry me?'

For what felt like an eternity her expression remained set and it felt as though his heart, too, stilled as he waited. The room around them was silent, not a sound to be heard. He concentrated on her mouth, those lush lips, willing her to answer. Slowly…excruciatingly slowly…her lips lifted at the corners…curved into a smile…and parted.

And he shouldn't have been surprised, but he was. Because she went up on tiptoes, threw her arms around his neck and kissed him, quite thoroughly, accompanied by a chorus of gasps and sighs from their audience.

And Dominic could breathe properly for the first time since Liberty had announced she was not with child and he could marry whomever he chose.

He chose Liberty Lovejoy.

And she said yes…in deed if not in so many words.

# *Chapter Twenty-Two*

The ball was finally over. The guests, other than their families, had all gone home and the Beauchamps and the Lovejoys repaired to the family parlour for their first opportunity to discuss the betrothal. Publicly, of course, all his family had congratulated him. They had put on a good show…but was it just a show, or would they really be happy for him and welcome Liberty into the fold? The hard ball of anxiety that had lodged in Dominic's stomach over the past weeks had dissolved, leaving one tiny knot of unease, one unanswered question, behind.

Would following his heart mean a rift between him and his beloved family?

Dominic tucked Liberty close to him as they sat side by side on the sofa and the Beauchamps, Lovejoys—and Mrs Mount—assembled. Olivia, of course, piped up the minute the door closed.

'Well! I do think you might have told *me* what

you planned, Dominic. Liberty *is* my friend, after all. I could have helped.'

He should have expected no less and he noticed Father and Rosalind exchange wry smiles.

'I neither needed nor wanted your help, Livvy,' he said. 'But thank you for the thought.'

Olivia pouted. 'Hope and Verity knew! And even Mrs Mount and she's not even family.'

'I had to confide in them, Liv. I wasn't confident Liberty would come tonight otherwise.'

'She was exceedingly stubborn.' Hope was sitting next to Alex, casting occasional coquettish glances at him through her lashes while Alex pretended not to notice. 'Poor Mrs Mount had to feign illness before she would give in.'

'Well, I still think—' Olivia fell silent as Hugo placed a hand on her shoulder.

'All has worked out for the best, my sweet, so you must concede that Dominic didn't need your help. He knew what he was doing.'

'Eventually,' said Alex.

Dominic frowned at his brother, receiving an innocent smile in return as Alex continued, 'You're slipping, Liv. It must be motherhood. Hugo and I knew which way the wind was blowing *weeks* ago.'

Olivia sucked in a deep breath, ready to retaliate, and Dominic saw his father getting ready to intervene, but it was Liberty who spoke.

'Are you disappointed you weren't told, or disappointed in Dominic's choice, Olivia?'

The slightest of tremors in her voice told him how much courage it had taken for her to ask such a direct question, especially when she had already confided in him how nervous she was at facing his family. Especially his father. He took her hand and squeezed.

Olivia paled at Liberty's words and she shot out of her seat and sat on the other side of Liberty, putting her arm around her shoulders.

'How could you even *think* I might be disappointed he chose you, Liberty? When I think of those haughty girls on that ridiculous list of his—no! There is no comparison. You are perfect, just as Dom said. It is just that I feel like I'm the only one who didn't know.'

'You always did want to know everything that is going on, Olivia, and you haven't changed.' Father stood and moved across to the mantelpiece, commanding the room as was his wont. 'If it's any consolation, your stepmother and I knew nothing either, not until the very first guests were already walking up the stairs this evening. That is the first time we knew Liberty's identity.'

Both Rosalind and Father had trusted Dominic when he had asked them to throw a ball for a special announcement without revealing any details. He prayed they did not now feel that trust had been betrayed. Liberty's fingers tightened on Dominic's and he heard her intake of breath.

'Is that why you said what you did to me when I arrived, Your Grace?'

Dominic stared at his father. Had he been unwelcoming?

'What did you say to her?' he demanded. He had to challenge him—he would not stand for any member of his family, even his father, upsetting Liberty. He had deliberately not revealed her identity earlier because he had wanted neither his father's help nor his hindrance. Nor had he wanted to know if Father disapproved because his approval or disapproval had been irrelevant, in the end.

Liberty was Dominic's choice and his alone.

He held his breath, awaiting his father's reply, but it was Liberty who spoke.

'He said it was a pleasure to meet me again and that he and the Duchess were honoured that I accepted their invitation.' She smiled up at Dominic. 'Honoured! Your father made me feel welcome and that helped to give me the courage to face this evening.'

Dominic caught his father's eyes and sent him a silent apology. Father ghosted a wink in reply and that last knot of tension in Dominic's stomach unravelled.

But Liberty hadn't finished. Her cheeks turned

pink as her gaze took in every person in the room, one by one.

'I was convinced Dominic was about to announce his betrothal to someone else and I wanted to be anywhere but here tonight.' She beamed then at her brother and sisters, and Mrs Mount, who had still come to the ball, but rather later than planned. 'Thank you all for not giving up on me.'

'That's all right, Sis,' said Gideon. 'We did it for ourselves more than you—how else could we get rid of Romeo?'

'Is that your dog, Liberty?' Rosalind asked, over the chuckles raised by Gideon's remarks. 'I hope he likes other dogs because there will be several around when you come to the Abbey in July.'

Liberty looked questioningly at Dominic. He hadn't even thought that far ahead. The Abbey was his childhood home and he couldn't wait to show Liberty around, although they would make their home at one of Father's minor estates.

'The entire family will all be together for the first time since Olivia and Hugo married, four years ago,' said Dominic. He lifted her hand and kissed it. 'I cannot wait for you—and Romeo—to meet the rest of them.'

She smiled at that. 'I am sure he will be on his best behaviour,' she said to Rosalind.

'Well, now.' Father crossed to where Rosalind was sitting and helped her to rise, then he led her across to Dominic and Liberty, who stood up also. 'I said it in the ballroom, Liberty, but I want you to be in no doubt… I am delighted to welcome you to our family. I can see you have made my son a happy man and that's good enough for me.'

He placed his hands on her shoulders and bent to kiss her cheek, then murmured something into her ear. Something Dominic could not hear.

'Goodnight, everyone.' He and Rosalind went to the door, then Father held it open, making it clear to the rest of the company it was time to leave. One by one they said goodnight to Dominic and Liberty and trooped out. Gideon was the last to go.

'We'll wait for you in the entrance hall, Sis,' he said.

And then they were alone. At last. Dominic wrapped Liberty in his arms, but still the question burned in him and he had to ask.

'What did Father whisper to you?'

Liberty beamed up at him. 'He said he knew it was me, from the night of Lady Stanton's ball.'

'And I was very pleased,' came a deep voice from the doorway, 'that you saw sense, my Son. After all, why spoil the Beauchamp tradition of following our hearts?'

'Why did you say nothing?'

His father never normally shied away from manipulating events to suit himself.

'Because it was your decision, Dom. It was for you to make your own choice—head or heart. I'm happy it was the right one. Eventually, as your brother would say. Goodnight.'

They were alone again. And now there were no more unanswered questions. Except… Dominic frowned.

'What is it?'

'You never did answer my question, Berty.'

'Which question?'

'Will you marry me?'

She smiled and traced his lower lip with her forefinger. '*I* thought I answered you most explicitly, Lord Avon. But, if you want unequivocal, then you shall have it.'

She slipped her arms around his neck, went up on tiptoes and, for the second time that night, she kissed him. Very thoroughly. Until his senses swam and his blood was on fire.

'Oh, yes,' she whispered against his lips. 'Yes. Yes. Yes.'

* * * * *

# MILLS & BOON

## Coming next month

### MRS SOMMERSBY'S SECOND CHANCE
Laurie Benson

'How can I help?' he asked, tilting his head a bit as he looked at her with a furrowed brow.

'I'm stuck.'

'Pardon?'

'On the hedge.' She motioned to her back with her gloved hand. 'The lace on my dress is caught on a branch and I can't move. Would you be so kind as to release me?'

He glanced around the small wooded area she was in and even appeared to peer over a few of the lower hedges as he made his way closer to her. When he stood a few feet away, the faintest scent of his cologne drifted across her nose as it travelled on the soft breeze.

Clara was petite in stature and had to look up at him as he stood less than two feet from her. Facing him, without the busyness of the Pump Room, she was able to get a better look at him. His firm and sensual lips rose a fraction in the right corner, softening the angles of his square jaw. Although he was clean shaven, there was a hint of stubble on that jaw and on his cheeks. She appreciated impeccably groomed men so it was surprising that she had the urge to brush her fingers against his skin to see what that stubble felt like.

He leaned over her and her breath caught as his lips

drew closer to her eyelids. His finely made arms, defined through the linen of his blue coat, came around hers. He could have easily stood to the side of her to free the bit of fabric, but being surrounded by all his quiet masculine presence, she was glad he had decided not to.

'You truly have got yourself caught.'

He looked down at her and flecks of gold were visible in his blue eyes. 'I know I haven't spent much time in your presence, however, this is the quietest I think I have seen you,' he said with a slight smile.

'I don't want to distract you.'

'You already have.'

She lifted her chin and now their mouths were a few inches apart. The warm air of his breath brushed across her lips. The last time she had kissed a man was ten years ago. And even then, she couldn't ever recall her pulse beating like this at the thought of kissing her husband.

*Continue reading*

MRS SOMMERSBY'S SECOND CHANCE

Laurie Benson

*Available next month*

www.millsandboon.co.uk

LET'S TALK
Romance